# DON'T STAND SO CLOSE

www.**transworldbooks**.co.uk

# DON'T STAND SO CLOSE

## CLOSE

Luana Lewis

BANTAM PRESS

LONDON • TORONTO • SYDNEY • AUCKLAND • JOHANNESBURG

TRANSWORLD PUBLISHERS
61–63 Uxbridge Road, London W5 5SA
A Random House Group Company
www.transworldbooks.co.uk

First published in Great Britain
in 2014 by Bantam Press
an imprint of Transworld Publishers

A CIP catalogue record for this book
is available from the British Library.

ISBNs 9780593072301 (cased)
9780593072318 (tpb)

Addresses for Random House Group Ltd companies outside the UK
can be found at: www.randomhouse.co.uk
The Random House Group Ltd Reg. No. 954009

The Random House Group Limited supports the Forest Stewardship Council®
(FSC®), the leading international forest-certification organisation.
Our books carrying the FSC label are printed on FSC®-certified paper.
FSC is the only forest-certification scheme supported by the leading
environmental organisations, including Greenpeace.
Our paper procurement policy can be found at
www.randomhouse.co.uk/environment

Typeset in 11/14pt Sabon by Falcon Oast Graphic Art Ltd
Printed and bound in Great Britain by
Clays Ltd, Bungay, Suffolk

2 4 6 8 10 9 7 5 3 1

For Genna Leigh

# Hilltop, Friday 7 January 2011, 3 p.m.

At first, she ignored the doorbell.

The sound rang out, echoing through the entrance hall, crashing through into the living room and clattering and bouncing inside her skull.

She stood at the window looking out at her garden, at a world that blazed white. A layer of snow coated the ground and the tangled arms of the trees and the Chiltern hills beyond. It looks like Narnia, she thought, as though Aslan might stride out from the forest at any moment.

The quiet was unnatural. Unnerving.

The snow had begun to fall at nine o'clock that morning. The newspapers carried warnings: *A Wall of Snow*. Airports cancelled flights. Her husband had left for work as usual.

The doorbell rang again. Longer, louder and more insistent.

She felt exposed, in front of the wall of windows stretching across the back of the house. Her home was a white concrete edifice, a modernist triumph of sharp angles and tall windows. Nobody should be able to get past the entrance to the driveway without the intruder alarm sounding an ear-splitting warning. And yet someone had. The snow was the problem: it must have piled up so high that it had covered the infra-red eye of the sensor.

She pulled at the neck of her jumper. It was too tight and her throat itched. Her mouth was dry and her palms moist. It was three o'clock and darkness would come soon. Her husband would not be coming home. Inches of snow had turned to ice, had made the steep approach impossible.

She checked the locks on the patio doors. A draught whistled around the edges of the black steel doorframe, as if the cold was trying to force its way inside. The house was Grade II listed, nothing could be done, the doors and the windows could not be changed. She tested the locks once more and then pulled the heavy drapes closed.

The doorbell rang again. And again.

She paced the living room. A half-empty bottle of wine stood open on the coffee table. She breathed. In for three, out for three. She pressed her hands against her ears.

A normal person would go to the front door and see who was there.

Stella walked through to the large square entrance hall. A chandelier with myriad round glass discs spiralled down above the staircase. She flicked a switch and light bounced off the pale grey walls and shimmered, everywhere, too bright. She was disoriented, as though she had stepped inside a hall of mirrors and could not get her bearings. She would not panic. Nobody had ever tried to harm her at Hilltop. People intending to do harm did not announce themselves, or wait to be invited inside. But she could not think of a reason why someone would ring her doorbell in the middle of a snowstorm.

She checked the monitor mounted on the wall next to the

front door. A young woman was outside. She stood on the doorstep, her arms wrapped around her chest, shifting from one foot to the other. A beanie hat was pulled down low over her long fair hair. A short leather jacket, covered in studs and zips, barely covered her midriff.

Stella lifted the handset. 'Yes?' she said.

'I'm freezing. Can I come inside?' Snowflakes churned around her as she shouted at the intercom. She shivered with cold and she didn't look like much of a threat. 'Could I use your phone?'

She looked up into the camera. Her face was lovely on the screen, with cat-like eyes and high cheekbones.

'I'm sorry,' Stella said. 'No. Try one of the neighbours.' She placed the receiver back on to the cradle.

She waited until the screen faded to black and the person outside disappeared and then she returned to the living room and took up her place at the window. But she was uneasy and the spell was broken. The snow that covered everything – the lawn, the trees and the hills beyond – no longer seemed magical. She hated being alone. The daylight hours were difficult, the nights almost impossible.

The air shattered as the doorbell rang again.

The police would hardly be impressed if she called them out to complain that a young woman had rung her doorbell. And she didn't want to disturb her husband. But she so wanted to call him and ask him what to do. Her BlackBerry was right beside her. She picked it up. Ran her fingers across the keypad. Put it down again. She would not call him, she would deal with this herself. She was getting better. Of course, she wasn't. She was alone and helpless and useless. She wanted Max. If she had her way, she would have him home all day.

9

Max deserved a better wife. He had rescued her and then it had all predictably gone to hell.

She returned to the front door, a rising anger competing with her nerves. The intercom screen showed the same young woman, with her beanie pulled down almost to her eyebrows and the absurdly short leather coat that provided no warmth.

'*What is it?*' Stella said.

She babbled as she looked up into the camera: 'I used to live here,' she said. 'I came up from London to see my old house. I didn't know the snow would be so bad. It's all frozen and it's really steep going back down the hill. Can I *please* come inside?'

Stella realized that the girl outside was very young. She couldn't be more than fifteen years old. Fourteen, maybe. A child.

'I'll call a taxi to take you back down to the station,' Stella said.

'You can't. They've shut down because of the snow. *Please.* The tube isn't running either, I'm stuck here. I can't go back down the road or I'll break my neck.' Her voice was rising with outrage and distress. 'Can I just come inside?'

The girl was shaking with cold. Her lips were a purple gash, startling and dark against the pale skin of her face. She looked as though she was about to cry. Stella felt sorry for her. Not sorry enough, however, to risk opening the door.

'No,' Stella said. 'Go and try one of the other houses. You've got an entire street to choose from.'

'Please,' the girl said, 'I'm so cold. Why can't you just let me in?' She pouted at the camera and she stomped her white trainers on the black marble tiles.

Stella slammed the receiver back against its white plastic

cradle. She watched as the girl tried in vain to keep warm. She paced up and down, leaving a haphazard pattern in the snow around Stella's front door. She wrapped her arms around herself and bounced, up and down. At a certain point, she stopped fighting. She sank to the floor, her head on her knees.

The cold must be unbearable, like torture.

The minutes passed as Stella sat in front of the fire on her grey linen sofa. She pressed her bare feet into the soft, Chinese deco rug. She stood. She walked around the navy border, placing one foot in front of the other as though she was on a tightrope. She stopped at the yellow and orange parrot embroidered in the right-hand corner. She did not understand why the girl insisted on waiting outside her door.

Her thoughts came fast and fragmented. One day it would be different. She would be free of her chains. But she was losing time. She found it harder and harder to remember what she had been like before.

The house was silent.

Almost forty minutes had passed since the bell had rung for the first time. The girl at the front door must have decided to brave the steep hill that was Victoria Avenue. She was right: if she tried to make her way down, she might slip and fall. But after all – and here Stella tried to make herself feel less guilty – what was the worst thing that could happen to her? She might end up with a wet backside. And once she made it down the hill – wet backside and all – she could walk along the High Street and she would be inside the cosy inn within minutes. The Royal Oak: good wine, an open fireplace and exposed beams. The television above the fireplace had sort of melted along the bottom but no one seemed to notice it was a fire hazard. Stella could feel the soft sheepskin throws against her skin. She could taste the Bloody Mary – poured from a jug on the counter, slices of lemon arranged on the wooden board next to the glass pitcher. Max had described it all. He often walked down there alone on a Sunday evening. Stella had never walked with him, but maybe she would go, for the first time, when he came home to her the next day. He must be desperate for her to leave the house, though he hid it well.

The silence had become a pressure, pushing against her eardrums, and the darkness drew closer.

Max would not force her back into a world that terrified her. But she had been hiding a long time. More and more often she feared it was too late. Whichever way she looked at it, she was a recluse.

With any luck, the girl had gone to pester the neighbours, families with children of varying ages whom Stella had never met.

Or she might still be outside, waiting.

The silence and the waiting became unbearable.

Hilltop was her home, she was safe inside. If she went down the road paved with paranoia and self-pity she knew where it would lead – into a padded cell most probably. She *was* safe. Nothing had changed; no one could get in. It was just a girl.

Hilltop was her own private kingdom, her palace and her prison.

Stella returned to the entrance hall. She tilted the shutters and peered out into the silvery-grey landscape. Heavy snowflakes swirled everywhere, as though a million goose-down pillows had been sliced open in the sky. With each passing second, the light grew weaker. The girl sat with her back to the polished steel front door, her knees pulled up to her chest and her head down. She was a child: helpless and cold.

A part of Stella was excited, the part she usually kept locked down tight. A little of her old self stirred in her chest. She needed to take a risk, to shatter the invalid's life she had created for herself before it was truly too late. She needed to know that she could still be of use, to someone. She was tired of being inside, immobilized, waiting for something to happen, tired of waiting to get better while other people went on with their lives and her husband stayed away. She punched in the code, turning off the motion sensors. She rested her left hand on the door handle. There was a human being outside, alone and suffering. With her right hand, she reached for the deadbolt. She opened the door.

The blackened sky was shot through with violet. Icy air raged inside and heavy snowflakes blew through the open doorway then melted as they landed on the heated floor.

The girl was covered in white. Ice crystals had settled everywhere, in her hair and on her shoulders, and they clung to her leggings and her shoes.

She blinked up at Stella. 'It's fucking freezing out here,' she said.

Her blue eyes were defiant and full of mistrust. She stayed where she was, unsure whether she was to be allowed inside. She made no sudden movements and she did not try to force her way in. She waited to be invited.

Stella took a step backward and nodded. With stiff, frozen fingers, the girl picked up her bag and scrambled to her feet. She stepped across the threshold.

Stella shut the front door behind her, locked it and then

turned to get a better look at her uninvited guest. The girl was like a frightened deer. Strands of damp hair clung to her face. Her jacket hung open, revealing a cropped T-shirt and a hint of pale, goose-pimpled flesh. Bony knees protruded through tight black leggings. She held on to the strap of her rucksack and rocked back and forth on her grubby white running shoes. The girl pulled off her hat, her fingers still angry and red. She shook out her long wet hair and, as she did so, she caught sight of the colossal chandelier. She stared up for a moment, wide-eyed.

At five foot four, Stella was not particularly tall, and the girl was a head shorter than she was. And that was with the extra inch she gained from the running shoes. Stella felt foolish for being afraid.

'My toes are burning,' the girl said. 'And I can't feel my fingers.' She glared at Stella as if she were responsible for her pain. She curled her fingers into a fist, then released them; watching her hands as though they belonged to someone else. Her eyes glistened and Stella thought she might be about to cry.

'Why don't you take off your shoes,' Stella said, thinking about frostbite.

The girl bent down and tried to undo her laces, but her fingers were rigid and it took ages before she managed to loosen the double knots. As Stella waited and watched, the girl pulled off her trainers and placed them side by side on the front door mat. She wasn't wearing socks and her toenails were painted black.

'You should take that off too.' Stella pointed at her jacket. Up close, she could see it was no more than thin plastic.

The girl shook her head; no.

'Come inside, there's a fire – it's warmer,' Stella said.

She walked towards the living room, pointing at the doorway, as if encouraging a timid animal to follow. She felt energized, or perhaps she felt anxious, it was hard to tell the difference. The girl followed, barefoot and still clutching at the strap of her bag. She didn't look as though she felt at home in her old house. She stood motionless next to the sofa with her damp hair and her damp clothes.

Stella felt bad for leaving her outside so long. She lifted the tartan blanket from the back of the couch and shook it out. She ventured a step closer, holding the blanket out in front of her. When the girl didn't back away, Stella draped the blanket around her shoulders and wrapped her up tight. The girl's stiff fingers took hold. Stella saw it again, the suspicion in her eyes, and she backed away.

'Sit in front of the fire,' she said.

The girl sat, perched on the edge of the sofa, her back to Stella, staring at the small flames. The shivering went on and on. Stella hovered behind her, unsure what to do next.

'I should phone your parents and let them know you're here,' she said.

'My toes *really* hurt.'

Stella wondered if she might end up having to find a doctor for this strange, reckless girl who wandered about half undressed in the arctic conditions. She walked round and sat on the opposite end of the sofa. She noticed how beautiful the girl was. Exceptionally so. Her deep-set eyes were the colour of the sky on a clear, sunshine-filled day. Her hair had begun to dry, forming soft golden waves that caressed her cheeks. Her skin was velvety smooth. Her top lip was a shade too thin, but her bottom lip was fuller, pouting. She was so young.

'Why are you staring at me?' the girl asked.

'I'm Stella. What's your name?'

'Blue.'

Blue was the colour of her eyes. Blue did not sound like a real name.

'Is Blue your nickname?'

'It's my real name.'

'And what's your surname?'

She rubbed at her dry lips, tinged blue with cold, and hesitated, her eyes flickering around the room from left to right. 'Cunningham,' she said.

Stella had no way of knowing if she was lying.

'We need to get you home,' Stella said. 'We need to let someone know you're here.'

'I'm not going home.' The girl spoke with a certain determination that concerned Stella.

'Why not?' Stella asked.

'I had a fight with my mother. She won't let me back in.'

'Blue, even if you had an argument with your mother, she'll still be worried about you.'

No response.

'Well – I still need to call someone to let them know you're safe. Is there someone else I could call, besides your mother?'

Blue shook her head, not looking at Stella, staring at the fire. The shivering had lessened, but now and again a small quiver passed through her shoulders.

'We do need to find a way to get you home,' Stella said. Her words sounded empty, repetitive, lame.

'I didn't really use to live here,' the girl said. 'I made that up.' She turned to look at Stella. The colour of her eyes seemed to shift, so that the blue was deeper and more intense, the colour of cold, hard tanzanite.

Stella tilted her head from side to side, trying to release the muscles that had seized up in her neck and across her shoulders. 'Then why have you come here?' she asked.

If she panicked, if she breathed too fast, if she allowed her heartbeat to thunder out of control, she was lost. She should have gone upstairs when she heard the doorbell, shut the door of her bedroom, swallowed a sleeping pill, ignored the goddamn noise. There was a tightness in her chest, it was impossible to take in enough air.

'I came because I need to see Dr Fisher,' the girl said.

'My husband?'

'Yes.' Blue's mouth set in a stubborn line and she began to scratch at the skin on her forearms.

# Session Four

At the beginning of the session, he sat all quiet and serious, while he waited for her to say something first. His eyes were hidden away behind the black frames of his reading glasses and she couldn't see what he was feeling. He always wore suits and ties. As far as she could tell he had two: a navy one and a tan one. His shoes were black and shiny and expensive-looking, with square toes. Under his shirt there was a slight curve to his belly. She didn't mind at all. She also liked that he wasn't too tall and that he had a beard. She didn't know why, but these things pleased her.

He was still watching her.

'I hate these chairs,' she said.

He didn't say anything, yet.

'Why do you put your chair so far away from mine?' Her voice sounded a little whiny. 'I don't really hate the chairs. I could curl up in this chair and stay here all day and not go back home. I'd just stay here with you.'

She leaned forward, pulling a strand of her hair into her mouth. Men were always looking at her. He looked at her too, in that same way, she was sure of it, but he pretended he didn't. He shifted in his chair, changing over his crossed legs to the other direction. He leaned back and rested his chin on his hand. She looked up at the clock. Five minutes gone. That meant forty-five minutes left. She squeezed her bottom lip with the fingers of her right hand. He was still watching. She wondered if he stared at all his patients so hard. She liked his lips – they were sort of thin, but in a sexy kind of way. She had been in therapy of one kind or another for as long as she could remember. So far, he was her favourite.

She was wearing her school shirt and the top two buttons were undone. She played with the next button, slipping it open. She leaned slightly forward, watching for his reaction. He cleared his throat.

'I think about you a lot,' she said.

'I'm your doctor,' he said. 'Our relationship has boundaries that are very important. Do you understand what I mean?'

'I think about you kissing me. I think about it a lot. I don't know why, that's just what I think about.'

His hands were tightly clasped in his lap, like he was afraid of what might happen if he let go. 'This is not a seduction,' he said. 'It's a therapy session. You shouldn't get the wrong idea.'

But she already had lots of her own ideas.

'It could be a seduction,' she said.

'There are other kinds of relationships you can have,' he said. 'I mean, other than sexual.'

She slipped her hand inside her shirt and stroked the velvety skin between her breasts. She slid a finger under the cup of her bra to find her nipple.

'You need to stop the acting out, or we will have to end the session,' he said.

She removed her fingers from her shirt. She sat on both hands. 'Fine. What do you want me to talk about?'

'Only you can know for sure.'

'Give me a break.'

'You're angry now? Shall we take a look at that?'

She shook her head. 'I'm not angry with you.'

She picked at a loose thread on the arm of her chair. She liked having his full attention, but fifty minutes was much too short, too little time. She sighed. He massaged his forehead with his left hand. Was he left- or right-handed? She watched his hand, still stroking his forehead, and pictured his fingers stroking her. She shifted, uncrossed her legs and pressed hard against the base of the chair. She wanted him to fall in love with her, to take her home with him, to look after her, always. She was pretty. Much prettier than most women. Why should he not want her? Lots of men his age wanted to be with her that way, she had proof. And now she wanted him. She slid from the chair on to the floor, giving him a small smile as she moved. She sat on the floor at the bottom of the chair, pulling her knees up to her chest. She didn't say anything.

'I can't read your mind,' he said. 'You have to tell me what you want my help with.'

She lifted her arms up above her head and stretched.

'How are you feeling right now?' he asked.

'Wet. How are you feeling?'

'I'm going to have to end the session for today if this goes on.'

He was nervous. She could see it in his eyes and she could hear it in his voice, all tight and squeezed up. She held on to her knees and rocked, looking up at him. The buttons of his shirt were done up all the way to his throat. He wore a pink tie. He also wore a wedding ring. She wondered what it was like, when they had sex. She hated his wife. It wasn't fair, she was probably some woman who had always had everything: parents who loved each other, and a nice house to grow up in with cats and bloody dogs. A really big, clean house with no shouting and screaming and definitely no drinking. With a bedroom that her parents had decorated for her with pink girly stuff, a bed with a pink duvet and matching pillowcase, a pleated bed frill, a pink wallpaper strip with fairies. She could see it all. Dolls and soft toys. And his wife-to-be would grow up all safe and liking herself and she would go to university and meet a man like him.

It wasn't fair.

But then she was beautiful and she was young. And some men liked young girls. Being pretty could get you a lot. She wanted him. And not just for fifty minutes once a week.

'You asked me how I felt,' she said. 'And now you're going to punish me for telling you the truth.' She *was* pissed off.

He softened, she could see. 'Do you think that sex is going to help you? To get the relationships you want?'

'Maybe. I don't know.'

'Who taught you that the only thing important about you, the only thing of value, is your sexuality?'

'Nobody taught me anything.'

'And you have feelings about that?'

'I don't want to talk about my feelings.'

'So you put a wall between us. A wall of sexuality. And we never get to know the real you, under that barrier.'

'It's not a wall. I want to be close to you. I don't want any wall.'

She crawled towards him on her hands and knees, until she

was at his feet. He didn't move, legs crossed and hands folded in his lap.

'You know our agreement,' he said. 'No acting out. No touching.'

'Please,' she said. 'I just want to rest my head against your knee. No one's ever touched me, or hugged me, never.' OK, that was all lies.

She leaned forward, touching her forehead to his leg. The linen of his trousers felt a little rough against her skin. She could feel the hard edge of his knee as she pressed against him. She closed her eyes.

# Grove Road Clinic, April 2009

Stella pulled out the file marked *Simpson* and skimmed her notes one more time. The family had first come to the attention of social services, and then the Courts, more than a decade earlier; now the case had been handed to her as a twisted mess of accusations and counter-accusations between two warring parents. There were several professionals involved already, and a general air of pessimism prevailed about ever making progress in a case where hatred between the parents obscured every fact and where the child remained a pawn between two factions. Court proceedings had already been lengthy and acrimonious and the state was paying a high price for their domestic warfare.

Nobody knew the truth. Not social services, not the solicitors, not the children's guardian and certainly not the judge – which was why he had asked for a psychological and psychiatric evaluation of both parents.

Stella had summarized two lever-arch files of background documents in preparation for her first appointment with Lawrence Simpson. His daughter had been taken into foster care three months earlier, after she had called emergency services to tell them she had found her mother unconscious in the bathroom after a drinking binge.

According to the most recent statement he had filed, Simpson claimed his ex-wife was an unfit mother and he was seeking sole custody. The mother had a history of alcohol problems and had admitted a relapse, but she was keen to seek treatment.

This most recent incident was not the first time the child had been placed in care: there were three previous incidents, all when she was between the ages of six months and three years old. Each time was related to the mother's substance abuse. Simpson had sought custody before, when his daughter was still a toddler, but in spite of the mother's difficulties, the relationship between mother and child was always described as warm and loving, and Simpson had not succeeded. For the last few years, things seemed to have settled down, and the case had been discharged from social services until the mother's most recent relapse had set the process in motion once more.

Simpson said his ex-wife had a drinking problem long before she met him. But, according to the ex-wife, she had turned to drink when faced with his ongoing abuse, physical and emotional. The ex-wife's credibility was not particularly good. She had been unemployed for several years, after being fired for stealing codeine-based painkillers from the pharmacy where she had been all too briefly employed. She had several admissions to National Health Service rehabilitation facilities.

Details about the relationship between Simpson and his ex-wife over the years were patchy. It seemed that they had separated and re-united several times, but had been living apart for at least six years. Mother and child had lived on benefits in a council flat in a dodgy area where schools were poor. Simpson, on the other hand, had gone from strength to strength after their marriage broke down. He was a general practitioner with a thriving practice in an affluent area, he had a new, steady girlfriend and a three-bed semi.

Stella's boss, Max Fisher, would see the mother and would give an opinion as to whether she suffered from any psychiatric illness, as well as a prognosis regarding her substance dependence. He had asked Stella to formulate a personality profile for the father, a request that pleased her because she thought it reflected a certain level of confidence in her ability. Max had been a consultant for over ten years, while Stella had been qualified for just over two years; it was both a learning curve and a thrill to work alongside him in such a complex case.

Max thought, as a team, they might be the first to succeed.

Stella laid out three blank questionnaires on her desk and placed a pencil and eraser next to the forms. She took a slow breath. She was always both nervous and pleased to meet a new client. Her job involved pronouncing on whether or not people were fit to look after their own children and always, for a moment or two, she felt a fraud: young and inept, hiding behind her title and the posh consulting rooms.

The Grove Road Clinic was housed in three grand red-brick Edwardian buildings. Anne, the practice manager, had created a slick and professional suite of offices, all equipped with antique desks and sleek laptops. The cream walls were adorned with a mix of oil paintings, mainly of flowers and boats. Shutters and double-glazing throughout the building created a tranquil atmosphere, far removed from the busy road outside. It was a great place to work.

A winding, carpeted staircase took Stella from her office

on the first floor to the waiting room downstairs, where the reception area was gently jasmine-scented.

'Your next client is waiting,' Anne said. She tended to hover around the reception desk, keeping an eye on the comings and goings of both patients and staff. She was a study in controlled perfection, with perpetually sleek hair and glossy nails. Her blouse was, as usual, low cut and invited attention to her breasts, which in Stella's opinion were suspiciously firm and upright. Anne arranged her pens, telephone and iPad in lines far too precise and she made Stella apprehensive for no good reason.

She pointed towards the waiting room with the air-conditioning remote control. 'Dr Simpson has been here for twenty minutes,' she said.

Anne managed to imply that Stella was late for her appointment, when in fact the client was early and Stella was precisely on time.

He was waiting for her on the red-leather chesterfield, his arms and legs tightly crossed and his slender body tensed from head to toe. Next to him was a stack of magazines: the latest issues of *Hello*, *Vogue* and *Men's Health* artfully arranged in a spiral by Anne. The light reading matter was untouched.

'Dr Simpson?' Stella asked.

He nodded, unsmiling and ill at ease. Most of her medico-legal clients responded this way on meeting her for the first time, and she did not take it personally. They were required to see her, forced, essentially, by the judges of the family courts. There was tremendous pressure on these parents to present in the best possible light and so they feared her.

Simpson's angular face was clean-shaven. His fair hair was sharply cut and combed to the side. He wore a navy suit with a pristine white shirt and a yellow tie. His black brogues shone. She would note this for her report; he was 'well-groomed' to say the least.

'I'm Dr Davies,' she said. At the mention of her title, she thought she saw him flinch.

He stood and extended his hand, slowly. His eyes flickered up and then down, over her black suit jacket, her skirt and her heels. His handshake was firm and warm. Stella smiled. 'We're on the first floor,' she said.

As he followed her up the stairs, she couldn't help but wonder where his eyes rested. She held open the door to her office and he took his time stepping over the threshold.

She had arranged two chairs at right angles to each other, along the two sides of the desk. 'Take a seat,' she said.

The moment he sat down, he resumed his position from the waiting room, with his arms and legs tightly crossed.

'Before we start, I need you to sign a consent form,' Stella said. 'Please read it carefully. This gives me permission to release the contents of my report to the court.'

She handed him the standard form on a clipboard. He frowned at the page and then signed. His expression was rather acid as he handed it back to her.

'Is it all right with you if I record our interview using my Dictaphone? That way I don't need to take notes.' She smiled once again, pretending she did not notice his displeasure.

'No, it's not all right,' he said.

Stella had never had a client refuse this request. Her clients were told by their solicitors that everything discussed in the interview would be taken down for the report anyway, so there seemed no reason to refuse other than the desire to make her life more difficult.

'It saves me time taking notes as I talk to you,' she said, hopefully.

'No recording,' he said. He glanced around the room as though checking for covert surveillance equipment. He seemed restless, uneasy. It was clear that he found it difficult not to be in charge. He was used to being the person behind the large desk. Stella could relate; she too liked to be in control.

'No problem. I'll type as we talk. I type much quicker than I write.' She kept her tone light, but there was no glimmer of a smile to acknowledge her banter.

She needed to win him over somehow, to find a way to engage him. The shape of his personality – or the personalities of any of her clients – could not be truly known or understood without some level of cooperation. Simpson could, if he wished, say nothing and give nothing away. And then Stella would have to base her opinion on a negative space, on his desire to remain unknown. This would be of little help to either judge or child. Her biggest challenge was to find a way in, a way to earn his trust and to convince him that it was in his best interests to talk to her. She had to convince him that this was his opportunity to tell his side of the story.

She decided to begin with the pen and pencil questionnaires. That way he would not have to answer probing questions straight away.

She pushed a sheet of paper towards his side of the desk. 'Right,' she said. 'Let's start with this one – the instructions are on the top.' She pointed. 'It's straightforward, just true or false answers. But it takes quite a while to complete, about an hour. There are just over five hundred questions.'

She could not help but feel a spark of satisfaction at the look of dismay on his face. It was her turn to score in their subtle battle of wills. Simpson would cooperate, he would complete the questionnaire – he had to if he wanted a chance to gain custody of his daughter, and they both knew it. He lifted the pencil, albeit grudgingly.

He took a very long time over each question.

'I can't say true or false to this statement – it doesn't apply to me,' he said.

'Just pick the one that is closest to the truth for you.'

He delayed, frustrated, Stella guessed, at having to choose between two options that did not reflect his state of mind precisely. But after ten minutes, he seemed to be marking the answers more readily, and she could see he was progressing more quickly down the endless rows of statements.

At one point he laughed, a bitter sound. 'This is ridiculous,' he said. Nevertheless, he made his choice, colouring in a small, dark circle with the tip of his pencil.

'Would you like a cup of tea or coffee?' she asked.

She was not without empathy. She could imagine how the process could feel like a violation, particularly if he had been wrongly accused of being an abuser. And besides, she needed a coffee herself.

'I'd appreciate that,' he said. He seemed grateful for her small act of kindness and Stella sensed a minuscule thawing of the ice. He liked his coffee black, with one sugar, he said.

Stella did not think he was the type to steal her purse while she was out of the room. She did, however, close her laptop and take her file of notes with her.

# Hilltop, 4 p.m.

'Why do you want to see my husband?' Stella asked. Her whole body prickled with suspicion.

'I just need to.' Blue huddled under the blanket, digging herself deeper into the sofa, as though she were trying to put down roots.

'How do you know my husband?'

'I can't tell you.'

'You can tell me. You just won't.'

Stella sat on her sofa, annoyed and also helpless in the face of the girl's stubbornness. She could not force her to tell the truth. She considered what to do. She could call Max and ask him if he knew her. But for some reason, she decided to wait before involving him. She sat still and did nothing for the time being, aware of the tension running from her neck all the way down her spine. She pushed her feet harder against the Chinese rug. She did not take her eyes off Blue, because she did not trust her.

Now that she had let the girl inside, it might not be so easy to get her to leave.

'My husband isn't home,' Stella said. She didn't tell the girl that he was away for the night. She wondered if Blue had come alone – or if she had brought someone with her, someone who waited outside. Opening the door was a mistake. She was lucky no one had rushed at her in the few moments it had been wide open.

She was speculating, imagining, catastrophizing. The girl's motives might not be sinister. She had to stay in control.

'Where is he?' Blue asked. 'Dr Fisher?'

Stella did not answer. She too could withhold information.

'When is he coming home?'

'Later,' Stella said.

Blue sighed and looked irritated. Stella got the feeling she wasn't too good at delaying gratification.

'Can I stay here with you?' Blue asked. 'Until he gets back?'

Physically, she looked like a young adult, but she was childlike with her audacity and her impatience.

'Not if you don't tell me the truth about why you've come here and how you know him.'

'But it's dark outside. And I don't have money to get home.' Blue tucked her legs underneath her and pulled the blanket tighter around her shoulders.

'I'm more than happy to give you money for transport,' Stella said.

'I won't go. I'll just sit outside the door and freeze to death.' She pouted.

'Suit yourself,' Stella said. 'Or maybe you could change your mind and phone your mother.'

They sat in silence on opposite ends of the sofa, both refusing to budge. Stella wondered if she would have to sit there the whole night, watching over Blue, until Max arrived home in the morning.

After a while, she considered that kindness might work

better than the silent treatment. 'Are you still cold?' she asked. 'I can make you something hot to drink.'

Blue nodded. 'Do you have any hot chocolate?'

'No. Tea?'

'OK.'

Stella stood, relieved to put some distance between them as she traced the familiar path to the kitchen. The open-plan design allowed her to keep watch over the girl as she took down two mugs from the open shelves. Blue twisted around on the couch; she watched Stella as intently as Stella watched her.

Stella lifted the kettle and filled it with water. She reached into her glossy cupboards to find teaspoons, sugar, milk. Her thoughts drifted and scattered. The white mugs were the first thing she had ever bought when they had moved into Hilltop. Max wanted to keep his flat in Hampstead fully furnished, so they had started from scratch, with nothing. She could feel her heart beating, she could taste the adrenaline surging. She kept a box of pills next to the box of tea bags, just in case. The orange light clicked off, the kettle was boiled. And even as she tasted the bitterness of the pill on her tongue, her taut muscles eased and her body responded to the promise of calm that would soon come.

Stella walked back to the living room carrying a tray. She already felt lighter, a sensation of gently flowing or floating. Her hands were quite steady. She placed each mug on a coaster on the glass and chrome coffee table. Blue tossed off the blanket, leaned forward and heaped two teaspoons of sugar into her drink. Stella didn't take sugar but, impulsively, she added a heaped spoonful to her tea and stirred. Droplets of scalding tea splashed on to her table. She held on to the mug with both hands and felt her palms begin to burn. Blue's hands trembled as she lifted her mug.

'Well?' Stella said. She attempted to sound kind yet authoritative. 'Why did you come out here in the freezing cold to see my husband?'

Blue took a sip of her tea, gazing at Stella over the rim of her mug. She took her time, placed the mug slowly back down on the coaster. 'I think he's my father,' she said.

'What?' Stella was confused.

The blue eyes were watchful. The girl took another cautious sip of her hot drink.

Stella composed herself. 'What makes you think he's your father?' she asked, calmly.

Blue took her time, thinking about her answer. In the delay, Stella had already decided she did not believe her.

Eventually, Blue said: 'I found something to prove it.'

'Found what, exactly?'

'My birth certificate.'

'Where?'

'In my mother's bedroom. It was hidden – at the back of a drawer.'

'Did you bring it with you?' Stella asked.

'No.'

'Well, that's a surprise.'

'Don't you believe me?' Blue asked.

Stella didn't answer and didn't look at her. She stared ahead at the crackling fire. Her tea had cooled and she drank it, even though it was too sweet and too milky, not the way she liked it at all. Her body felt pleasingly light, as though she drifted along the top of a gentle wave.

'I'm not a liar,' Blue said. She leaned forwards and put her hand on Stella's forearm. Stella wasn't sure if her touch was a plea or a threat. When Stella did not respond, Blue tightened her grip. Stella became aware of drops of sweat beading along her hairline and her top lip. She pushed the girl's hand away.

'Have you ever met my husband?' she asked.

'No.'

'So besides apparently seeing his name on your birth certificate, what else do you know about him?'

'My mother said he's a doctor.'

'Did your mother also tell you his home address?'

Blue nodded, too quickly, and Stella regretted the leading question.

'I didn't think you'd let me in if I told you the truth,' Blue said. 'That's why I said I used to live here. I'm not a liar.'

Max had blue eyes too – but his were a cloudier, greyer shade than Blue's. And Blue's hair was so fair, her skin so pale. So unlike Max. Stella tried to remember if her husband had ever mentioned a Nordic girlfriend. Not that she could recall. But then Max was not short of either charm or previous relationships. She wondered how he might react, and whether he might like to have a daughter. They had never discussed having children. They both knew Stella was in no fit state to be a parent.

She tried to stay rational. The girl was a teenager – any liaison that might have produced her would have taken place long before Stella and Max had even met. But she didn't feel rational, she felt jealous. And resentful and confused about why Max might have kept this from her. About another woman sharing his child.

Blue began biting her thumbnail, her small white teeth chipping away at the red polish. It looked as though she might draw blood, the way she attacked her own skin.

'Don't bite your nails,' Stella said.

Blue stopped. 'I'm hungry. Do you have anything to eat?'

Stella almost smiled, it all seemed so absurd. 'Not really,' she said. 'There's not much in the house.'

'Could we get a takeaway or something?'

'In this weather? No. No one can get up the hill, most places are closed.' Then she regretted what she'd said; she had only emphasized her vulnerability and her isolation. They were trapped. Together.

'You must have *something* to eat,' Blue said.

'I can make you a sandwich,' Stella said. 'I think I have some ham, or tuna.'

'I'm a vegetarian.'

'I see.'

'I don't like to think of killing animals.'

'Good for you.'

'What about peanut butter?' Blue asked.

Stella did have peanut butter. She stood, once again feeling a release of the tension that had built up while she sat next to the girl on the sofa.

Blue wriggled underneath the pink-and-green checked blanket and pulled it up around her face. She stretched out, resting her head on a yellow silk cushion. Her long blonde hair flowed over the arm of the couch.

Perhaps the girl had come to steal. Stella thought about everything that should be locked away: jade ornaments that had belonged to Max's mother, silver picture frames and, most importantly, her diamond earrings, her graduation present. She decided she couldn't be bothered. Everything could be replaced, nothing was important.

Out of habit, Stella listened for the sound of Max's key turning in the lock; the sound that signalled the end of a day's

35

solitude. On his way home, he might stop in at the Tesco opposite the station to pick up the items she had asked for: milk, bread, Perrier water, kitchen roll – whatever banalities she needed. She no longer cooked for him. It would take him a few more minutes to drive down Station Road and then up the hill towards Hilltop. A couple of days a month, he finished too late to make it back from London to Buckinghamshire and so he stayed in the Hampstead apartment. On those nights, Stella took an extra sleeping pill.

Blue's eyes were closed.

Stella laid down the knife she was holding. She approached the sofa, moving slowly. The girl's breathing was even and she seemed to be asleep. Stella hoped the drowsiness wasn't the result of hypothermia. Again, she felt guilty for leaving her outside in the cold so long. She couldn't be sure that Blue meant her any harm. Perhaps she was in trouble, in need of help. Stella picked up Blue's bag from where she had dropped it, next to the sofa. It wasn't heavy and there wasn't much inside: a thin leather purse, small and square, with a five-pound note and a few coins. That was it. Nothing that might identify her and no mobile phone. So she couldn't even have tried phoning the taxi company. And as for her claim about being Max's daughter – Stella had no idea what to make of it. Basically, the only thing she really knew about the girl was that she was a vegetarian.

Blue lay still and pale on the sofa. Her lips were no longer a harsh purple but had faded to a delicate pink. Stella reached out and touched the girl's forehead with her fingertips. Her temperature felt normal, if slightly cold. She tucked the blanket tighter around the girl's small body. Still, she did not move. A strand of soft, golden hair had fallen across her face and Stella smoothed it away.

\*

Stella left the living room and crossed the hallway into her study. She could see nothing through the window; the garden was in complete darkness. She flicked a switch and the snow-covered ground was flooded with yellow light. There was no one outside. No one that she could see. She pulled the curtains closed.

She left the door slightly ajar, so she could see if Sleeping Beauty stirred.

She tried to reach her husband, but his mobile went straight to voicemail. She left a message, casually asking that he call her back.

She needed to talk to someone. Now. And it wasn't as though she had many options. She hesitated. The number was still saved in her phone.

He answered after three rings. 'Harris.'

Stella coughed.

'Hello?' He sounded rushed and impatient; harsher than she remembered.

'Peter, it's me.' She cleared her throat. 'Stella.'

'Stella?' He must have deleted her number. Under-standably, he was surprised to hear from her.

'I'm sorry to disturb you,' she said. 'I need some advice. Professional advice.'

'What about?' His tone was cool and crisp. She felt she was talking to a stranger. But at least, if he thought it un-reasonable, her asking for his advice after all this time, he didn't say so.

'There's a girl in my house. A stranger. She came to my front door earlier and I let her in. She kept ringing the doorbell and – it's freezing outside. She's young. I was worried she'd get hypothermia or something. Anyway she's inside now, she's passed out on the sofa, and I'm not sure what to do. I'm alone in house with her.'

He must think her a fool. He must think that she was looking to get herself hurt.

'Where the hell are you?' he asked.

'We live just outside London. Max and I. We're married.'

'Congratulations.'

She couldn't see his face, she couldn't tell what it was he meant.

'It's lovely out here,' she said. 'And it takes less than an hour to get into central London.' Her words sounded absurd. She dug her fingernails into her palm and stared at her wedding band. 'I didn't ever go back to work,' she said.

She ran her fingers along the leather top of her desk, a small fifties beauty from Belgium, the legs in polished steel. She had bought it years ago from her favourite antique shop in Camden Town. Peter's voice made her feel sad for her old life.

'How about you?' she asked. She pictured him as she had seen him last: cropped grey hair and stocky build, in his jeans and his black raincoat, standing outside the door of the Hampstead flat.

'Not married. Still living in London. Still a DI with the Met. So – there's a problem with a girl?'

'I think she's about fourteen or fifteen,' Stella said. 'She rang the doorbell saying she wanted to come inside, that she used to live in our house. Now she's admitted that was a lie. And I'm not convinced she's told me her real name, either. I'm not sure what to do.'

'Have you talked to Max?'

'He's away,' she said. 'For the night. I can't get hold of him.' She began to ramble. 'We're snowed in. There's almost half a metre of snow piled up all over the driveway. That's how she got past the sensor.'

Stella moved the mobile phone over to her other ear; her face was hot and the handset was sweaty.

'How long has she been at your place?'

'About two hours. I left her waiting outside for almost an hour before I let her in. I had to let her in. I was worried she might die of cold.'

'Did she say where she's come from?'

'London. And – something else,' Stella said. 'She knew Max's name. And she claims that Max is her father. Her long-lost father. She says she just found out.'

'I see.' And the coldness was back between them. 'Is that why you called me? Because you're pissed off with Max?'

'No. I called you because he's not picking up his phone and my gut is telling me something is wrong.' Although her gut wasn't too reliable, it was always telling her something was wrong. 'There's something about her – I don't trust her.'

She waited. He did not offer to rush over and help her. She could hardly blame him. 'Are you still there?' she said.

'Yes. Do you think her mother knows where she is?'

'I don't know. She said something about a fight.'

'What advice are you looking for?' he asked.

'What do you think I should do?'

The silence was ripe. When he spoke, his words were tight and cold.

'My advice would be to call your local police station. Get them to check her name and description and see if she's been reported missing. Or,' he said, 'you could wait for your husband to answer his phone and ask him what he thinks you should do.'

'Right,' she said.

'Or – you could make up your own mind.'

'I see,' she said. 'Well, that's clear. Thanks.' Her own voice was small and useless. She didn't hang up.

'Are you frightened?' he said. The sudden kindness in his voice was painful.

'I feel pathetic.' It must be obvious to him now: how weak she was, how helpless. He would know that she had not moved on at all. He would remember how different she used to be.

'You're not pathetic,' he said. 'You said something about sensors – so there's security in the house?'

'There's an alarm system. Sensors on all the windows and doors.'

'And –' he paused – 'do you think she's alone?'

She swallowed, feeling a sick twisting in her gut. 'I have no idea. I suppose if she was with someone – they would have forced their way in when I opened the door.'

Then he relented, just a little. 'If you give me some details, I can check for any reports of girls her age missing across London. But that's it.'

'Thank you. She says her name is Blue Cunningham.'

'Blue?'

'Apparently. And it's not a nickname.'

'What does she look like?'

'Caucasian. Blue eyes, long blonde hair – halfway down her back. She's petite – maybe five foot one – and thin. She's wearing black leggings and a leather kind of shortish coat. White T-shirt, beanie hat. White Nike trainers, no socks. I would guess she's in her mid-teens, but she could pass for older.'

'Any distinguishing features?'

'I'm not sure. Not that I've noticed. She's beautiful.'

'If I find out anything useful, I'll call you back.' Already, he sounded distracted. He sounded as though he wished she hadn't called him, hadn't involved him in another of her dramas.

Abruptly, Stella bashed at the red button to disconnect the call. She didn't want to consider what he thought of her now.

She was trapped inside her home with a stranger. Overnight. She didn't think she could make it that long. Already, her anxiety threatened to triumph over the drugs. It wasn't safe to take any more pills. She had to stay alert.

# Session Five

She said: 'I had a dream about you last night.'

His expression didn't change and he didn't say anything.

'I thought therapists were *supposed* to be interested in dreams,' she said.

She watched her hand moving slowly up and down along the arm of the chair. She rubbed the raised crimson flowers until they disappeared under her fingertips. She felt far away, removed from her own body, as though she was looking at someone else's hand moving back and forth. The strange, disconnected feeling was not unfamiliar.

She was sitting in an oversized wing-back armchair. The curtains were drawn and the soft light in the room came from a lamp in the corner. These fifty minutes in his office were her favourite part of the day.

He sat opposite her and his chair was exactly the same as hers, with the same crimson flowers on a beige background. A matching pair. She felt hot and fidgety. He was too far away. Even if she stretched out her legs she couldn't touch him. She wondered if he thought she was pretty. She didn't care about boys her own age, she only wanted him.

'So, do you want me to tell you about my dream?' she asked.

'If you'd like to,' he said.

'I wish my dreams were real.'

'There's a big difference between dreams and reality. You know that.'

The air between them crackled with anticipation and excitement and a strange sort of hope. Her skin prickled and tingled; he made her nervous and excited all at the same time. The sky had clouded over and the room had darkened.

'I dreamt you touched me,' she said. She was half embarrassed, half excited.

He shifted around in his chair and crossed his legs tight. She stifled a giggle.

He didn't say anything more. He wasn't a big talker. She was dying to know what he was thinking when he looked at her. He was much older than she was, but she didn't mind. Maybe that made her weird, being interested in someone so old. She didn't care.

She let herself slide down and inched across, closer, until she was sitting on the floor at the base of the big chair, staring up at him. She put her thumb between her teeth and bit down gently.

She reached up and found his fingers, and wriggled her own in between until their hands were intertwined. She looked down at the swirling patterns of the carpet, full of longing.

# Grove Road Clinic, April 2009

Stella was relieved to be away from her reluctant client for a few minutes. She took shelter in the compact, well-equipped kitchen along the hallway. The small space, not more than two metres long and even narrower than that, was another of Anne's many triumphs. The modern kitchen included all the essentials: hob, fridge and coffee maker; it was always neat and clean and well stocked with snacks for the staff, healthy stuff, nuts and dried fruit, as well as a selection of biscuits. Stella needed a stiff combination of sugar and caffeine to get through the next two hours so she opened the tin and found a biscuit covered in thick chocolate. She poured her coffee into an elegant yet bland cream-coloured mug. She took a sip. Anne always put too little coffee into the filter and she could barely taste it; she would have to start all over again.

'A question, Stella.' Max was standing in the doorway looking bemused as she poured the entire pot of coffee down the plughole. 'I've been referred a case where they're looking to confirm a diagnosis of Asperger's in a fourteen-year-old. How would you feel about taking that one on?'

Max Fisher, psychiatrist and now Stella's boss, owned the

Grove Road Clinic. He had managed to secure financing for the building four years earlier, just before the recession hit, and he had worked hard to lure Harley Street specialists away from the city centre to work in his state-of-the-art facilities. Initially, his plan had been to attract residents in the surrounding areas stretching from St John's Wood to Hampstead, where they weren't short of disposable income and had good health insurance. The practice offered cutting-edge diagnostic equipment and a range of specialties: ultrasound imaging, physiotherapy, psychotherapy, gynaecology, even speech therapy. But the ever-increasing business closures, job losses and redundancies had changed the landscape of their work and there were fewer patients than Max had hoped for. Four years later, the clinic was not quite paying its own way, and Max put all his energies into keeping the place afloat. Contracts for medico-legal work, funded by government agencies, had become more central to the survival of his clinic than he could have foreseen. That was when Stella became important.

She replaced the empty coffee pot on to the counter and pushed her hair back from her face. 'Sure. I used to work in the complex-needs clinic in Camden. I've had experience in assessment of social-communication disorders.' Her words sounded rather stilted and self-conscious. He had that effect on her.

'How soon could you offer the appointments?' he asked.

'I'll need the next two weeks to write up the Simpson report. So any time after that.'

'That's great,' he said. He always sounded as though he was genuinely grateful she had agreed to do her job. 'I'll tell Anne to draft the letters – if you'll just give her your available appointment times.'

She nodded. 'Sure.'

Creases appeared around his eyes, when he smiled at her.

She did not see her feelings for her boss as being a problem. They were simply another reason she was always happy to come to work, a consolation for all the overtime she worked. She wanted to impress him, to please him.

Lawrence Simpson was where she had left him: diligently filling in the questionnaire, his head down. He did not look up as she walked in.

'Thank you,' he said, as he reached for the mug, his expression earnest as his fringe flopped on to his forehead.

While she was out of the room, he had put on a pair of reading glasses and, wearing these, he looked far more vulnerable. From her chair at the opposite side of the desk, she peered over at the questionnaire. He was halfway through the answer sheet. He must have worked more quickly while she was out of the room. Perhaps he did not like being scrutinized. Or perhaps he could see better with his glasses on.

He looked up and caught her eye. She smiled at him, hopeful that the mood of their meeting had begun to shift away from the tense, oppositional manner in which it had begun. She opened her laptop to start formatting the report. Simpson sharpened his pencil and then pressed on with the questionnaire without further complaint. It took him seventy minutes to finish the personality test. Stella put it aside to score later.

He declined to take a break, and so they went straight on to the clinical interview. Stella decided to change the way they were seated. She came out from behind the imposing desk and invited Simpson to sit opposite her, on one of the more comfortable chairs placed in the centre of the room.

'What's your understanding of why the judge has asked for a psychological assessment?' she asked him.

'My ex-wife has proved, over and over again, that she is not a competent parent. I'm assuming you know the background – she had problems looking after our daughter right from the start. She's an alcoholic. She also suffers from borderline personality disorder. I want a chance to take over, to do it properly, to give my child a stable home.'

'But, in your opinion – what are the problems that you might have had in parenting?'

'I suppose I knew the relationship wasn't right from the beginning but I didn't want to admit it, especially when she fell pregnant. It wasn't planned – stupid, I know, given my profession – but I was excited to be a father and I loved that baby from the first second. I practically delivered her. My ex-wife couldn't cope with a child. She was too emotionally fragile herself, too needy. She wanted all of my attention. I was working ungodly hours as a registrar and trying to pay the mortgage. I was exhausted and irritable, I fully admit that. But when I came home I wanted to focus on the baby, because I was worried about what she was getting – or not getting – from her mother. I'm assuming you've read all the documents? It started in the first few days – the baby was starving and she was completely unreasonable, refusing to supplement with a bottle. The health visitor had to intervene or God knows what would have happened. There are so many examples I could give you.'

He sighed.

His ex-wife had a rather different version of events. According to her, Simpson was jealous when she focused her attention on the baby. He was angry at the length of time it took her to breastfeed the colicky newborn and would snatch the child from her and insist on giving it a bottle. He wouldn't allow the baby to sleep in their room because he hated that his ex-wife wanted the child close to her at all times. And he wouldn't allow her to go to the baby if the child cried during the night. He insisted on sleep training, allowing their daughter to cry herself to sleep for an hour or more, from the time she was three weeks old.

'Dr Simpson, so far you've talked about your ex-wife's problems. But we're really here to focus on you,' Stella said.

There was a slight tightening of his lips, a pulling down.

'Your ex-wife has made several serious allegations and that's the reason why the judge has asked for this assessment as part of custody proceedings. Do you have any insight into the difficulties *you* have that may have contributed to problems in your marriage or problems in parenting?'

In response to her question, Simpson continued his monologue. 'She couldn't stand my devotion to my daughter. And so she punished me, first by drinking and then by trying to take my child away from me. She knows damn well she's not capable of being a decent parent. I can offer my daughter a good life. A home we own, a garden, private schools. My ex-wife has been evicted from properties twice in the last two years for non-payment of rent, for God's sake.'

Stella interrupted. 'You think that your ex-wife started drinking to punish you?' His view of the world seemed rather egocentric.

'Her father was an alcoholic too. I'm sure there's some kind of genetic component.'

'I see,' Stella said.

Simpson was in his comfort zone while talking about his ex-wife's problems and he was performing what appeared to be a well-practised character assassination. Unfortunately for

Stella, his sole purpose was to malign his ex-wife, not to reveal anything of interest about himself.

'My ex-wife was very beautiful when she was younger,' he said. 'You wouldn't believe it to see her now. She's let herself go in every way.'

He never referred to his ex-wife by her name. Stella had seen her as she was now: bloated and defeated. She had to wonder if this might have something to do with her life with Simpson.

Stella decided to change tack. She interviewed Simpson about his personal history, his childhood and his schooling. But this exchange turned out to be bland and boring as all hell – for both clinician and client. Simpson refused to talk to her about anything meaningful or close to his heart. His childhood was apparently 'good' and 'completely normal'. He had a 'great' relationship with both parents. School was 'fine', he enjoyed it. Etcetera. He gave her nothing, no access to his inner life.

Stella found that she had begun to take a deep breath before asking each question. Each enquiry, any attempt to get to know him, seemed to be perceived as some sort of attack. He was intensely, impossibly, guarded. She felt drained. It was stressful for her too, being with someone who hated every minute of their interaction and who resisted all the way. She reminded herself that the interview, frustrating as it was, was all good data – of one sort or another.

She put her hand over her eyes, closing them for a brief second. At that moment, a terrible piercing sound shattered the genteel atmosphere of the Grove Road Clinic. A sound so loud it was painful.

Stella was disoriented. It took her a few seconds to realize it was the smoke alarm.

'We need to go to the nearest fire exit,' she said.

She knew she shouldn't do it, but she couldn't resist the urge to pack her laptop into her bag. The thought of losing all of her work was unbearable.

Simpson followed her out of the office, but at the top of the staircase he stopped. Instead of following her to the end of the passageway, he took the stairs instead. Stella carried on, towards the fire exit. By the time she heaved open the exit door and looked behind her, he had disappeared.

She climbed down the metal staircase along the side of the building. She was cold; she had left her coat in the consulting room. Anne was already at the meeting point at the bottom of the stairs. She looked even chillier than Stella, in her low-cut top. She seemed to be on the telephone to the fire department. Paul, the psychotherapist, was outside too, in his white socks and sensible sandals.

'Where's Max?' Stella asked.

Paul shook his head. 'No idea.'

'He left for a meeting,' Anne said, covering the mouthpiece.

The three of them waited, impatient to be let back into the building. Stella had never heard the siren go off before and she feared there might really be a fire. Max would be devastated. And she wondered what on earth her client was up to, more uneasy about her case file than his safety. She should have grabbed it as she left the office. He could be reading through her notes as the staff waited, helpless, outside the building.

The alarm stopped. Minutes later, Simpson appeared at the front door of the clinic.

'There's no fire,' he said. 'But there were two incense sticks burning in one of the rooms on the ground floor and the smoke set off your fire alarm.'

He held up the two offending incense sticks as proof. Anne looked accusingly at Paul.

'I've never had a problem with incense sticks before,' Paul said.

'It's quite safe,' Simpson said. 'I've checked all the consulting rooms. You're perfectly safe to come back inside.'

When Stella and her client resumed their positions in the first-floor office, his posture was more open, his arms relaxed and placed casually along the armrests, both feet solidly on the floor.

'Are you all right?' he asked Stella. He was staring at her, looking right into her eyes. Intelligence and curiosity flickered in his gaze.

'I'm fine,' she said. It was a strange sensation, and mildly embarrassing, to have been vulnerable in front of a client, for him to have seen her confused and rushing for the fire exit. But the pay-off appeared to be that he had dropped his aloof and irritable stance and she was allowed to glimpse a gentler side. He seemed happier, now that he had performed an act of heroism. Or, maybe, if she took a more cynical view, if he saw himself as her protector, then she must be the powerless female and that was what made him happy. Regardless, his need to be the good guy was a lot more charming than the guarded stance he had taken up until that point.

Just as Stella had retrieved her interview schedule, there was a light knock on the door and Anne stepped inside, without waiting for an invitation. 'I just wanted to thank you, Dr Simpson,' she said.

'Glad I could help.'

'We have warned him about those incense sticks,' Anne said.

Stella was annoyed to have her intrude on the assessment session. The support staff at the clinic knew better than to disturb any of the clinicians when they were with clients, but Anne tended to act with impunity. Stella wondered sometimes about the nature of Anne's relationship with Max Fisher. Anne's French-manicured fingernails played with the diamond-encrusted bee that dangled from the thin gold chain around her neck and hung just above the V of her blouse.

'Thanks, Anne,' Stella said in a tone that indicated she should leave the room as soon as possible.

Anne gave her client the once-over. 'Can I offer you a cup of tea or coffee?' she said. As she spoke, she ran her fingers through her hair, the sharply cut bob that swung just above her shoulders. Stella felt for the chunky plastic clamp from Boots that she had used to pin her own hair up that morning. She couldn't remember the last time she'd been near a hairdresser. Her suit, too, could do with a trip to the dry-cleaners. Between her student loan, rent and utilities, she barely came out even.

She noted that Anne had not bothered to offer her a cup of anything.

Stella admired Simpson's self-control as he kept his eyes firmly locked on Anne's face. 'Dr Davies has already been kind enough to make me one,' he said.

Stella imagined that Anne looked disappointed as she made her gracious exit, leaving behind her a lingering, musky scent.

'I hope you don't mind,' Simpson said, 'my having a look around the building. I just know how these things go. We could have been waiting outside for an hour while the fire department turned up and searched the place. We would all have lost an afternoon's work, and I can't afford to take off much more time. You have no idea how many appointments I've got to attend for the court case.'

Stella nodded. 'It's fine. We all appreciate your help.'

'You're sure?'

'Of course. Thank you,' she said. She decided that the time was right, with his eagerness to impress her and his guard down, to move on to the more challenging part of the interview.

'Dr Simpson,' she said. 'I need to ask you about some of the more difficult material in the background documents. Some of the accusations your ex-wife has made against you.'

He nodded. 'As long as you actually listen to my answers,' he said.

He didn't change his open posture, but his fingers tightened around the arm of the chair. The tension was back.

'Of course.' She flipped open her case file to a page she had marked with a Post-it note.

'Your ex-wife has said in her statement that you physically abused her, over a number of years. She claims that it started when she was pregnant, and that you would hit her on her torso and upper arms, so that the bruises could be hidden under her clothes.'

Simpson gave a bitter laugh. 'Unbelievable,' he said.

'Are her allegations true?'

He shook his head.

'Do you want to say anything more about this?' she asked him.

'Why should I? It's a pack of lies.'

Stella turned to another page she had marked. 'In 2003,' she said, 'your ex-wife presented at Accident and Emergency with a broken nose. She told nursing staff that you had punched her. After she was discharged, she changed her mind. She said she'd fallen in the bathroom after a night of heavy drinking. Within twenty-four hours she had withdrawn her complaint and I understand you were back together.'

'Exactly,' he said. 'That's exactly what she does. It proves my point. She acts out, to punish me, then when she sobers up, she begs me to go back to her. Have you ever lived with an alcoholic? You have no idea. It's basically a living hell.'

'There were some suspicions that there was pressure on your ex-wife, from you, to withdraw her initial statement.'

'Look,' he leaned forward, his face twisted, 'I don't have to sit and listen to this crap. I've been tormented enough with these false claims.'

'I'm not doing this to torment you,' Stella said. 'I'm raising this so you have a chance to respond, to give your version of what happened. Whatever you say will be documented in my report, so you get a chance to have your views on record. So is there any comment you'd like to make?'

Simpson leaned back and looked away from her, towards the examining bed against the wall. She could see the tightness in his jaw as he clenched his teeth.

'It's no use,' he said. 'There's no point. This has been going on for years. It doesn't matter what I say.' He had softened, a sadness rising up in him.

'I think it does matter,' Stella said. 'But I can't force you to open up.'

He looked at her, held her gaze for a few moments. 'Imagine what it's like,' he said. 'Imagine how you'd feel if someone made up the most vile, the most disgusting things imaginable and said you'd done them.'

Stella nodded. There were a few moments of calm silence between them.

'There were a few more things I wanted to ask you about,' Stella said. She kept her eyes on her notes. 'According to your ex-wife, when she first asked you to leave the house, she would come home to find windows had been smashed and there was damage to some of her property – her computer was full of water damage, her tyres were slashed. She blames you for these incidents and she thinks you were trying to frighten her or punish her, to intimidate her into letting you back into the home. Do you want to respond to that?'

He spoke slowly and deliberately. 'These accusations paint me as a monster,' he said. 'And there is nothing I can do about it.'

'So you deny all of it?'

'All I've got to say is this.' He was making eye contact again and his voice rose as he kept it steady, trying but not quite succeeding in controlling his anger. 'You need to understand that the drinking made her less and less able to look after a child, even to meet her most basic needs. I hope you've read the social worker's report, because it's all there. When she was a baby – the only way I could have prevented her being shunted off to foster care was if I had stayed home and given up my medical training. Maybe I should have. But I was terrified of losing my career and losing our house if I couldn't pay the mortgage. I was out there, slogging to put a roof over our heads. I did what I could. As soon as I was on my feet, I applied for custody. I poured her bottles of drink down the sink when I found them. I restricted the money I gave her so she couldn't spend it on drink. Of course it didn't work. Her need for alcohol is her one and only priority. Not me, not our daughter.'

He wiped at his eyes with the back of his hand. Stella wanted to pass him the box of tissues but she hesitated, he was so easily offended. She looked down at her notes and flipped to the third section of background documents. The ex-wife had claimed that he did not give her enough money to buy food or clothing for their daughter and would not allow her access to their joint bank account. She had to ask her parents for financial help. She claimed she had once had to beg him for money for sanitary pads.

Stella knew she could not risk being too strongly influenced by his ex-wife's claims. The problem was that once an allegation was made, it was repeated over and over again in the mountain of background documents: in the social worker's report, the guardian's report, the case summary – until it became its own truth. She felt herself sinking, being sucked into the same vortex of contradictions every other professional had faced while working on the case.

Simpson had composed himself. His eyes were dry again. He began to speak. 'I blame myself for the fact that my daughter has once again had to be put in a foster home. I should have seen it coming. I should have fought harder. Of course her mother is never going to change. Of course she's not. How many times must my daughter lose her home, or be placed in the care of some stranger?'

He sat back, pushing his fringe away and taking a breath to calm himself. 'I lost that first house because every cent I had went into fighting custody proceedings. But I've clawed it all back – I have my own practice, a new house, a stable relationship. Gemma and I have been together for over a year and there have been no problems at all. What more do I have to do to convince you people?'

Stella was beginning to grow impatient with his tendency

to answer every question by launching into a list of complaints about his ex-wife. 'Well,' she said, 'if the situation is so clear-cut, why do you think the judge has asked for a personality assessment? There is concern about your ability to parent. There is concern about potential risk factors.'

'If you've decided to believe everything my lunatic of an ex-wife has to say, I haven't got a hope, have I?' He stood up.

He most certainly did not like being challenged. She was disappointed. He had withdrawn again so quickly and the prickly, closed façade was back in place. Completely.

She was left looking up at him, powerless to engage his cooperation and feeling somehow foolish. He was tall, around six foot two, and while not powerfully built – more on the sinewy side – she felt small looking up at him. She was aware of the difference not only in their respective sizes, but in their ages. He must have fifteen years on her. She felt young, an impostor. She had been *Dr Davies* for all of two years and sometimes the title still felt like a fraud.

'I've tried to explain,' she said. 'This interview is your chance to talk about yourself, not only to give your opinion about other people. I would like you to allow me insight into your personality. But you're not doing that.'

She looked at the clock. The two-hour session had come to an end.

Simpson had noticed her checking the time. 'I know my way out,' he said.

She stood, straightening her skirt.

Stella was eager to score the personality test because she thought it was the best chance she had of salvaging any useful information from their fraught first appointment. She suspected that Simpson would come under the profile known as 'faking good', in that he would not admit any psychological problems, even those milder ones commonly experienced by everyone from time to time. But she was curious – there just might be something that could give her insight into his personality profile. Something he had not intended to reveal. She entered his responses – more than five hundred of them – into the computer programme and waited while the report was generated.

She was disappointed. Simpson had succeeded in staying out of sight. So far as the validity scales indicated, the profile was invalid. It could not be interpreted. Stella could comment, of course, on his reticence in the clinical interview and his guardedness. All of the data so far pointed to someone who had no wish to be known and who refused to give any insight into his inner life. Someone who might have something to hide. He would succeed in his efforts, to some extent, but in reality he wasn't doing himself any favours. If he was determined to do so, he could conceal his emotional difficulties, but then he also deprived himself of the opportunity to showcase his strengths. And his behaviour with her didn't bode well for his future cooperation with professionals around the wellbeing of his daughter.

Stella stood up and stretched. She flipped open the shutters and looked out of the window at the four lanes of traffic outside. It was rush hour and the cars were at a standstill, bumper to bumper. She was frustrated. This had been an opportunity to demonstrate her skills and to shed some light on a case that others had found impenetrable. She would talk to Max, see if he had any ideas about how she might approach the second interview. She knew in her gut, the strength of her report would hinge on being able to engage Simpson, on gaining his trust. If he relaxed a little, got to know her – if he understood that she was fair – perhaps she was in with a chance. She wondered if his stand-offish, guarded behaviour might be driven by an undiagnosed anxiety disorder; an irritable depression, even. Because there were moments when he seemed – decent. He had appeared so pleased to have rescued the clinic from Paul's incense sticks.

Stella ran through the background documents again in her mind. Some of the claims were horrifying. One image in particular kept coming back to her. His ex-wife had described how Simpson had punched her belly while she was seven months pregnant. But then again, these were allegations from an unreliable, substance-dependent witness who was fighting tooth and nail for custody of her only daughter.

Stella had to convince Simpson that it was in his best interests to let her in. She believed him when he said he loved his daughter and wanted the best for her. But his love alone didn't mean he was capable of providing her with a home where she was physically and emotionally safe.

She packed the test materials away and straightened up her desk. She closed the blinds. She would write up her findings so far over the weekend, in preparation for her supervision session with Max on Monday. And she would have to think creatively about how to approach the next appointment with Lawrence Simpson.

## Hilltop, 5.30 p.m.

Stella had laid out plates, glasses and serviettes, but had decided against putting out any cutlery, just in case. Blue chose the chair at the head of the vast kitchen table and began to pick unenthusiastically at the sandwich Stella had prepared.

Stella sat next to her. 'How about a thank you?' she said.

'Thank you,' Blue said, ungratefully.

'You don't seem very hungry,' Stella said.

'You can't force me to eat.'

'I'm not interested in forcing you to do anything.'

Blue kept her eyes down as she pushed the sandwich from one side of her plate to the other. She hadn't eaten more than a mouthful. Stella supposed the request for food had been a ploy, to ensure she was allowed to stay in the house a little longer.

Blue yawned. 'I'm still tired. Why did you wake me?' She looked resentfully at her host.

'It's getting late. I need to phone someone to let them know you're safe,' Stella said.

'I told you – there's no one.' Blue shifted the sandwich to the opposite side of her plate.

'There must be someone,' Stella said.

Blue shook her head.

'Well, we need to find a way to get you home.' In truth, any hopes Stella may have had for a swift departure were fading. She was less and less optimistic that the girl would leave voluntarily.

'I told you – I'm not going home.' Blue pulled off the crusts and discarded them. 'Have you got any Coke?'

'No.' Stella poured them each a glass of water from the jug on the table. 'How old are you?' she asked.

'Eighteen,' Blue said.

'I don't think so.'

'Sixteen.'

'It would be so much easier if you told me the truth.'

The scene in the kitchen had begun to resemble an interrogation, but somehow Stella had ended up in the wrong place. She sat directly under a bright enamel industrial pendant lamp that hung over the long white kitchen table, casting a harsh light that hurt her eyes.

'I'm not a liar,' Blue said. She was digging her nails into her forearm and staring at the floor.

'Be careful, you'll hurt yourself.' Stella pointed to Blue's short, ragged-edged nails with their chipped red polish. Blue stopped and pulled the sleeves of her top over her hands.

'Does your mother know you've come here to see my husband?' Stella asked.

'No.'

'She might think something has happened to you. We have to contact her.'

Blue peered up at Stella from under her fringe. Stella imagined a flicker of guilt in her expression.

'You don't even know my mother,' Blue said. 'Why should you care?'

'My husband won't be home until much later. We can't leave your mum waiting that long. I need to know your home telephone number.'

'I don't have to tell you anything.'

Stella, tired of watching Blue dismember her sandwich, went to retrieve the half-empty bottle of Chardonnay from the living-room coffee table and poured herself a glass. It was not a good idea to drink on top of her pills, but what the hell.

Blue stared at Stella and at the glass of wine. 'You don't have any Coke but you've got wine,' she said. She appeared to be making some sort of accusation.

Stella took another sip.

'It's not even six o'clock,' Blue said.

'I don't usually drink at this time,' Stella said. 'I'm in shock – you, turning up at my front door, and saying that my husband is your father. Do you know someone who drinks too much?'

The girl nodded.

'Is it your mum?' Stella asked.

'Vodka,' Blue said. 'She thinks it doesn't smell but I still know.'

'Is there anyone else that looks after you? Grandparents?'

'Just me and my mum,' Blue said. She stretched her arms above her head so that her T-shirt rode up even further, exposing more of her flat belly and then her sharp hipbones. She reached across the table to lift up Stella's glass. 'Does he like this wine?' she asked.

Stella wondered if Blue had inherited her beauty from her mother. Again, that unreasonable flicker of jealousy. She wondered if Max might be happy to have a daughter, and whether Blue might have more claim to his heart than she herself did. She hoped this girl was not his.

'How many bedrooms does this house have?' Blue asked.

'Quite a few.'

'It's so quiet,' Blue said. 'I don't like this place, it gives me the creeps.'

'I'm sorry to hear that,' Stella said.

'How long have you been married?' Blue asked. She rocked back and forth, teetering on the back legs of her chair. It was extremely irritating to watch her.

'A little more than a year.'

'You're younger than he is.' Blue looked thoughtfully at Stella, examining her face. 'His hair is sort of grey,' she said.

'I thought you said you'd never met him?'

'I saw his photograph. On the internet.'

Blue took a sip from Stella's glass. 'Mm,' she said. She lifted the bottle of wine and filled the glass to the brim.

'I don't think you should drink that,' Stella said.

Blue took a long drink. Stella wondered if she was responsible for the girl, simply because she had lied her way into her house. She supposed she was, especially if she did turn out to be Max's daughter. Max might care about the girl. He might expect Stella to keep her safe. The rounded slippery plastic of her chair felt hard and uncomfortable against her back. She was sure Max would not abandon a daughter, if he knew one existed.

'That's enough wine,' Stella said, more forcefully. It had been a long time since she had taken responsibility for anything or anyone.

Blue paused, long enough to give Stella a defiant look, before taking another swig. She kept drinking until she had polished off almost all the wine, then she lifted the bottle as if to pour herself a refill. Stella reached across, took hold of the neck of the glass and yanked it away. Wine splashed across Blue's lips and down over her precious jacket.

'I said: that's enough.' Stella banged the glass down on to the table top.

'Bitch,' Blue hissed. She wiped her hand across her mouth. She pushed her chair back hard, so the metal legs made a terrible scraping, screeching sound against the slate floor. She stood behind Stella, leaning over her. Stella's heart rate picked up, missed a few beats. She gripped the edge of the table. She did not move or show fear.

Blue leaned in close, her breath sour with wine. 'Are you two in love?' she asked.

'That's enough,' Stella said. Now it was her turn to push back her chair. She stood up. She enjoyed the fact that she was a head taller than Blue. 'I've called someone – from the police. I've told him you've run away. He's looking at the police reports to see if any girls matching your description have been reported missing. You haven't given me any choice.'

Blue shoved Stella's chair so hard that it fell backwards. She left it where it lay.

'Blue, what—'

Blue ran over to the sofa, bent down to retrieve her bag and then slung it over her shoulder as she made her way to the front door. She fumbled as she bent down and tried to pull on her still damp trainers.

Stella stayed a few paces away from her, at a safe distance.

It would be better if the girl left her alone. In peace. She might not even mention the visit to Max; it would be as though it had never happened. Blue's claims were so unlikely.

Blue did not look back at Stella, but she took her time

leaving. She fiddled with her laces, then with the zip of her jacket. Stella didn't want the girl to do something stupid. What if she did turn out to be Max's daughter? What if she hurt herself, or froze to death? She would soon be in agony if she walked out into the snow.

'At least let me give you a proper coat,' Stella said.

There was nothing she could really do to stop Blue leaving Hilltop. She could hardly hold her in the house against her will. But if the girl left and they couldn't find her – Max might not forgive her. And Stella couldn't take that chance.

'Maybe you shouldn't leave – yet,' she said.

Blue hesitated, her hand on the doorknob. 'Why not?'

'It's not safe out there. You know it isn't. Please. Just tell me your mother's name and her telephone number. I'll find a way to get you home in one piece.'

'Are the police coming?'

'I don't know. If we can contact your mother, then I can phone them and tell them they don't need to come out.'

Blue's fingers slipped away from the door handle. She pushed both hands deep into her pockets. Stella could see her clenched fists through the thin fabric. As Stella watched, the girl's colour seemed to change. She grew even paler and her skin acquired an odd, greenish tinge.

'I don't feel well,' Blue said.

'I'm not surprised. After all that wine.'

'I need the toilet,' Blue said. But she didn't make it that far. She doubled over right where she was, in front of the door, dry retching and heaving. When the spasms stopped, she was on her hands and knees, her long hair hanging down, covering her face.

Stella hesitated, then moved towards her. She knelt down and pushed Blue's hair away from her face and tucked it behind her ears. She rubbed the girl's back, feeling her bony spine. Then, placing her hands on the girl's shoulders, Stella pulled Blue back towards her. Blue relaxed. She let her head fall back against Stella's body. Her shallow breathing slowed and became regular. Stella stroked her hair and felt the girl grow calm. The feel of Blue's body against hers was warm and not unpleasant. This must be what it feels like to be a mother, Stella thought.

## Session Six

She lay on her back on the floor, staring up at the ceiling. There were loads of cracks all over the place. The rug underneath her was nice and thick, a Persian-type thing. Really soft. She wondered if anyone else had ever lain down on the rug before, instead of staying on the chair like a good girl.

She pushed herself up on to her elbows and then stood, taking a moment to steady herself. She walked slowly over to his chair. He sat very still, his hands resting on his knees. She knelt in front of him and laid her head down. He let his hand lie still and warm under her cheek and she felt happy.

After a while, he lifted his other hand and placed it gently on her head. She kept very still. She'd washed her hair that morning, putting on loads of conditioner so that it was soft, like silk. He stroked it, from the top of her head into the base of her neck, and then right the way down to the ends. His hand stayed on the small of her back.

She had to breathe, she took a deep lungful of air. She waited to see what would happen next. He didn't push her away. Again, he stroked her hair from the top of her head to the base of her neck, down to the place between her shoulder blades. She felt his fingers exploring her spine, moving down and then back up again, tickling her neck, pushing up into her hair; pulling slightly.

'You need someone to love you,' he said. 'You want to be close to me, but the only way you know how is like this. It's not right. In the end you'll be hurt.'

'I don't care. I want to.'

'You're too young.'

'I know you want to touch me. I know you do. It's not even my first time.'

'Don't talk like that.'

But his hand pulled harder at her hair.

She liked kneeling on the floor and resting her head against his knee. She didn't try anything else, she knew she had better not push her luck. He let her stay there for a long time. She was tempted to reach up along his inner thigh, to trail her fingers along – just to see what would happen. But she didn't. She waited. He might change his mind, he might make her leave. She knew he could get into bad trouble and she didn't want that. He was the best doctor she'd ever had. She would never tell. But she wanted him to want her so badly that he would risk everything to touch her. And she could wait a little while longer.

She felt his fingertips on her forehead. A slow, gentle touch. He ran his thumb along her cheekbone, and down, to her lips. She wanted to open her mouth and lick him, taste him, bite him. She waited, patient. Her whole body tingled. She had to be very strict with herself, she made herself stay very still, she wouldn't frighten him away. She wanted to open the buttons of his shirt and unzip his trousers. She was pleased about her self-control. She might be a lot younger, but she was the one in charge. His fingers lifted away from her face for a moment and her heart sank. But then he touched her again. His hands were back in her hair now, his fingers a pressure on her scalp. He pushed them all the way along, twisting his fingers into her hair until he reached the nape of her neck. He stopped and held her there.

She shivered.

She wanted to reach for him so badly, to know if he was hard. But she didn't. 'Time's up for today,' he said. 'I'll see you same time next week.'

She stood slowly. At the door, she turned back. 'Thank you, doctor,' she said, grinning.

## Bayswater, April 2009

Stella was lying in bed, half awake, when the mail thudded on to the coir mat at the front door. Her vision was still blurred as she peered at the small clock beside her bed: it was ten o'clock. She remembered she had a weekend of report writing ahead of her. The Smith report was due on Tuesday: three children, all under five, all in foster care, cocaine-addicted mother pregnant with the fourth. The local authority was paying extra to have the report done in half the time and of course she had said yes when Max asked her to take it on, even though she was already overloaded. She knew he was keen to have the double fee. And she liked to please him. She always said yes when he asked.

She huddled under the duvet and pulled it up higher around her face. Her cotton pyjamas were crisp against her skin. A man would be nice, she thought. Any man would do. If she couldn't have Max, it didn't really matter. Her bed, like everything else in the flat, was pretty horrible. It sagged in the middle where two of the slats were coming loose. The cheap stuff always looked so good in the catalogue. The lukewarm radiators didn't seem to have any effect even though she ran them day and night. And on top of that, the flat smelt strongly of damp. She should really put up some pictures, she thought for the thousandth time. It was the same thought she'd had every single day since moving in two years ago.

Her desire to check the mail finally overcame her reluctance to leave her bed. She was hoping her payslip from the Grove Road practice would be in there. She was always paid on the last day of the month; Anne was in charge of the payroll and naturally was highly efficient.

She didn't have far to travel from her bedroom to the front door, about six steps. As usual, she almost bumped her head against the paper lantern lightshade that hung low and crooked above her head. She picked up the post from the worn-out mat and flipped through the envelopes – mostly junk, the usual array of catalogues addressed to the previous tenant. She dropped those into the recycling and flipped through the rest. The gas and electricity bill had arrived. And, happily, a thick cream envelope of the kind favoured by the Grove Road Clinic. A couple more years and she would have enough money saved for a deposit to buy a small flat. Max might take her on as a full associate if she made herself indispensable.

Feeling more cheerful at the thought of future disposable income, Stella pulled on a pair of socks before steeling herself to brave the bathroom floor in order to splash some soap and hot water on her face. She did not look up at the ceiling where yellow globules were thriving due to a complete and utter lack of ventilation. Unfortunately, she could not avoid a sighting of the mould growing in black spots all around the windowsills. There was so much flora germinating in the bathroom it was beginning to look like a rainforest.

She pulled a brush through her hair and a halo of

static-filled strands sprung up around her head. She tried a few more brush strokes but this served only to worsen the situation. She couldn't be bothered with make-up; she looked more or less presentable without it. Not that a coat of mascara and some lipstick would hurt, and she could make an effort to wear something other than jeans and a white shirt – but she wasn't likely to see anyone worth glamming up for this weekend.

She would go down to the Caffè Nero and order a strong coffee from the good-looking Italian barista with warm eyes. The walk would get her brain going. Stella grabbed her bag and checked for phone, purse and Kindle. She banged the door of her apartment closed behind her and walked across the intricately patterned maroon carpet to the old-fashioned lift. She had to wait an age for the tiny antique car to climb up to the top floor. Thick black ropes swung slowly in opposite directions as the lift inched upwards. When it arrived, she heaved open the iron doors.

Outside her building, it was a gorgeous day in London. Although there was still an edge, a chill in the air, and spring had not yet arrived, the sun on her skin felt good.

She was disappointed when she was served by a trainee barista, a woman. She couldn't face her flat or her laptop for a little while longer and so she sat at a table at the window, looking out at all the people strolling along Westbourne Grove in the sunshine. She imagined she might see Max, alone, walking towards her; the familiar beard, the grey at his temples. She would invite him to join her, they would go back to her flat. A young couple, smiling, passed the window walking close and holding hands. Stella felt somehow bereft. The couple was followed by a tired-looking Filipino nanny, pushing blond twin boys in a cumbersome double buggy.

Stella stared as more people passed in front of her, her thoughts drifting as she sat in the dim café, stirring, bright light outside. Then she sat up straight, narrowing her eyes so that she might see better. Lawrence Simpson was walking along the pavement outside. He came closer and closer to the window where she sat. He stopped and looked straight inside, straight at her. Stella didn't know if he could see in through the tinted window, he might be staring at his own reflection. He wore a formal black suit and although his shirt was open at the collar, he seemed strangely overdressed for a Saturday stroll. He pushed back his foppish fringe in a gesture she remembered from her office.

He walked on, his face impassive, with no sign of recognition.

Stella watched the man's straight back moving further away, his left hand in his trouser pocket. She was no longer sure of what she'd seen. The interior of the café was dark while the street outside was so bright. Chances were it wasn't him at all, just someone who looked like him: tall and thin with straight, fine hair.

Why was she thinking about Lawrence Simpson, anyway? She felt unreasonably guilty, for letting him intrude into her thoughts and into her weekend, as though she had done something wrong. Was she attracted to him? She honestly did not think that was the case. Perhaps it was because he was a doctor, someone whose orbit travelled so close to the world of the clinic, and they had more in common than was usually the case with her medico-legal clients. Stella had to admit that she was more interested in getting to know what made Simpson tick than she should be. She was thinking about him even while not at work. She might even be more intimidated by him than she ought to be.

She waited ten minutes to ensure that, whoever the man was, he was long gone.

Stella's living room was the same size as her bedroom. She had crammed in a small sofa, a television on a stand, and a tiny dining table for two. She opened her laptop, propping her notes on the chair next to her. She began to write up the final section of the Smith report: *Opinion*.

It was such a glorious day. She thought about what her friends might be up to. Izzy and Mark would be nesting, finishing off the nursery. Hannah and the other singles were meeting up in Regent's Park to enjoy the unexpected sunshine. Stella wanted so badly to ditch her report and join them, but she wouldn't because she would not let Max down.

She had written nothing besides the heading. *Opinion*.

The forensic work was intellectually challenging, but not without emotional strain. She believed she could help, she believed she could make a critical difference to the life of a child. That was her job, as she saw it: to act in the interests of the child. But often that meant writing things in her reports that caused the parents intense pain. And while it might be true that most of the people who landed in her office had screwed up, no one was born bad. All of her clients had their own traumatic histories.

Sometimes clients were grateful – even when the news was bad. Sometimes in their hearts they knew they could not care for a child. Sometimes, they were angry – but not as often as she might have expected when she started out. She liked to think that, ultimately, many of her reluctant clients appreciated the thoroughness and accuracy of her reports. She put in many more hours than she was supposed to. She made sure she gave the parents a chance to put forward their side of the story. She was proud of that, proud that she always went the extra mile.

# Hilltop, 6.15 p.m.

Blue had her back to Stella and was still leaning against her chest.

The girl smelt sour.

'I think you need a hot bath,' Stella said. Gently, she pushed the girl away and stood up. She held out her hand and Blue took hold and pulled herself to her feet; the girl was so light. She seemed a little unsteady as she began to climb the curved staircase and Stella stayed close behind her.

The only bathtub in Hilltop was in the bathroom attached to the master suite at the top of the staircase. As Stella led Blue through the door of her bedroom, she tried not to dwell too long on how it felt to have a stranger invading her sanctuary. The cast-iron, French antique bath was spectacularly deep, as good as any drug at helping Stella to relax, and she hoped it might have the same soothing effect on Blue. She balanced on the side of the bath and turned on the taps full blast while the girl rested on the armchair.

Stella once had visions of sitting in that same chair, a glass of wine in her hand, talking to Max while he soaked in the bath.

Blue looked drained. Her face was now so pale it was ghost-like, with shadow half-moons, like bruises, under her eyes. But her eyes were wide open again, and fixed on Stella, in a permanent state of watchfulness.

The tub filled quickly as water thundered from the spout. The water pressure in the house was spectacular. Stella added bath foam to the water and then a generous amount of lavender bath oil. 'It's ready,' she said.

For the first time since entering the house, Blue took off her jacket. She did so with some reluctance, taking ages to fold it and place it carefully over the back of the armchair. Then, facing Stella and with no hint of self-consciousness, she pulled off her cropped T-shirt. She stood in her bra, a delicate white lace. Stella stiffened, trying to hide her unease. She couldn't help but look at Blue's body: her milk-white skin, her pink nipples showing through skimpy lace, the curve of her hips. Blue stepped out of her leggings, pulling them off and tossing them on to the floor. Half wary, half defiant, she reached behind her to undo the clasp of her bra. She stripped off her underwear.

Naked, she stepped gingerly into the deep water. She sank down into the bubbles and lay back, looking up at the rainbow crystals of the chandelier.

Stella felt as though she had been hypnotized. She forced herself to look away, to find something to do. She picked up Blue's clothes from the floor and dropped them in a pile on the chair. She looked in the cupboard under the basin and found two fresh towels. She placed them over the towel warmer. She rubbed the condensation from the mirror. In front of her was a dull, fearful person she did not recognize. She was thirty-two, but the person looking back at her was much older.

She looked down and washed her hands. She massaged them with chamomile hand lotion. She was careful to avoid her engagement ring: a two-carat round-cut diamond set into a platinum band. Proof of her husband's commitment to her, of his loyalty. The ring had belonged to Max's mother; it was beautiful but not to her taste.

She turned back to Blue. 'I'll get you a glass of water,' she said. 'Take as long as you like.'

'Don't leave me,' Blue said, turning her head.

'Are you still feeling sick?'

'No. But I don't want you to go.'

Stella knelt down next to the bath. 'You need to use the shampoo,' she said.

'I'm too tired.'

'I'll do it for you.'

Stella scooped handfuls of warm water over Blue's fair head. She rubbed lavender-scented shampoo into the girl's scalp, massaging it into a lather, keeping a firm pressure against her head. Stella felt calmer.

'Are the police going to come?' Blue asked.

'Are you in some kind of trouble?'

Blue rested her arms on the sides of the roll-top bath and Stella could see her scars, patches of thickened white lines along her forearms. 'You seemed frightened, when I talked about the police. Has something happened? If you tell me, maybe I can help you.'

'I don't like the police. I don't trust them. I haven't done anything bad.'

'I wish you would trust me,' Stella said.

'Why should I?' Blue submerged her head under the water, her eyes closed. A stream of small bubbles passed through her lips, rising to the surface as her hair fanned out around her small face. Stella waited, holding her breath, until Blue emerged, gasping.

'Cool bath,' she said. It seemed she'd cheered up a little.

Stella was growing impatient; tired of the cat-and-mouse conversation. The air in the bathroom was humid and it was difficult to breathe, as though she was inhaling water instead of air. She needed to get out. She stood up, her knees stiff and sore from kneeling on the hard floor.

'I'll be just outside,' she said. 'I won't close the door. There's nothing to be frightened of. There's no one else in the house.'

Blue nodded. She leaned back, loosening up, and once again closed her eyes.

Stella sat stiffly on the edge of her bed. She had developed the ability to be still, to slow her thoughts and to lose herself in the small details around her, to focus on anything but her inner life. The bedroom was vast. The fire in the hearth had not been lit recently and only a few twisted black logs were left behind. The bookshelves on either side of the art deco mantelpiece were filled with novels. Her textbooks were downstairs in the study and she hadn't opened a single one of them in all the time she had lived at Hilltop. The windows were framed by heavy yellow silk curtains. In daylight, Stella could see out over the tops of tall pine trees and beyond to the undulating hills.

On the first night she had spent with Max in this house, she had covered the walls and the ceiling of this bedroom with tiny fluorescent stars. With the curtains closed, the stars had glowed everywhere around them. Stella had curved herself around Max, tracing his vertebrae with her fingertips. She wished everything between them could be as she had always hoped. She still believed things might change.

From where she sat, she could see Blue's fair head resting against the side of the bath.

## Session Seven

She had chosen her underwear carefully: a pink bra and a matching thong. As she walked to her appointment, she could feel the lace chafe between her legs, and she smiled, at the thought of his hands, his arms holding her. She unfastened the top two buttons of her school shirt. She was wearing perfume – she felt older, sexier.

He watched as she undid all of the buttons, letting the shirt fall open. The cups pushed her breasts forward and she knew her nipples showed through the lace. She looked down at his trousers. She could see she had won. She gave a small smile, tipping her chin forward as she unzipped her skirt and let it fall to the floor. She turned around, so that he could admire the full effect of her thong. Quickly, she unhooked her bra, shrugging it off her shoulders and letting it fall. She turned back to him, walked over and sat down on his lap. She placed her lips against his and kissed him softly. His beard tickled. He smelt good. Just as she had imagined. She pushed his hair back from his face, looking into his sad eyes.

'This can't happen,' he said.

She whispered: 'Tell me what you want me to do.'

With one hand he unzipped himself, with the other, he pushed his fingers inside her.

Next time, she thought, she would make him take her to a posh hotel with a really big bed. Or maybe to his house; she would like to see his bed. She smiled at the thought of the receptionist outside.

'I want to make you happy,' she said.

## Grove Road Clinic, April 2009

Stella knocked on Max's door. She waited. No answer. She knocked again, both irritated and disappointed, because she was fairly confident the office was empty. He was going to be late for her supervision session. Again.

She went downstairs to find Anne. 'I'm supposed to have supervision with Max,' she said. 'But he's not in his office. Do you have any idea where he might be?'

'He'll be in late today,' Anne said, knowingly. She began playing with the thin gold chain around her neck and she gave Stella a rather smug smile.

'How late?' Stella glared at her, as though Max's tardiness was somehow her fault.

'I'll give him a call,' Anne said. 'You can wait in his office.' As usual, she managed to give the impression that she owned the place.

Stella stopped by the kitchen. She threw out the cold dregs of coffee and made another, much stronger pot. She bit into a white-chocolate-chip biscuit. Max was often lax about her supervision sessions: he cancelled at short notice, started late or ended early. She had put up with his casual approach without complaint, and for the most part it was worth it. He was a brilliant clinician with several years more experience than she had. She looked at her watch. Fifteen minutes of her hour with him were already lost.

Max's office was the largest in the building. The front windows overlooked Grove Road. Cream shutters masked the view of heavy traffic and double-glazing ensured the room was cocooned in silence. A second window, at the back of the office, overlooked the small garden, most of which had been swallowed up by an extension for the clinic. Stella could see the skylight in the roof of Paul's office, and beyond that the courtyard with a fountain in the middle. Anne had been in charge of garden design.

A medical examining bed covered with a fresh white sheet of paper stood under the window, and a screen with floral fabric was folded back at the side. When Stella used his office, she made sure to fold out the screen so the bed was hidden. She didn't like the office to feel too cold, or too clinical.

She saw herself, Max on top of her, on the examining bed.

'Stella.'

The sound of his voice triggered goosebumps along her arms. She felt her face flush as she turned.

'I'm so sorry I'm late,' he said. He did look genuinely remorseful.

'It's fine.' As usual, she let him get away with it. She was both grateful for any small part of his attention and resentful he did not give her more.

He placed his battered-looking briefcase down next to his desk; it was the same one he had carried ever since Stella had first known him. Like Max, it seemed to get more attractive with age. Max loosened his tie and sat down in the wingback chair opposite hers. Not classically good-looking, he was slightly shorter than average and what was left of his hair was cropped short. But his blue eyes were warm and full of life and when he looked at Stella she felt she was the most interesting person on the planet. This was the effect he had on everyone, patients included. And he was fully aware of his charm, hence his ability to get away with being late, being careless at times, and still maintaining tremendous goodwill.

He leaned forward. 'So, which case did you want to discuss?'

He should know the answer to that question. Clearly he had not prepared for their meeting. Stella liked to believe that the reason he didn't place too much emphasis on her supervision was that he trusted her clinical judgement and he knew she could work on cases independently. She knew she should be more demanding. She knew it was as much her own responsibility as his to ensure she got the supervision she needed. But in truth, she liked working autonomously and she also liked her status as his star pupil. And so, their relationship worked.

'Lawrence Simpson – care proceedings,' she said.

'Yes. Tell me.' He always rubbed his temple when he was concentrating. Stella told him about the difficult interview with Simpson and his refusal to disclose any meaningful information about his childhood or his relationships.

'That's all valuable information in itself,' Max said, as she knew he would. 'His defensiveness, his unwillingness to reveal anything about himself.'

'I know, but it doesn't give me anything new to add to what they already know about the case. It's frustrating. I want to know who he really is. I owe it to the child to find out more. I want to make him let me in!' She laughed; she sounded childish.

Max did not make fun of her zeal. He was thinking, rubbing his temple harder. As he took off his glasses and rested them on his knee, Stella felt a familiar blend of anxiety and affection.

'You could try a different approach,' he said. 'A test that isn't self-report, so it doesn't depend on him being willing to reveal anything about his personality in a straightforward way, through direct questions. I think you should try the Rorschach. If you administer it, we can rate the protocol together afterwards.'

'Great,' she said.

His glasses were back on. 'Was there any other aspect of the case you wanted to go through?'

She sensed he wanted her to say no. Her resentment flared again.

'What do you think about some sort of collateral information? Asking to interview a family member, or asking to meet with him and the child together, to observe contact?'

'It's a good idea and we've already set that up with the mother. But I doubt he'll agree. When we first sent out the interview schedule we requested an observation of contact and he refused – on the grounds that there have never been any concerns raised about his care of the child. Contact between the two of them is unsupervised, so the judge evidently agrees with him. If you ask for that now, you run the risk of antagonizing him further, and making him shut down even more. If I was you, I think I'd see how the second interview goes before we put pressure on him to let us observe him with the child. But don't be too pessimistic, he might loosen up once he spends more time with you. You can handle him.'

He smiled at her.

'I know,' she said. 'But I think he knows that the less he says, the more shaky the conclusions in my report will be. I don't want my entire opinion section to be based on conjecture. And I don't want it to be so brief it's unhelpful.'

'Your reports are excellent – there's so little I have to query or change. And you're talented and you've been doing this work for a couple of years now – so I think you've earned the right to be a little more confident than you are. I might just relax a little. Try to enjoy the next interview a bit more. Your client might be picking up on your anxiety and your need to get inside his head. If you . . . loosen up a bit, it might help him relax.'

Stella nodded, wondering if she was being rebuked for being uptight.

'There's something else I wanted to discuss,' he said. 'Are you in a hurry?'

'No.' In fact there were still twenty minutes left of her scheduled supervision session.

'You know about the developments with the legal funding authorities?' he asked.

'A little bit.'

'I've just been to a meeting of the expert witness consortium. It's clear that funding for these cases is going to become much more difficult to secure. Within the next year, there is likely to be a cap on the hourly rate we charge – in fact, the plan is to halve what we're charging now. And if we don't agree to work for the lower rate, we won't get the work. And not only that – they want to put a cap on the hours as well. I'm getting some ridiculous requests, asking us to complete a psychological assessment of an entire family in sixteen hours.'

'Why would someone agree to undertake a complex report in less than half the time they need?'

He gave her a tired smile. 'Because at the moment that's the mainstay of our work.'

'Of course.'

Max had put a tremendous amount of energy into forging links with family law solicitors in central London. Funding for most of these cases was assured through the state and the contracts had been lucrative.

'Does this affect my job?' Stella's work was entirely focused on the medico-legal arm of the practice. Up until this point, she had thought she was indispensible.

'We need to start thinking more creatively about how we can diversify,' he said.

'Meaning?'

'You and I probably need to look at taking on personal injury work, so that we have a fall-back if the cuts in fees for family cases become untenable. If we can secure those kinds of cases, with private funding, we can charge double what we charge now in family cases. But we need to market ourselves more aggressively and we need to start networking. I've already asked Anne to draw up some marketing materials and I'd like you to work on the presentations with me. We need to raise our profile and expand what we do – and we need GPs as well as psychiatrists and health insurance providers to see us as a centre of excellence.'

'OK. Sounds good.' Stella found herself tongue-tied and inarticulate, as was so often the case when she was around him. She would be able to think more clearly and to take in the implications of what he had said once she had left his office.

Max always made a point of presenting a positive front; she knew he wanted to nurture the morale of his employees. He managed to exude a robust energy, a combination of optimism and ambition. But while his plans sounded exciting and full of potential, Stella sensed that underneath all of his words he was afraid. She saw signs of strain on his face, and a certain evasiveness, an apprehension in his eyes when he smiled.

# Hilltop, 7.30 p.m.

Blue's cheeks were flushed a rosy pink after the hot bath. She had a large towel wound around her chest and her wet hair hung loose. After the striptease in the bathroom, Stella wondered if the girl might have other surprises in store for her. But for the moment, Blue held tight to her towel. The two of them remained very still. Blue at the doorway to the bathroom, Stella on her bed.

Stella had no idea what to do with the girl.

Blue moved first. She walked over and sat down on the bed next to Stella, unexpectedly close, so that Stella could feel the girl's thigh pressed against her own and could smell the scent of lavender that still clung to her hair.

Stella was aware of each part of her body, where her thighs touched the mattress, where her hands pressed down, where her feet touched the floorboards. She held herself rigid, a tightness knotting in her neck and her shoulders.

She felt Blue relax and lean into her side. The girl seemed to have no sense of where her own body ended and Stella's began.

Stella shifted, leaned away.

Blue was staring at Stella's hands, at her engagement ring.

Stella wanted Blue out of her bedroom. She wanted her out, immediately. But she had better be patient. She didn't want to frighten the girl, or worse, to make her angry. She had no idea who Blue really was. She reminded herself how Blue must have suffered, locked outside.

'How are your fingers and toes? Are they still burning?' she asked.

Blue shook her head. 'No.' She peered down at her feet, where all ten toes appeared to be a healthy pink. She held out her hands for Stella to inspect.

'They look good,' Stella said. But Blue's nails were horribly short, with jagged, bloodied edges. She had bitten them right down to the nail bed.

'You have so many nice things,' Blue said. She inspected the room: the fireplace and the books, Stella's dressing table with her perfume, her hairbrushes and her leather jewellery box.

'Thank you,' Stella said.

Blue's eyes lingered on Stella's wedding photograph on the mantelpiece.

'What kind of house do you live in?' Stella asked.

Blue didn't answer. Instead, she twisted round to stare at the bed.

'Which side does Max sleep on?' she asked.

'That's none of your business,' Stella said.

'Why? He's got to sleep somewhere. I'm just asking.'

Stella declined to answer.

Blue shook out her wet hair. It dripped down her back, leaving marks on Stella's pale green bed linen.

'You should get dressed,' Stella said.

'I need to comb my hair out first or it will get all knotted,' Blue said.

'Fine.' Stella got up to find a comb.

The art deco dressing table had rounded drawer fronts with large brass handles, and a round mirror that stood on a black glass top. Blue was watching her in the mirror, vigilant, guarding whatever motives or secrets she might carry. Stella chose a wide-toothed comb that would not pull too hard on Blue's wet hair and held it out to her.

'Can you do it?' Blue spoke in the pleading singsong voice of a small child.

'Come and sit over here then.'

Blue sat on the low chair in front of the dressing table. She turned her back to Stella and faced the mirror, staring at herself. She seemed pleased by her reflection. Stella too was mesmerized by the angles of her face and the hollows under her cheekbones, by her delicate, pouting mouth and the creamy skin of her shoulders. Carefully, Stella took up handfuls of wet curls. She tried to pull the comb through gently, with short strokes, so as not to cause any pain, but every now and again she had to give a little yank. Blue did not complain.

'I haven't seen any kids' stuff around the house,' Blue said.

'No.'

'Have you got any children?'

'Nope.'

'Are you going to have any?'

'I don't know.' She could understand that Blue would want to know, if she really believed Max was her father.

'Does Max want children?' Blue asked.

'I don't know.'

What Stella did know was that she was in no fit state to be a mother. In her heart, she didn't think it was going to happen for her. Once she had wanted a career rather than children, now it seemed she might end up with neither.

'That's weird,' Blue said.

'What's weird?'

'That you don't know what your own husband wants.' Blue pushed her fringe back from her small, chiselled face and looked up at Stella with bright violet eyes. The name could not be a coincidence.

Stella switched on the hairdryer. The noise, harsh and loud, made conversation impossible. Blue's hair reached halfway down her back, and once it was clean and dry, the colour was extraordinary: shades of blonde ranging from almost white to the colour of beach sand.

Stella put the hairdryer down carefully on the glass table-top. 'All dry,' she said.

Blue picked up Stella's hairbrush and started to brush her hair, staring at herself appreciatively as she did so. The girl was such a strange creature, such an uneasy combination of sulky teenager and seductress. There was something appeal-ing about her; something compelling.

Blue placed the hairbrush down next to the hairdryer. She ran her hands over her hair, smoothing it down, and check-ing her profile. Several strands of her hair had been left behind in the hairbrush, and Stella placed it carefully back in the drawer, leaving them in place. She could collect them later, for DNA testing if the girl persisted with her claims about Max. Max could use his contacts at the labs.

Blue showed no sign of moving from the dressing table, let alone leaving Hilltop. She seemed unperturbed to be wearing only a towel. Stella could feel her staring again, with her unnerving, intense gaze.

'What time is he coming back?' Blue asked.

'I told you – later.'

'When is later?'

'I'm not sure.'

Blue sighed.

She stood up and stretched, lifting her hands above her head, arching her back. The towel stayed in place. She made her way back into the bathroom and left the door wide open behind her. She made sure to show off her behind to full advantage as she bent to pick up her clothes. Much to Stella's relief, she was fully dressed when she re-emerged, jacket and all.

For a brief moment Stella hoped that she might have grown tired of waiting and decided to leave. She would happily give Blue the money for the taxi fare all the way back to London; she would phone every taxi company in the area and pay double if they agreed to take the girl home.

But Blue walked over to the fireplace and stood with her back to Stella, in front of her wedding photograph. She picked up the silver frame and studied the picture.

'Where is his stuff?' she asked. 'There's nothing of his in the bathroom – no shaving cream or aftershave. There's nothing in here, either. Only your stuff.'

'It's none of your business where his stuff is,' Stella said. She grabbed the picture frame and placed it safely back down. She couldn't tolerate the girl and her games and her lies for much longer.

'I know nothing about you,' Stella said. 'I don't even believe you've told me your real name.'

'*Why won't you say when he's coming home?*' Blue's voice was rising, now she was a whining, petulant child. 'Does he even live here?'

'Of course he lives here, he's my husband.'

Stella had made a mistake, opening the front door. She blamed the benzodiazepines; the drugs had been in her system so long they had saturated her bloodstream, dampened her functioning, made her lower her guard. She stood squarely in front of Blue, right in between the girl and her wedding photograph. 'Look at me,' she said.

Blue looked out from under her fringe, sullenly.

'You don't really believe that my husband is your father, do you?'

Blue put the tip of her thumb in her mouth and bit down. She seemed to be growing younger by the second. 'Maybe. I don't know,' she said.

Stella took hold of her wrist, wrenching her thumb out of her mouth. 'You had better answer me. Who are you? What's your real name?'

'I told you – my name is Blue.' The girl was frightened now, and Stella was glad. She tightened her grip around her small wrist.

'And your surname?'

'Cunningham. Blue Cunningham. I promise you.'

She tried to pull away, but Stella held on, pushing her fingers into the soft flesh of the girl's arm. She knew she was hurting her.

'You've lied to me. About everything.' Stella grabbed her chin, forcing Blue to look into her eyes. This girl is terrible trouble, Stella thought. And she wants to drag me down with her.

'You're scaring me,' Blue said.

'Good. Who brought you here? Is your boyfriend waiting outside? Is he waiting for you to let him in? Are you going to rob me?'

'I don't have a boyfriend.' Tears oozed from her eyes

and made their way down her cheeks. Stella felt very little sympathy.

'Why are you here?' Stella was growling at her. The girl had manipulated her, lied, taken advantage. She felt a fool. 'I'm calling the police right now,' she said. She didn't know what else to do, what else to threaten her with. She had no way of knowing anything.

'Please don't,' Blue said.

'Why are you so frightened of the police, Blue?'

'I'm not.'

'Have you done something bad?'

'No, nothing like that. I promise.' She wiped at her wet cheeks with the back of her hand, sniffing.

She was small and delicate. Weak. And Stella was glad. For once, she felt strong. She felt she could hurt her. If she had to, she would strike first, before the girl could do any damage.

'WHY ARE YOU HERE? ANSWER ME!' It felt good, to scream at her; to frighten her.

What could the girl want from her? Stella felt dizzy, the floorboards under her feet threatened to give way, she almost lost her balance.

Blue's eyes were luminous against her pale skin. The tears kept coming, rolling down her cheeks and wetting her face, her nose was streaming.

Stella caught a hold of herself and let go. She had left a red mark in the shape of her fingertips around the girl's tiny wrist. Blue made a big show of rubbing her arm and of feeling sorry for herself.

When she looked at Blue's small, lovely face, she didn't believe that she could have come to do harm. Blue was afraid.

And then the moment of rational thought, of empathy,

passed and Stella wanted to shake the girl in front of her. Hard.

Blue was sobbing, she could not speak. She covered her face with her hands.

'I think you'd better sit down,' Stella said. She guided Blue towards the bed.

Blue sat. Then she pulled back the covers, wriggled her legs underneath. She propped herself up against Stella's pillows. As creepy as it was to see her there, at least she had calmed down. And she looked harmless; more than ever like a young child.

'Our house is small,' Blue said. 'Nothing like yours. It's so ugly, the carpets are brown, the walls – the paint has disgusting marks all over it. It's not even ours, it's a council house. I mean – it's not so terrible really – when it's cleaned up. And I have to look after my mum, sometimes. She drinks. She can get through a whole bottle of vodka in one night.

'She gets migraines. Sometimes, in the mornings, she can't get out of bed. She's really pretty though – when she's feeling better she gets dressed up and I help her, I blow-dry her hair, I help her colour it. We share clothes sometimes.'

Blue began to bite her nails. Flakes of red polish dropped on to the bedcovers.

'There's this man – I don't even know why she likes him. He says things to her – horrible stuff. He tells her she's fat and she's old. I heard him tell her he wouldn't fuck her if she begged him.'

The words were all the more monstrous, coming from Blue's lovely mouth.

'But then he does,' Blue said. 'And I can hear it. He hurts her. Sometimes it's bad and we have to go to the emergency room. Mostly it's just bruises.'

Stella came closer, looked down at her small head with her golden hair. 'Blue – does this man ever hurt you?'

Blue shook her head. 'Can I watch TV?' she asked.

Stella managed a smile. She almost felt fond of her. Protective, even. Blue. Curled up in her bed.

# Session Eight

She turned up for her next session right on time, just like nothing extraordinary had ever happened between them.

The secretary smiled in the same fake way she always did and gave her a look that was like: *You're a nutcase and don't we all know it, poor thing.* You could tell she was the kind of person who hated all the people who came up to her desk and hated answering the phones. But when *he* came out, her smile changed. For him, her smile was real. Ha ha. She should only know.

'You can go through now,' the secretary said, still with the fake smile. She pointed to his office as though she was stupid or something and after all her appointments wouldn't even remember which way to go.

She knocked on the door and waited.

She had a fantasy of how it would be now that they were lovers. As soon as the door closed, he would reach out for her, pull her on to his lap, kiss her, stroke her hair.

He opened the door with his usual straight, nothing face. He pointed at the usual chair. She walked past him and waited while he turned his back to her and closed the door. Time had slowed down. He sat down the way he always did, crossing his legs, his notepad on his lap. He did not reach out to her. It was as though nothing had happened, as if the time before – between them – had been erased.

Her face flushed, it blazed.

He was silent, waiting for her to begin. She scratched at the flowers on the arms of the wingback chair with her fingernails. She crossed her legs, her right leg kicking back and forth.

'How have you been this week?' he asked.

He was acting as though nothing had ever happened. She didn't understand.

'I'm not sorry about what we did,' she said.

'What do you mean?'

'I mean it. I'm not sorry. I've been happy this week. Happier than I've ever been. I've been eating properly, taking care of myself.'

'I'm glad you're feeling better,' he said.

'Stop it.' She kicked her leg, back and forth, frustration building inside.

Silence. Then he said: 'I can't read your mind. Tell me what's going on inside.'

She coughed and cleared her throat. 'I want you to touch me again, like last time. Don't pretend. I know you want to.'

She saw him take a deep breath. 'You need to try to draw a line between fantasy and reality,' he said. 'Between what really happened and what you wish would happen.'

'I know what happened.' She wanted to cry but she didn't want him to see. He was making her so angry. 'I can describe it to you in detail, if you like.'

'That won't be necessary,' he said.

'Because you remember.' She leaned forward, so he had a good view down the front of her shirt. She ran both hands through her hair, pulling it back from her face, then scooping it all forward over her right shoulder. She twirled the ends with her fingers.

She couldn't stand it, to be still, to be apart from him and also so close. She jumped up, ran over to him and put her head in his lap. She held him tight, her arms around his waist.

It wasn't the way she imagined it would be, when she got what she wanted. Being with him. She glanced up: his head was back, his eyes closed, his hand pushed down on her head. It smelt the same way it always smelled. He was far away from her. When he finished, she wanted to gag. She pushed her hand against her mouth.

She lay with her head in his lap and hoped he would say something. Something kind, something loving. He put his hands on her shoulders, pushing her away. She sat cross-legged on the floor and fastened her top. The thong was chafing, she stood up and pulled at it.

'This is the last time,' he said.

She bent down, brushed the top of his head with her lips. She wanted him to kiss her back, on her lips, she wanted to feel his beard against her face. He pushed her away. 'Don't,' he said.

She checked the clock. 'I still have ten minutes left until the end of the session.'

She walked back to her chair and sat down, still so angry. She wanted to make him happy, but he looked miserable. She wasn't leaving until her time was over.

He zipped himself up.

This wasn't what she wanted. She was frightened he didn't care about her at all. He would pretend there was nothing between them.

'Do you love me?' she asked him. 'Answer me. You have to give me an answer.'

'Of course I care about you,' he said.

'I want to be with you,' she said. 'I love you. You're the only person that can help me. The only one.'

She wouldn't let him do this to her again. He wouldn't be able to pretend that he hadn't touched her, hadn't been excited by her, hadn't loved her.

## Grove Road Clinic, May 2009

Stella placed the first card down on the desk, a black and white inkblot.

'Have you ever taken this sort of test before?' she asked.

Simpson shook his head and stared sullenly at the card in front of him.

'This test is a bit different,' she said. 'Could you tell me – what might this be?'

She picked up the card and offered it to him. She gave him a small smile of encouragement, but he did not see it, because he refused to look at her.

'Absolutely not,' he said.

'Can I ask what the problem is?' Stella said.

'I'm not engaging in this nonsense.'

'I can't force you to take the test if you don't want to,' she said. 'But it's a standard personality test. We use it all the time here.'

With the palpable, precipitous rise in his anxiety, his oppositional side had come right to the fore. He pushed himself as far away from her as he could, his body jammed against the stiff back of the chair, his legs tightly crossed. 'I'm not going to complete some ridiculous activity that looks like something a child would enjoy.'

Stella realized that the Rorschach had brought out the most defensive, mistrustful side of her patient. He had no way of knowing what his responses might reveal about him, and she guessed that this lack of control terrified him. Perhaps the test had not been a good choice after all. *It's all grist for the mill. Every response, each behaviour, gives you information*, she heard Max say.

'I know a bit about your field,' he said. 'I majored in psychology in my undergraduate degree. I've spoken to someone who advised me not to take this test.'

Stella would not have been surprised if Simpson had done some research into which tests were routinely administered in custody evaluations – he was that type, intelligent and somewhat obsessive. And the inkblots had got a lot of ill-informed bad press.

She would not argue with him. She was not going to enter into an intellectual debate or a power play.

'I'm not prepared to take this test without a lot more information,' he said.

She placed her clipboard down on the desk. She knew full well she could quote the entire test manual to him – statistics, norms, the lot, not to mention the extensive research backing up the test – it would make no difference whatsoever. He was trying to manipulate her. He was desperate to even the playing field, but the reality was that he was the patient, mandated to be there, and she was the professional, the expert witness. The power lay with her, whether he liked it or not.

'It's your choice,' she said. 'I'm not going to argue with you – or try to force you. But you understand that the judge has asked me to carry out a full assessment. Have you thought about how it will look if you don't cooperate? What do you think the judge will think of your refusing to take the test? Or refusing to complete this assessment?'

It sometimes helped to make reference to the judge, to impress upon parents the importance of cooperating in the assessment process. Sometimes, Stella supposed because she was young, petite and female, clients underestimated the influence of the psychological report. Particularly clients like Lawrence Simpson. But she saw straight away that her question was a mistake. Simpson's eyes turned cold and the muscles in his jaw rippled as he clenched his back teeth.

'Please, don't talk to me like a child,' he said. He paused deliberately between each word. 'I've had it with your condescending, superior attitude. I've put up with a lot – I don't mean just from you – from all the others involved in this case. How DARE they put me in here with someone half my age, practically out of secondary school. How can you imagine that you know better than I do what's best for my child?'

Stella took a deep breath. 'I didn't mean to offend you,' she said.

He gripped the arms of the chair. His knuckles turned white.

'The test takes about an hour and a half. I had planned to use this entire session to complete it. So if you're not comfortable to do that, well – in that case I suppose we're finished. Unless there is anything you wanted to ask me?'

'No.' He looked almost disappointed that she had dropped the rope, that there would be no power struggle.

Stella retrieved the inkblot and placed it back in the cardboard folder along with nine others. She glanced up at the clock on the wall with the large numerals. They were only ten minutes into the appointment. She was intensely disappointed. The Rorschach had been her last shot. She, like all the others, had failed to crack the case.

'Is there *anything* that you would like to tell me, that you want me to include in the report?' she asked.

'I love my daughter,' he said. 'All I want is to give her a good home, a good education, an opportunity to do something with her life.'

While his anger had spiked quickly, it was abating fast too.

'All right. I'll make a note of that and make sure it's included,' she said.

She closed her laptop. There was no point prolonging the agony. If Simpson had made up his mind not to cooperate, there was nothing she could do about it.

'So we're finished?' He was still in his chair, hesitating.

'We are. I'll walk you out.'

She stood, straightening her black wool knee-length skirt and automatically fastening the button of her jacket. She was conscious of him watching her; conscious of how quickly he had moved from anxiety, to anger, to dismay.

'I'm an asshole,' he said.

She couldn't bring herself to disagree.

'I'm screwing this up. I'm going to lose my daughter because I'm fucking this whole thing up.'

'Did you want to give the test a go?' she asked.

'After you,' he said, motioning for her to leave the office first.

At the bottom of the staircase, her heels clicked against the wooden floorboards as she walked briskly to the front door. She held it open for him, welcoming the burst of noise from the ever-present traffic outside that punctured the heavy atmosphere inside the clinic.

Simpson paused at the top of the steps and offered her his right hand. Stella did not want to touch him, but she forced herself to hold out her hand to take his. She had no desire to risk wounding his fragile pride. His handshake was firm and confident and his skin was warm and dry.

## Hilltop, 9.15 p.m.

In the bathroom, the scent of lavender lingered in the steam.

'Tell me what's happened,' Peter said.

Stella hadn't expected him to call her back, but she was pleased he had. She spoke quietly. 'Nothing much. I've had to let her stay.'

'I'm phoning you because there's a report just come in – there is a fifteen-year-old girl who might be missing. She lives on an estate in Ladbroke Grove, with her mother. Her name is Blue Cunningham.'

Stella opened the door a crack. Blue was still in her bed, thumb in her mouth, eyes fixed on the screen. The television was blaring.

'What do you mean, she *might* be missing?'

'They're still checking with friends at this stage and they're having a look at her laptop. It might be that she's just gone out somewhere without telling anyone. Her mother looked in on her and saw her sleeping this morning when she left the house. She also spoke to her on the landline at around ten, when the girl said she wasn't feeling well and wasn't going to school. So she was still at home at that stage. But when the mother called again at around lunchtime, she didn't answer the home phone or her mobile. The mother made her first call to the police when she got home at around eight, after she'd called round to a few of her friends and couldn't find her.'

'Has this girl run away from home before? Did the mother give a reason she might have run away?'

'She hasn't gone missing before, but she does have a history of behaviour problems. Apparently she's been caught smoking cannabis on the school premises and she's been excluded a couple of times – disrupting classes, truanting, that sort of thing. And she self-harms – with razorblades.'

'I think I've seen the scars.'

'She used to be on Ritalin. At the moment she's taking – hang on.'

Stella heard rustling noises.

'I'm back,' he said. 'Aripiprazole, Epilim and diazepam. And she hasn't taken her meds with her.'

'*All* of those?'

'Yep. That would mean some pretty serious symptoms, wouldn't it?'

'Either that,' Stella said, 'or a psychiatrist who is very liberal with his prescription pad. It sounds like they think she has either a mood disorder or a psychotic disorder. Maybe she has bipolar disorder that's been difficult to control, that could be why the mood stabilizers are prescribed. And bipolar symptoms can look like a psychotic disorder in phases where the person is manic – so she might have had some kind of delusional, out-of-touch-with-reality episodes. But it's a little strange. She seems so young for that diagnosis. Do you have the clinician's details?'

'The name isn't in the police report. I'll try to find out who it is.'

'Maybe she's having some sort of withdrawal,' Stella said. 'She's been feeling sick, nauseous.'

'Stella – I have to say – if it is her, I think this girl is a risk. I'm a little concerned.'

She knew Peter. If he said a *little* then what he meant was: *extremely*. He was much gentler, much less formal this time, and that worried her most of all.

'She has behaviour problems. If she self-harms with razor-blades that involves a potential for violence.'

'Great.' Stella stood in front of the double vanity unit. She stared at her toothbrush, her toothpaste, her perfume. Max's side was empty. Acid churned in her gut and pushed its way up into the back of her throat. The after-effects of the wine and the adrenaline, she supposed.

'I want you to take a photograph of her and send it to me,' Peter said.

'I'll try. I don't know if she'll let me. She freaked out when I mentioned the police. Maybe she's committed some sort of crime – robbed a house in the area and run off, or something. Who knows.'

'Try. I've let her local police station know but I don't know how fast they'll act. It would help, to have a photograph.'

'OK.'

'And keep an eye on her.'

'Pete – where are you?'

'Stella,' he said. 'I'm not coming out there.'

'I didn't ask you to.'

The last time he had tried to help her, she hadn't been very cooperative.

'Send me the photograph as soon as you can. I'll see what I can do.'

He still cared, she could hear it in his voice.

Stella filled a glass of water and opened the mirrored cabinet above the basin. Inside were several white cardboard boxes full of tablets in blister packs. She reached for the box on the far left, swallowed her antidepressant, then placed the box back in its place. She reached for the next box and placed a small, bitter tablet on her tongue. Then she spat it out. The diamond-shaped pill dropped into the basin, dissolving around the edges into a puddle of blue. She ran the tap, flushing it down the plughole.

She needed to be able to think.

All of the drugs she took were legal: prescribed by a psychiatrist. She needed diazepam in the morning, or she would never leave the bedroom. And she needed another dose at night, or she remained sleepless, seeing shadows around her bed where there were none. The psychiatrist said it was fine to continue this medication regime for years, there were no risks. Max agreed with him. Of course Stella did not believe a word of it. She was overmedicated and she knew it: physically and psychologically dependent. The tranquillizers, in particular, were a hard habit to break.

She hated herself for being so weak.

So much medication. Blue could be a danger to herself. To others around her. Stella couldn't make it through the night, alone with the girl, sleepless and fearful. She wasn't going to sit around and wait for Peter to make up his mind about whether he could forgive her for cutting him out of her life, or for the Met Police to make their way up to her through the frozen countryside. She had to do something.

Stella placed the mug of tea down on the bedside table

and smiled at Blue. She hoped this might appear to be a reassuring, comforting smile.

'Drink this,' she said. 'You'll feel better.' She retrieved the remote from the bedcovers and turned off the television.

'I'm sorry about before,' Blue said. 'I didn't mean to make you angry.'

'I'm sorry too,' Stella said. 'I'm sorry I lost my temper.'

She had been careful to make the tea just the right temperature; she had added a little extra milk to make sure it wasn't too hot. Then she had put in two heaped teaspoons of sugar and stirred well. She had tried a sip herself and she was confident that the sweetness and the milk masked the bitter aftertaste.

Stella watched as Blue lifted the mug, brought it to her lips and took her first sip. Thankfully, she was being quite cooperative, really quite docile.

'It's good,' Blue said.

Stella smiled, pleased.

She had no idea when Blue might have taken her last dose of medication. A physical withdrawal might leave her edgy and unpredictable. She might relapse, into psychosis or a manic state. Stella felt justified in giving her a low dose of an anxiolytic to ensure she stayed calm, to help her sleep. To help Stella stay sane.

Stella could still see redness on the skin around Blue's chin and her own fingerprints, imprinted like a bracelet around the girl's wrist. She sat down next to her, right on the edge of the bed.

'Look, Blue,' Stella said. 'I've let you into my house and I've been kind to you, right?'

Blue nodded.

'So I think I deserve something in return. I'd like you to

answer some questions that might actually sound a bit silly.'

'Fine.' Blue already sounded sullen.

'Do you know what day it is today?' Stella said.

'Friday.' The wariness in Blue's eyes eased away in response to the innocent question.

'And the year?'

'2011.'

'Do you know where you are now?' Stella continued.

'Inside your house.'

'And which country are we in?'

'England.'

'Just a few more,' Stella said. 'Can you tell me the name of the Prime Minister?'

'David Cameron.'

'And do you remember my name?'

'Stella. Stella Fisher.'

Stella was confident that the girl was oriented to time, place and person. There was nothing floridly psychotic about her. She didn't know exactly how long Blue had been off her meds, but there was no sign of seriously disturbed thinking. Yet.

'Blue, do you take any medicine?'

Blue nodded.

'Do you remember the name of the pills you take?' Stella asked.

'No.'

'Try.'

'There's a lot. My mother gives them to me, I don't look at the boxes. Epi-something. Like epilepsy, but I don't have epilepsy. And some other stuff.'

Stella felt a sense of relief. Blue seemed to be telling her the truth. She hadn't lied about her name. It was very likely she was the missing girl. Once she had a photograph, Blue could be returned home without delay.

But why would a psychiatrist prescribe so much medication for a fifteen-year-old? Diazepam was highly addictive. Stella could vouch for that. And if Blue stayed on the antipsychotics for long enough she could develop neurological problems – grimacing, tongue thrusting, odd tics in her arms and legs. It could become difficult for her to move or walk. And the damage would be permanent – irreversible. It didn't seem right. Unless. Unless Blue had exhibited some seriously disturbed, even dangerous, behaviour.

'Do you remember how long it's been since you took your last dose?' Stella asked.

'Uh-uh.'

'Did you know that it can be bad for you to stop taking those pills suddenly?'

Blue shook her head.

Then she turned to Stella and smiled, tremulous and wide-eyed and nervous all of a sudden. Stella could not read her at all.

'It's true that I came to see Dr Fisher,' Blue said. 'But I lied when I said I'd never met him.'

Stella sat up straighter and stiffer on the edge of the bed.

Blue took another sip of tea, her eyes never leaving Stella's face.

'How do you know him?' Stella asked.

'He's my doctor. Or he used to be.'

'I see.' Stella kept her tone even. She wasn't going to react with shock or surprise to the girl's lies and her ever-changing revelations. She was relieved that Max was not the girl's father after all, that Blue had no permanent place, no role to play in disrupting their already complicated union. It made sense that Blue was a patient. And no doubt a deeply disturbed one, given her medication.

'What was Dr Fisher treating you for?' Stella asked.

'He was my mother's doctor. I went to see him too, sometimes. He tried to help us. I used to hurt myself but I don't do it any more.'

'I see. Did something happen at home – something that made you decide to come and find him tonight?' she asked.

Blue shook her head. 'No,' she said. She hesitated. 'I just wanted – to ask him to help us.'

'Help you how?'

'I don't really know.' She placed the mug back down on the bedside table. It was still half full. She lay back against the pillows, closing her eyes.

Blue had changed her story so many times that Stella had lost track. Stella felt as though her inner compass was shattered; she no longer trusted her instincts. When she looked at Blue she felt both sympathy and fear, in equal measure. But fear was her master. She reached for the mug and offered it to Blue once more. 'Finish your tea,' she said.

Blue drank, obedient.

'Blue,' Stella said. 'Can you describe Dr Fisher's office for me?'

'Yes.'

'Well?'

'I walk there, after school. From the tube. It's on Grove Road. First I have to tell the receptionist I'm there. Then I wait in the waiting room. His office is upstairs, on the first floor.'

'Where do you sit, when you're in his office?'

'He has a big desk but he doesn't sit behind it. We sit in the armchairs, there are two, they're exactly the same. Big. With red flowers on them.'

Blue yawned. Her eyelids drooped, they looked heavy, as though she was struggling to keep them open. She reached out, hesitantly, for Stella's hand and Stella did not pull away. Such an odd girl; her mood fluctuating so quickly, from guarded, to oppositional, to affectionate.

Stella shuffled up next to her. They sat quietly for a few moments, facing the blank television screen on the wall. Blue edged closer and rested her head against Stella's shoulder. Stella was too tired to resist. She couldn't remember the last time she had touched another human being. She relaxed. She wrapped her arm around the sad, troubled girl, holding her tight and feeling her soft hair against her face, enjoying the fresh smell of lavender.

Blue's chin sank forward on to her chest, her head flopped forwards, her hair covered her face.

Stella was so tired. She wished that Max was home, to take care of her. She wondered what Max thought of Blue and her moods and her charms. Apprehension flipped like a fish, turning over and over inside her gut as she thought about the girl and the way she had hunted down Max's home address; about her fantasy that Max would act as her saviour.

## Central London, May 2009

The party was downstairs, in a cave-like, subterranean room. Along one side was a bar, packed with people. Along the other side, a series of booths were tucked into the arches that ran beneath the city, each one snug with an oval table, scatter cushions and billowing scarves overhead.

There were eight of them around the table. Stella sat on the end because she had been the last to arrive. As usual, the District and Circle Lines were down for the weekend. There was a couple down the opposite end Stella hadn't met before – friends of Izzy and Mark's from antenatal classes – but the rest of the group she knew well; most were from her doctoral programme. It was Izzy's thirtieth birthday, and she was also forty weeks' pregnant. She had chosen a North African bar and restaurant, where there would be belly dancing for all. She was determined to induce labour.

Stella was drinking some sort of cocktail with fresh lemon and mint and lots of ice, and something pinkish swirling along the bottom. They raised their glasses: to Izzy and Mark and their baby. To being thirty. All of them, soon.

The music was loud, a Middle-Eastern, pounding, energetic beat. The belly dancer's bustier teemed with sequins. Her veils billowed as she swayed and turned, sending ripples through the flesh of her belly. Izzy, despite the size of her own belly, sprang up to join her. She grabbed Stella's hand and pulled her on to the dance floor.

Stella liked to dance. She pulled at her hairband, letting her hair fall loose down her back. She felt light and uninhibited, as though they were back at university again, not qualified, not responsible for anyone else – just having a good time. They danced in a circle, the oud playing a slow tune, building up to something; the belly dancer leading the way: grinding and rolling her hips to the flute, the drums and the tambourines, clapping her hands, jiggling the chains around her hips. Faster and faster, impossibly fast. Stella was laughing, clapping, spinning. They all were.

And Lawrence Simpson was standing at the bar, and he had seen her.

Stella looked away, laughed at something Izzy said about the belly dancer's hips. The music was loud, relentless, reverberating against the low brick ceiling. She retreated to her table and lifted the bottle of sparkling water. She filled the glass in front of her, bubbles rushed to the top and over the sides, she saw too late the rim was marked with a faded ring of some other woman's pink lipstick. And Simpson was at her elbow, looking down at her. She could see from his smile and the expression in his eyes that he was pleased to see her on neutral ground.

'Dr Davies,' he said. There went his hand again, flipping back his fringe, his nervous tic.

'Dr Simpson,' she said.

'So you remember me?'

'Of course I remember you,' she said. 'You've spent hours in my office.'

'Has the psychotherapist tried to set your clinic on fire lately?' he said.

She gave a small laugh, to be polite. It was bad luck that they should run into each other outside of the office. She'd never been to the restaurant before and London was so vast – what were the chances? She wondered if he'd been watching her, dancing. She pulled her hairband off her wrist and tied her hair back from her face. The back of her neck was damp with sweat. She tried to relax her shoulders.

He gestured towards the crowded bar. 'I'm with a colleague,' he said. 'You won't be insulted if I don't introduce you – under the circumstances.'

The music was throbbing and pounding, he had to lean in close to speak to her. His aftershave was fresh and subtle. 'I came over because I thought it might be helpful if we talked again.'

The music had slowed. Stella could hear each distinct chord of the string instrument: slow and suspenseful, building to a climax.

'It's not a good idea for us talk here. We shouldn't have contact outside the office.' She had to talk loudly, to be heard.

He leaned closer. His lips practically grazed her ear. 'If you just give me a minute of your time,' he said. 'I wanted to apologize.'

It was the last thing she'd expected him to say. He looked contrite and entirely sincere. Perhaps some of his oppositional attitude, his bravado, had been based in fear. Fear of the court process and fear of losing his daughter. Perhaps the way he behaved in her office was not the most accurate reflection of his personality in the outside world.

She nodded. 'I appreciate your apology,' she said.

The waiter had arrived with plates of food and the smell was wonderful. Stella was starving but she could hardly tuck in with Simpson leaning over her. He wasn't budging from her table. Her drink, with two straws protruding from the top of the tall glass, stood in front her. The ice was beginning to melt. The others were tucking into the starters: pita bread, humus, and yoghurt and cucumber dips. Stella dragged her eyes away from the swiftly diminishing feast.

'Do you have children?' he asked.

She didn't answer.

'I don't expect you to tell me,' he said. 'But I imagine you don't. It's impossible for you to understand what it's like – my daughter's been shunted off to foster care again, and it's not because of anything I've done wrong. I've never had a chance to look after her, her mother won't allow it. The system works against fathers – you must know that from the work you do.'

Stella was starving, and slightly lightheaded from the dancing and the cocktails. Her head was at an awkward angle as she craned her neck to look up at him.

'I can't talk to you about the case outside of the office,' she said. 'Every meeting, every discussion we have, needs to be recorded for the court.'

He was still leaning over her, both palms flat on the table. His body language was very different from the withdrawn, arms-crossed pose he'd clung to in her office. She could see that he was in pain.

'I didn't make it easy for you the other day,' he said. 'You were trying to do your job. Would you consider giving me another chance? I just want to give my side of the story.'

She caught a whiff of beer. She knew there was every

chance she might lose another two hours of her valuable time if he turned up completely sober, having changed his mind; if she was confronted with the sullen version of Lawrence Simpson, as opposed to the contrite one. But still, there was a chance.

'Fine,' she said. 'Telephone the receptionist at the clinic and make an appointment for this week. I'll fit in an extra session for you, so there's no delay in submitting the report. But you'll have to fit in with whatever appointments are available now, there's no flexibility. The report is due in ten days, it has to be submitted before the final hearing.'

'I appreciate that. Can I ask – do we have to meet at your clinic in St John's Wood? My offices are in south London. It would be a great help if we could meet there. I've had to take a lot of time off work for all of these appointments and it takes me half a day to get across London to your place.'

'Yes, it has to be at the clinic,' she said. 'All my files, all the test materials are there. And it wouldn't be appropriate for us to meet outside of the office. I think you know that.'

He laughed at her stilted words. '*It wouldn't be appropriate*. I thought you'd say that. Predictable. But worth a try?'

'Sure.' He was irritating her. She didn't like being mocked. She was entitled to enjoy a night off with her friends. And she had to eat something soon.

'Make sure you telephone the clinic to make the appointment,' she said.

'Thank you. I really am grateful. I know I can be my own worst enemy. I tell myself you won't just believe everything you read about me but it's hard to go into a meeting knowing you might think I'm a twisted, sick, wife-beater. I'm ashamed, about something I haven't done. It does my head in sometimes.'

He lingered at her side. She didn't want to be rude, but she did want to draw a line. She looked away and took a sip of her drink. She hoped he would get the message without her having to ask directly and risk injuring his fragile ego.

He peered at her drink. 'Let me buy you another cocktail. To make it up to you for being such a sulky bastard.'

He wasn't unattractive, when he smiled, when he showed his vulnerability; perhaps there was even a sense of humour, lurking beneath the sullen exterior. And if she refused the offer of a drink, he would no doubt feel slighted; he would view it as yet another blow to his pride. So Stella sat, annoyed, but also feeling sorry for him as he motioned to a passing waiter.

When he turned back to her, he knelt down so his eyes were level with hers. She felt horribly uncomfortable, and exposed. He was invading her space, breaching the boundaries between them.

'You're someone I could be attracted to,' he said. 'And you see me as—'

'This conversation really is not appropriate in the middle of court proceedings,' she said.

His eyes hardened, and mocked her again as he laughed. 'Must you always act so formal?' He hadn't moved any further away.

'It's not an act. Our relationship *is* a formal one.'

A smiling waiter in a fez placed two luscious drinks down on the table in front of her. Fresh mint over crushed ice and straws at the ready.

Finally, Simpson stood up and took a step back. 'I'm sure you could do with a drink or two, the things you have to listen to.' He lifted his glass. 'Let's drink to the best interests of my daughter,' he said.

She didn't move.

'Come on,' he said. 'I'm not a leper.'

She lifted hers, clinked it against his, took a sip.

'There,' he said. 'That wasn't so bad.'

She was unable to force a smile.

'I've disturbed your party.' He looked around at her friends, his eyes resting on Izzy's pregnant belly. Then he disappeared into the throng of people at the bar.

Hannah caught her eye across the table and raised her eyebrows. Stella shook her head: *It's nothing, he's no one.* She couldn't tell Hannah he was a client, she wasn't about to break confidentiality.

Stella lifted the drink Simpson had paid for and gave it to Peter, who sat opposite her. He accepted it gladly.

She wasn't sure whether or not to write up the out-of-office encounter in her report. She would ask Max what to do. She was so thankful not to be facing the vagaries of the case on her own. She picked up her BlackBerry and scrolled through her contacts until she was looking at Max Fisher's telephone number. She would love an excuse to call him over a weekend. She was also too embarrassed to bother him; the meeting with Simpson was hardly an urgent matter. She would talk to him about it on Monday.

Peter held out a bowl of warm, soft pita bread.

The belly dancer sashayed closer, her body a marvel of curves, undulating; gold chains shimmering around her waist. She turned away from them, then looked back over her shoulder, her smile a seduction. Her hips and her belly quivered, so near to Stella's face she felt herself flush.

Stella wondered if Simpson was still lurking, watching her.

*

On Sunday morning, Stella woke up next to a man; his body warm and solid against hers, his arm heavy across her waist, her back moulded into his front. He woke too and pulled her closer.

'Morning,' she said. She had slept well.

'Morning.'

'So,' she said.

The curtains in her room were flimsy and didn't keep out any of the morning sun. She lifted his hand from around her and moved away, rearranged herself, moving further apart so that she lay on her back, facing the ceiling.

She had drunk more than usual the night before; those cocktails were deceptively sweet. It had become impossible to talk, as the music became faster and louder, as the basement room was crammed with more and more bodies. She couldn't remember what they'd said to each other, if anything. Peter had passed her plates of food. He had been sitting opposite her at the horseshoe-shaped table, then they'd been in a circle, dancing, laughing, ridiculous as they tried to copy the belly dancer. When they sat down again, he'd changed places and he was sitting next to her. Their shoulders and their hips were pressed together, and she had liked the feel of him. It was raining outside. He'd waited with her, to make sure she found a taxi. Next thing she knew, he kissed her and she had responded with an enthusiasm that took her by surprise. She remembered the way he had tasted, of her lemon and mint cocktail.

'Is it OK if I use your shower?' he asked.

'Sure.'

He stood, naked. She studied his shape as he turned away. She compared him to Max, who was older and most definitely not in such good shape. But it was Max who excited her.

Damn. She felt awful. She felt guilty.

She was still in bed when he emerged from the shower with her pink towel around his waist. 'Can I make you some coffee?' he said.

He was a decent human being. A kind man. She felt awful again.

'That would be nice,' she said. 'But I don't have any coffee. I don't have any milk, either. In fact, I don't have anything, really, in the kitchen. I haven't had a chance to go shopping this week.'

'Let me take you out for breakfast.'

'OK,' she said. 'There are loads of places on Westbourne Grove. Give me a couple of minutes to get dressed.'

She stepped out of bed, unselfconscious. He was a friend, there was no need to impress him. She rummaged around for her loose Sunday jumper and her jeans. She could feel him watching her. He came towards her, and stood very close. She contemplated letting him kiss her. She turned to him, reached up and stroked the hair on his temples. They were the same age, but he was completely, prematurely grey. She rubbed her forehead against the stubble on his chin, his skin rough against hers. The skin around her lips still chafed from last night. He reached for her, running his fingers down her arms, pulling her hands gently from behind her back.

She had to extricate herself before it got messy. 'Pete, this wasn't a good idea. I'm really sorry. I mean, I'm not sorry really, I had such a good time. I don't want you to think . . .'

He let her hands drop.

She knew how he felt about her. They had done a couple of modules together on the forensics programme at London

South Bank uni. They had hit it off straight away, had ended up sitting next to each other, having the same complaints about the tutors, revising for exams together. He was bright. Not as bright as she was, she had told him several times. She had known he was attracted to her, and she had been careful not to encourage him. He was an open, uncomplicated man. Too uncomplicated, too predictable. He didn't have that certain edge, the inner shadows that excited her. She was sure he'd had a happy childhood with loving parents who were probably still married and living in the Cotswolds.

No, that was all rubbish, irrelevant. The point was: he wasn't Max.

She watched as he pulled his trousers back on and buttoned his shirt. He looked across at her, his jeans still undone. She glimpsed herself, riding on top of him, his fingers squeezing her nipples. Something between them sparked again, and then died. She pulled her jumper over her head.

'Thanks, for last night,' she said. 'It's been a while. For me.'

There were a few moments of uncomfortable silence.

She could hear Hannah's voice: *What is wrong with you? You're an idiot.*

The silence grew longer.

He leaned forward and kissed her softly on the cheek. 'Why don't we skip breakfast,' he said.

She nodded. There was no point prolonging the parting.

There was a pull inside her, a mix of disappointment and relief.

She walked him the short distance to the front door. She hoped her devout Muslim neighbour would not emerge just in time to see her wave goodbye with no trousers on. But the corridor was empty.

He had to wait ages for the cranky old lift.

She stood in the doorway of her Bayswater apartment, alone, contented and also a little sad.

## Hilltop, 11.15 p.m.

Unsurprisingly, Blue remained in a deep and peaceful sleep. She lay on her side, her thumb resting near her mouth, her limbs limp and heavy.

Stella crept carefully away from her own bed. She walked over to the window and parted the closed curtains, just a crack. The trees and the hills beyond gleamed with the soft light reflected from the snow. The house on the hill was a far cry from the cramped Bayswater flat, but sometimes she missed west London and her piece of the city, high up on the sixth floor of an old mansion block. She missed the endless planes on the flight path to Heathrow, their twinkling red lights replacing the stars in the night sky.

At the top of the window, the light of the sensor flashed every few seconds, slow and reassuring. Stella made sure the heavy drapes were properly, completely closed.

Blue's eyes moved rapidly from side to side under the tissue-thin skin of her eyelids. She changed position, rolled over, her breathing still regular. Stella could still see her eyes wide open: determined and suspicious and seductive.

She reached for her BlackBerry, lifted it, framed the girl's face. The flash went off, but Blue did not wake. Stella emailed the shot to Peter.

She carried the low chair from the dressing table over to the bed and sat down to watch over Blue. She dozed off, then woke, afraid. But nothing had changed, the girl had not moved. Stella's neck hurt. She shifted in the chair, leaning her head against her arm. Her eyelids were so heavy, she was desperate to shut her eyes, just for a few moments, but she couldn't risk falling asleep in the same room with Blue.

She removed the key from the lock, and closed the door softly behind her. She locked it from the outside and tucked the key into her pocket. She felt a little better.

She didn't know what to do next. She was so very tired.

Downstairs the near empty bottle of wine stood lukewarm on the kitchen table. She unscrewed the lid and poured the last few drops into her glass. As she drank, she listened.

Dead silence from upstairs.

She never could hold her drink. Behind her eyes, images took shape. She was shivering, and cold, and her hand trembled. White wine splashed against the glossy white table top.

Nobody could get into Hilltop. Nobody could get out. Nothing would happen.

Stella struggled up, out of a thick and heavy sleep.

Bang, bang, bang.

She saw blue, blue eyes.

More goddamn banging. So loud. Like a hammer against her skull.

She opened her eyes and found that she was on the sofa, downstairs, grey linen coarse under her cheek. The fire in the hearth had gone out and there was a faint smell of charred pine and a chill in the room. She couldn't remember where she had left her phone. Maybe Max had tried to call her.

The banging was coming from the front door.

Maybe Max was home. Maybe the police had made it up the hill.

When she stood up, her head ached and there was a ringing in her ears. She had been stupid to drink on top of her pills. She looked hard at the monitor at the front door, a blurry image swam in and out of focus. She lifted the receiver to her ear.

'Stella – it's fucking freezing out here. Are you going to let me in?'

His face came into focus more sharply. Her head was clearing. 'Peter?'

She pulled back the locks and opened the front door wide. Cold air blasted inside. She didn't care; she welcomed it. The snow had piled up even higher in the darkness, inches more had fallen; he must have struggled to reach Hilltop. She could hardly remember the last time she had been so happy, so relieved, to see someone. She wanted to throw her arms around him and hold on tight. But something held her back.

He stepped through the door, his head down, his thick grey hair turned white with snowflakes. He was all trussed up in a black, waxy-waterproof coat. As he unfastened the buttons, the snowflakes fell to the floor, leaving tiny puddles around his boots.

How strange to see Peter in this place, so far removed from her previous life. How unsettling that he looked just the same while Stella felt she'd aged ten years. She tried to smooth down her hair and to straighten her sleeves, to pull down her top; she felt a wreck, standing there.

'What made you change your mind?' she said.

He took a long look around the entrance hall, and ended up staring at the chandelier. He was avoiding her eyes, she was sure of it. 'When did you move out to this godforsaken place?' he asked.

'It's not godforsaken. It's the Chilterns.'

She looked pointedly at his black boots with their thick soles, but he didn't remove them. He hung his coat next to hers, on the coat stand next to the front door. She tried to think of the last time she'd needed that coat, but she couldn't remember.

'Has the girl given you any problems?' he asked. She thought she detected a note of something else in his voice, only she wasn't certain what it was.

'Not really.' Stella wondered whether she had sounded totally unhinged on the phone earlier. 'But she still hasn't really explained why she's here – she keeps making up different stories.'

Peter was giving her that strange look again. Perhaps he thought she had been reckless, considering what had happened.

'I couldn't just leave her outside to freeze to death,' she said. 'I had to let her in.'

'Where is she now?'

'Upstairs. Asleep,' Stella said.

'Asleep?'

'It's late.'

'Yes. I suppose I imagined – something a little more fraught.'

He stood with his hands in the pockets of his jeans; stiff

and formal, as though they were strangers. Inside, she squirmed. She felt as though she was a suspect, under interrogation.

'And I've locked her in,' she said.

She reached into her pocket and felt for the key of her bedroom. It was still there.

'You locked her in?' He seemed taken aback by this.

'She's unpredictable. I didn't want her wandering around the house. And she wasn't exactly pleased when I mentioned I'd contacted the police.'

'Did you consider that could be viewed as child abduction? Are you sure she's asleep – that she isn't trying to get out?'

'Very sure,' Stella said. 'Because I gave her a sleeping tablet.'

Peter rubbed his hands over his face, and suddenly looked very tired.

'Don't look at me like that. It was only one – I crushed it up and put it in her drink. I was nervous, trapped in here with her. You said she was high risk. So I made sure she was out of action for a few hours. I needed some peace.'

She felt frustrated; he had no idea, he knew nothing about the way she lived.

Stella supposed he was wondering which one of them was more unstable, herself or the girl. She was beginning to wonder the same thing. She hoped Blue was all right. She listened, half expecting to hear the sound of Blue's fists beating on her bedroom door, but the house was silent.

'She's admitted that the story about being Max's daughter was a lie. But she now claims that she knows him, that she's his patient. Apparently it's Max she came out here to see.'

'Have you checked with Max?'

'No.'

'Why not?'

'She keeps changing her story every five minutes. I wasn't sure what to do.' She glanced up at him. He knew she was lying. 'I can't reach him. His phone has been turned off all day. He does that. Sometimes.'

Stella was feeling much calmer, much safer, now that Peter was with her. 'I'm sorry you had to drive out here in this weather,' she said. 'I'm very grateful. And also – surprised.'

His hands hung stiffly at his sides now. His eyes touched hers, then flickered away. He glanced at his watch. They had not spoken in more than a year. He might well resent her sudden intrusion into his life.

'I'm glad you're here,' she said. 'I'm glad you didn't change your mobile number.'

In fact Peter looked as though he would rather be any-where else but inside Hilltop. Nevertheless, he followed her through into the living room.

'When will your husband be home?' he asked.

*Your husband.* The words that should bring a feeling of pleasure, of warmth.

'Tomorrow morning – early,' she said. 'Today, I mean.'

She was too jumpy to sit down, and so she remained stand-ing at one end of the sofa. He stood too, at the opposite end.

'Coffee?' she asked.

'No, thank you,' he said. 'You're sure you're all right?' He had noticed the empty wine bottle.

'One minute I feel sorry for her, the next I don't trust her. I think she has some ulterior motive.'

Peter seemed not to know quite what to say to her.

He wandered over to the bookshelves at the side of the fireplace and began inspecting her books. She read almost anything. She had hours and days and months to fill, and new books couldn't come out fast enough. Her DVD collection was equally impressive. Each month she'd send a couple of boxes to Oxfam with Max and then re-stock the shelves. In Hilltop, time could feel like torture. On the days when she could no longer concentrate on novels or films, she had to face the truth: her life had become like watching paint dry.

'You organize your shelves,' he said. 'Fiction and non-fiction. And then non-fiction by subject. And also by size.' He was in front of the shelves on photography and interior design.

'I do,' she said. She wished he'd get on with it: the reason for his visit.

'Wouldn't that be classified as obsessive?'

'Rituals keep anxiety at bay.'

'What anxiety?' he asked.

'You know.'

'So. You and Max,' he said.

She nodded. She knew he was asking her a question, and that he wanted some kind of explanation, but she didn't want to talk about her husband.

'Has Max tried to get you back to the clinic?'

'He doesn't pressure me.' She rested her hands on the back of the sofa, stroking the rough fabric.

'What do you do with yourself all day?' he asked.

The Stella he knew was a different person, driven and ambitious. She loved her job.

'I don't go out much,' she said. 'I don't go out at all.'

'And his life goes on as normal?'

'Yes,' she said.

'Interesting,' he said.

'Why is that interesting?'

She was still hovering behind the sofa, deciding whether or not to sit down. If she remained standing, she could discharge more of her nervous energy, by tapping her foot, moving her arm along the back of the sofa, rearranging the cushions.

Peter always did have skewed ideas about Max.

'What about professional help?' he asked.

'Max took me to see a psychiatrist.'

'And?'

'It didn't go well. Lying on the couch with some strange man once a week didn't appeal to me at that point.'

'Did you try someone else?'

'No. He gave me a prescription and I take plenty of pills. They keep me functioning. They stop the flashbacks and the nightmares.'

Peter approached the sofa, cautiously, and sat down on one end – the exact spot Blue had chosen earlier. Stella walked round and sat down too. Not too close. He was looking directly at her now.

'You're still taking them, after all this time?'

'Max authorizes the repeat prescriptions. Neither of us think there's any point stopping the pills when I barely leave the house.'

'Isn't it unethical to prescribe drugs for family members?'

'It helps me stay sane.'

'Sounds an ideal set-up then,' he said.

'Oh, it is.'

Go to hell, she thought. Peter had always wanted too much, expected too much of her. Much more than her husband did. She should expect more of herself, she supposed.

'I take almost as many pills as that girl. I'm a walking

zombie.' It was a relief to say it out loud, to admit the truth.

And she had been cruel to him. She was wrong to have cut him out completely, and not only Pete, but all of her friends, all of the people who cared. She felt ashamed and she couldn't look at him, couldn't sit so near to him. She leapt up and, putting some distance between them, she wrenched open the curtains and flicked on the outside lights, illuminating her kingdom. The lamps along the patio cast yellow rays across the garden and the glow spread all the way across the lawn, reaching the edge of the snow-coated trees behind them.

He came to stand next to her, looking out at the garden, his hands in his pockets again. They stood very close and static crackled in the empty space between them.

'Why does he stay over in Hampstead?' he asked. He was more gentle with her now. He pitied her, and that was worse.

'The snow,' she said. 'He thought it would be safer. The roads were too difficult, in his car. How did you make it up here?'

'I borrowed a jeep.'

'Max kept the Hampstead apartment after we moved out here,' she said. 'He stays over there, sometimes. I think he probably needs to get away from me.' She cleared her throat. 'Any more questions?'

He shook his head.

She felt tears coming and she felt angry. At everything: at Max, at the girl upstairs, at her own weakness, at Peter. She paced around the blue border of the carpet. She stood on the parrot's face. She clenched her fists, feeling the power in her hands. She was struck by how vital Peter looked, how steady. He was a reminder of her old life, of everything she had given up.

'Do you still find me attractive?' she asked.

'Jesus, Stella.'

'Do you?'

'Of course I do.' He dug his hands deep into his pockets.

'You're lying.'

She stood right in front of him. She looked at his face, properly. What colour were his eyes? She had forgotten, or she had never noticed. She hadn't paid much attention.

His eyes were brown.

She leaned forward and kissed him, taking him by surprise. He kissed her back, tentatively, more gently than she would have liked. Her lips parted and she pressed herself close against him, trying to absorb something of his strength. She wanted to feel his hands in her hair, his arms tight around her. She wanted a taste of her old self. His lips against hers. If she could stay with him, where it was safe. The gold silk curtains tied back from the windows, the blanket of snow outside. His body, solid. She pressed harder against him.

His hands were on her shoulders. Firm. Not holding her, but pushing her away. He stepped back, holding her at arm's length, a strange look on his face. 'What are you doing?' he asked.

'Nothing.'

She couldn't explain the unexpected, urgent attraction. It must be the heightened tension in the house, the adrenaline, the stress of the unexpected visitor, all colliding, tricking her body into a heightened state of anticipation. Or, just maybe, the months of frustration, with her husband.

'I'm sorry, Pete,' she said.

'You don't need to apologize.'

'I do.'

'Let's sit down,' he said, moving away from her.

'No.' She was sick and tired of being kept at a distance. 'Please. Tell me why you came out here.' She looked into his eyes, trying to see what it was he wasn't saying. 'You're making me nervous. Has something happened to Max?'

'No. Nothing like that.'

He took his time, considering his words carefully.

## Session Nine

She sat in her chair, like a good girl. A good patient. Impatient. From the look on his face when she walked in, all stony and closed, she could see she had better not try anything too soon. She would have to wait.

For the first time ever, he started talking first.

'You know I want to help you get better,' he said.

She nodded.

'And I want to help you to come to terms with reality. Even if it's painful. There can't be anything between us, anything more than doctor and patient.'

She leaned forward, her blouse gaping open.

'You've had some very difficult experiences. And I think you're avoiding dealing with what's happened to you by fixating on me. By fantasizing about me. But I'm not the answer to your problems.'

She chewed on her thumbnail. 'Don't try and make out that I'm crazy,' she said.

'Having a fantasy doesn't mean you're crazy.'

Her mouth was *really* dry. She hadn't made up what had happened. It was real. Afterwards, she had changed her underwear and it was sticky – her juices and his, together.

'This has to stop,' he said. 'We can't work together any more. I'm not helping you. Not really helping, in the way you need.'

She swallowed again, her throat was tight. 'Can I have some water?'

He nodded. She reached for the glass on the small table beside her. With a shaking hand, she raised it to her lips and took a small sip, to wet her mouth so she could find her voice.

'This fantasy that you have about being with me – it isn't good for you. It's hurting you.' His voice was so calm and so cold.

'STOP TALKING!' She checked herself, tried not to scream. 'Stop it.'

Now her head was starting to feel fuzzy.

'If you can't stay with reality, if you can't deal with what is really happening around you, you know what the alternative is.' He was on edge. He kept looking towards the door. She must not scream again.

'You're scaring me,' she said.

'I'm not trying to scare you. I only want to help you, before you hurt yourself more than you already have. Can you understand how destructive this is?'

She put her head in her hands and she started to cry. She couldn't bear to look at him. He wouldn't stop talking and his words were like knives. And he wouldn't stop.

'I care about you. And I don't want you to get worse, to get seriously ill. But if these sessions aren't helping you, I have to do something different. I could carry on seeing you, I could increase the dosage of your medication, but if I'm honest, I don't think any of that is in your best interests. I think it's best if we stop these sessions and I find you another therapist. A woman.'

She didn't look up at him. She sank down, between the chair and the rug, drew her knees up to her chest and put her head down between them. She pushed the heels of her hands hard against her eyes. It wasn't a fantasy. He had loved her. And now he wanted to take it away and it was the only good thing she had left and she didn't understand why bad things always had to happen to her. He was supposed to love her, after what she had let him do.

His voice changed, it was softer and kinder. 'You have to admit to yourself that what happened between us was some kind of fantasy. Like a dream.'

She blocked out his words, not hearing. She focused on the sound of his voice, the softer, warmer tone, and her anger ebbed away. What started next was the feeling of wanting him; she felt a warmth spreading and pulsing. She wanted him to let her climb on to his lap, to hold her.

She sat with her head still between her knees, her eyes open, staring at the patterns in the rug and letting her eyes go out of focus so she wasn't really there at all.

'Do you understand what I'm saying?' he asked. His voice drifted towards her from far away, as though he were standing at the end of a long tunnel.

She closed her eyes, shook her head. She wanted to make him stop hurting her.

'Tell me,' she said. 'Anything you want me to do for you. Anything. I'll do anything.'

He looked sad and disappointed. 'This wasn't how I wanted it to end between us. I wanted to help you.'

She wanted to crawl over to him and slide herself between his knees, to move her hand up between his legs, until he would let her close to him again. But she was getting sick of this, sick of him always making her work so hard.

Making him love her all over again, every time. Having to wait seven whole days until she saw him for one measly hour. Sometimes she wasn't sure if she loved him or if she hated him.

## Grove Road Clinic, May 2009

'So – are we going to have a look at the Rorschach data?'
Max asked.

For once, he was in his office, at the right time. Although
he had looked a little surprised to see her at his door.

Stella shook her head. 'I wish we could,' she said. 'I
couldn't get him to take the test. He freaked out, he got really
paranoid about it. I think it was too threatening for him to
deal with a completely unstructured stimulus. He wouldn't
cooperate.'

'That's a pity.' Max looked at her over the top of his mug
of coffee. Unruly piles of paperwork were strewn across the
desk between them.

'I lost it a little bit – I was so frustrated at his defiance,
when he wouldn't cooperate, that instead of focusing on
building rapport, I said something smarmy about how he
should consider what the judge would think of him. So that,
of course, alienated him more and he ended up walking out
of the session. And I let him go. I'm not optimistic about filling my quota of hours on this case – there's hardly any
material to write up.' She hated disappointing him.

'Come on, Stella, I know how hard you work. You're an

excellent clinician and you're too hard on yourself. A bit perfectionistic sometimes.'

He rummaged around in the top drawer of his desk and swallowed a couple of tablets, washing them down with his coffee. 'Can I get you a coffee?' he said.

'I'm fine, thanks.'

He gave her a weak smile. He looked so tired.

'But that's not quite the end of the Simpson story,' Stella said. 'There's more. I'm not sure if it's good or bad. On Saturday night I was out with a group of friends, at a restaurant in Marylebone. Simpson was there and he made a point of coming over to my table to talk to me. Because I was in a group of people, I didn't want to cause a scene. I also didn't want to break confidentiality by identifying him as a client. So I ended up having a bit of a chat with him.'

'What did he say?'

'He apologized for being so difficult in the interview and he asked if I would schedule another appointment for him.'

'That's great,' Max said. 'Are you pleased?'

For some reason she felt sheepish, as though she had done something unprofessional. 'It was odd, bumping into him while I was with friends, in a bar. With a half-naked belly dancer in the background. He was really friendly actually, totally different to the way he behaved in my office. I got the feeling he would have sat down and had a meal with us if there had been an empty chair. I think he was pleased to see me, I think it gave him a thrill, to be able to get a look in at my personal life. He even got to see me belly dancing, for God's sake.'

Max ran his hand over his closely cropped head. He must have had a haircut over the weekend. His eyes glinted and he laughed. She grinned too. She loved to make him happy.

'It gave me the creeps,' she said.

'The real world does exist, you know. Things happen out there too, not just inside this clinic. You can't control every-thing, Stella. You over-think things sometimes.'

'And I should also say that he bought me a drink. At the time I just couldn't face making a scene over it. I know I should have refused.'

'Look, he was a little over-familiar, overstepping a boundary and treating you like a friend, like someone he met in a bar, and not as a professional. I'm sure that's what he does and you're not going to be the exception to the rule. On the positive side, if he apologized, it seems like he has some insight into his behaviour, and it sounds like he can see it's in his best interests to cooperate with you.

'And who can say that accepting that drink – his gift – didn't buy you some goodwill with a difficult-to-engage client? If you'd turned it down, and wounded his pride, you could have kissed any hope of rapport goodbye. Something small like that – acting like a human being instead of a snobbish professional – can be key to connecting with him. You can't simply be a blank screen and hide behind your pro-fessional credentials, you have to give something back sometimes. And if he imagines that he's succeeded in winning you over, or that you might be susceptible to his charms in some way, won't he cooperate a little more willingly?'

'I see your point,' she said.

'And they can't prove you drank it, can they?'

'I didn't, actually.'

He leaned forward and grinned at her again. She knew he had a sense of fun, that he was far from boring, that he questioned the need to keep a rigid hierarchical distance between patient and professional. As the familiar longing to be closer to him grew, so her nerves kicked in and the muscles in her face seized up. She found it difficult to hold her smile.

He leaned back in his chair, retreated, as though he had given up on her. She must appear humourless. 'It sounds like he was trying to connect with you. Do you agree?'

'I think he's so angry, and his pride has been so wounded by this whole process of having to go through a psychological assessment that he's trying to find some way to subvert our professional relationship, so that he can feel he has more control over the process. He even asked if I could travel to his offices, instead of meeting here at the clinic. I think he's desperate to convince me that we're somehow equals, to get me to like him, on a personal level.'

Her legs were so tightly crossed she could no longer feel her feet. She stretched them in small increments, trying to re-establish the blood flow. She wished she could be more relaxed around Max, wished she could enjoy him more.

'What about a clinical formulation? Do you have a hypothesis?'

'I think he's highly insecure and I think there's a strong possibility he suffers from anxiety. I think it's likely he's paranoid – he resents being forced into these appointments with psychologists and psychiatrists and he's preoccupied with what professionals will find out about him. The only way he will engage is if he believes he can manipulate the clinician into seeing his best side. I think he would like to be able to seduce me, so to speak, into being on his side. I think that even if he does turn up for a re-scheduled appointment, he will shut down completely if I try to explore any territory where *he* doesn't want to go.'

'Sounds to me like you're getting a good sense of him,'

Max said. 'I have to say I'm relieved he's re-engaging. Gregory's are a big law firm – if we impress them with this one, there'll be plenty more work. Let's focus on finishing the interviews, and then we can integrate our findings. And get the bills sent out.'

'How's it going with the mother and daughter?'

'Fine,' he said. 'All on track.' He placed his empty mug down on his side table and glanced up behind her head. She knew there was a clock on the wall. Her irritation mounted. She had only had thirty minutes of his time, instead of the hour she was entitled to. As always, he had cut their time together short.

'I wasn't sure whether to include all of this in my report: bumping into him in the restaurant, his approaching me, letting him buy me a drink.'

'It's a judgement call,' Max said. 'If you don't write it up, his solicitor may raise it in court and use it in some way to discredit you. Although I think that sort of personal attack would be extremely unlikely. On the other hand, from what you've said, nothing that happened in that meeting outside of the clinic has any relevance to his parenting ability, so there's no real reason to include it.'

'What would you do?' Stella asked.

'I'd advise you to write up exactly what happened, in as much detail as you remember, and keep the notes in the case file. But as he didn't really do anything noteworthy or in-appropriate, I wouldn't include it in the court report. If you have it in the file, then if it's raised at any point – which I very much doubt – you can hand over your notes. OK?'

She nodded, unsmiling. His brisk tone indicated that their session was over.

'When you've written up a draft I'll read your report in

detail and we'll go over it together before we submit it to the solicitors.'

In the end, he wouldn't let her down.

Stella collected her papers, packing them back into her bag and feeling self-conscious as she struggled to push the too-large files back into her bulging tote bag.

'Those are great tights,' he said.

She was wearing a knee-length black skirt and her tights had a slightly out-there zigzag pattern. She had been thinking about the supervision session when she chose what to wear that morning.

'Thanks.' Her mood lifted a little.

'You've got my mobile number. Don't hesitate to call me. Even if it's on a weekend or in the middle of the interview – if there's anything you're unsure about.'

Either he was being supportive and he cared, or he didn't trust her to handle a clinical interview with a challenging client. And, just maybe, he was hinting that he wanted her to contact him after hours.

Incredibly unlikely.

'Thank you,' she said.

'We're all going across to the Lamb and Eagle for a drink after work. Want to join us?'

'Sorry, I can't,' she said. In fact she could, she had absolutely nothing else planned. And she wanted to, very much. But she didn't trust herself to be around him, socially, and to act normal. Too many feelings simmered inside her, they were too difficult to control. She wouldn't be able to speak.

'Where are you off to?' He seemed genuinely to want to know.

'I have to get some work done on this report,' she lied.

'Nothing exciting then?'

How boring she must seem.

She backed away, heading for the door, though she would have liked nothing more than to move closer.

Max, Anne and Paul left the building together at six o'clock. Stella watched them go, through the wooden shutters of the office on the first floor. She felt irrationally angry at being left behind. Irrationally jealous. Max threw his head back and laughed at something Anne had said. She saw him rest his hand protectively on the small of Anne's back as they approached the crossing.

She could not imagine that Max would ever touch her. Professional distance – like a six-foot-high, reinforced concrete wall – was solidly, immovably in place between them.

She turned back to her computer and typed the heading she most dreaded: *Background Documentation*. She had yet another file of papers to summarize for the Simpson matter. She would try to be as brief as possible and to get it all down to twenty pages, double-spaced. Max had given her the history to write up because it was the most tedious part of the work. She accepted her place in the hierarchy: he was the senior consultant, he could pick and choose.

After forty-five minutes she got up and made another cup of coffee. For once, she felt grateful to Anne, who had put on a fresh pot before leaving. At nine, she shut down her laptop and packed it away.

She hated being the last to leave because it meant she was responsible for checking the building was secure. If a window was left open, if the building was burgled, if client files went missing, if the place burnt down – it would be her fault.

She locked the case files away in the tall metal cupboard, double-checking the doors were secure. She went through each room, checking windows and turning out lights. The building fell silent around her.

## Hilltop, 12.30 a.m.

'I wanted to talk to you in person,' Peter said. 'It's about the photograph you sent me.'

'Do you have any idea why she would come out here?'

'She is the girl I told you about – the fifteen-year-old. She lives with her single mother on an estate in Ladbroke Grove, but it turns out she's been in and out of foster care. Her last placement was around two years ago. The mother has substance-abuse problems.'

He was staring at her, waiting, watching for a reaction.

'That sounds right,' Stella said. 'She told me something similar.'

Stella spoke softly, as though Blue might be lurking on the stairs, listening.

'Stella. The reason I came out here to see you was because I'm certain that this girl is Lawrence Simpson's daughter.'

Stella almost laughed. 'No,' she said. 'She isn't.'

'His daughter has just turned fifteen,' he said.

'So have thousands of other girls. Millions, even.'

'Stella, the photograph you sent me – it is the same girl.'

'No. That doesn't make sense.' Stella shook her head. 'Blue told me that Max has been treating her. He would never take

151

her on as a patient if she was Lawrence Simpson's daughter. Not after – what happened. It's not her.'

Stella was calm. Flat. Detached.

'The name on her birth certificate is Lauren Simpson. Her mother started using the name Cunningham for both of them a few years back – it's her maiden name.'

It was sinking in, sinking through the fog. Her gut instinct had been right: the girl had brought danger with her. If Peter believed the girl was Simpson's daughter, she knew it must be true; he would never have come out to see her at Hilltop unless he was absolutely sure.

She closed her eyes and put her face in her hands. When she opened her eyes, the room was blurred and so was Peter's face.

'I wanted to tell you in person,' he said. 'The Met Police know but I have no idea how long it will take them to get someone out here.'

'Tell me the truth,' she said. 'Don't try and protect me. Honestly: do you think Simpson's involved in this? Do you think he sent her out here? Maybe he brought her here himself . . .'

She rubbed her eyes, but her vision wasn't any clearer.

'Stella, stop.' He reached out and put his hand over hers; it was warm, it covered hers completely. 'Listen to me. Absolutely not – that is not what's happening. I've followed the case. His daughter still has a guardian and I managed to talk to her earlier. Simpson has had an unblemished record for the past eighteen months. He didn't get custody but he was granted unsupervised contact. The guardian is happy with him. There's no reason he should screw that up. If he carries on the way he is, he has another shot at gaining custody because apparently the ex-wife is back on the bottle.

There is no reason I can think of that he would jeopardize what he's always wanted. But the question is – why would his daughter come out here?'

'It is her,' Stella said. 'She has his eyes.'

'Did she tell you anything more about why she wants to see Max?'

She shook her head. 'Not really – something about wanting him to help her.' She looked out, towards the garden. There was only darkness. 'Nothing about this makes sense. Max wouldn't take Blue on as a patient, not after everything that happened. He couldn't.'

'But he knows her,' Peter said. 'He was part of the assessment team, for the court case.'

'And that was almost two years ago and now he's married to me. And this girl lies constantly. She's also on some very strong medication – she may well be delusional. Maybe she knew Max wasn't here. Maybe she came out here to see me, to hurt me. Maybe she knows something about my report. We have to talk to her.'

She didn't wait for him to give her an argument. She ran towards the stairs. He had no choice but to follow.

Stella unlocked her bedroom door.

'Blue might be frightened,' she said, 'if she sees you when she wakes up. She's going to be groggy, confused maybe. Wait here.'

She barely looked at Peter. Her heart galloped in her chest, as though she expected a wild animal to lunge out at her.

'Blue?' She pushed the door wide open.

The air in her bedroom was musty and thick with sleep. Stella edged forwards, her eyes adjusting to the darkness. She stumbled over something at her feet. Something was wrong.

Or everything was wrong. The chair that usually stood in front of the dressing table lay on its side. Her dressing table was emptied and, around it, strewn across the floor, was a trail of cosmetics and shattered perfume bottles. The bookshelves were half empty, books flung out. Her cupboards gaped open and a mess of clothes and shoes spilt out on to the carpet. The room stank of perfume: lime and musk and pomegranate, all mixed up. It was as if there had been an explosion.

Stella groped her way across to the bed, hoping not to step on broken glass or to fall over some unexpected object.

'Blue? Are you awake?'

Blue was a bundle under the covers. She didn't stir at the sound of her name. Stella placed a hand lightly on her back, feeling for the movement of her breath. She closed her eyes, concentrating on her fingertips. And there it was: a small stirring, the girl's ribcage expanding and then falling, rising again, falling.

Stella pulled the covers back and touched the girl's bony shoulder. She shook her. 'Blue – wake up.'

Blue groaned. She pulled away, hauling the covers up around her head and trying to huddle her way back down into sleep. Stella turned on the bedside lamp. The empty mug was still in its place on the bedside table. Blue grimaced, screwing her eyes tightly closed and turning away.

'Come on.' Stella slipped her hands under Blue's arms and pulled her up to a sitting position, gently pushing her hair back from her face. Blue blinked at her, looking groggy as all hell.

'Are you awake?'

Blue nodded.

'What the hell happened to my bedroom?'

Blue's lips had lost their pale pink blush. She looked

terribly young and afraid. 'I woke up and I couldn't find you,' she said. 'The door was locked.'

'So you destroyed my bedroom?'

'I was calling you. I was scared. Why did you lock the door?'

'I needed to sleep,' Stella said. 'I just wanted to keep you safe.'

'I was banging on the door. Why didn't you come?'

'I didn't hear you. I was asleep, downstairs.'

'I thought you were kind of psycho. Locking me in here.'

'Blue, you came here to my house, remember? You lied to me to get in here. *Remember?*'

Blue nodded, looking down at her nails.

'I'm entitled to be a little suspicious of you too,' Stella said.

Her feelings towards the girl swayed and shifted and wouldn't settle. She looked at Blue's lovely, young face and felt a strange fondness. Blue was no threat.

And then the fear was back. She was afraid of what Blue might want from her.

Her eyes. Drops of sweat broke out across Stella's forehead, on her top lip, in the crease of her neck.

'I forgive you for locking me in,' Blue said.

Stella wiped the moisture from her face 'Blue, there's someone outside. You don't need to be afraid. He's a friend. And a policeman. '

Stella was expecting drama, a tantrum at the very least.

'Where's my jacket?' Blue asked.

'It's right here.'

When Blue had pulled on her jacket once again, she looked just the way Stella had first seen her when she had arrived at Hilltop the afternoon before, only now she seemed paler and smaller.

She wasn't sure the girl had heard her, had understood. Blue allowed Stella to take her by the arm, to steer her over the obstacles and out of the bedroom. She seemed sanguine about Peter's arrival; in the hallway she gave him a small, shy smile. Perhaps it was the tranquillizers, but she seemed calmer, more acquiescent.

Peter walked behind them, keeping a distance, as Stella and Blue descended the grand circular staircase, moving towards the hard concrete and marble downstairs. Nobody spoke; the atmosphere was charged and heavy.

At the bottom, Blue stopped next to the front door. She bent down and grabbed her shoes. 'I'm going home,' she said.

'We need to talk to you first,' Stella said.

'You can't keep me here. I'll tell them you made me have a bath in front of you.' She fumbled with her laces.

'Thanks, I appreciate that. But you can't leave – it's the middle of the night. It's freezing.'

Peter placed his solid frame in front of the door.

Blue looked warily at the two of them, as though they were the unwanted guests who had forced themselves into her home and not the other way round.

'Why is he here?' Blue asked.

'We're worried about you. We only want to talk to you.' Stella took a chance and reached for Blue's hand, catching it in mid-air, on the way to her mouth once more. She hoped they wouldn't have to restrain her.

Blue did not resist, she let Stella take her hand. At first her grip was shy and tentative, then she edged closer, taking hold of Stella's arm and leaning against her shoulder. Stella could see Peter taking it all in: the way Blue had staked a claim to her; the way she swung from sullen to seductive.

Blue allowed Stella to lead her into the kitchen.

It was strange, to have people in her home. On weekdays, Max would leave the house by six, whilst Stella was still asleep. On weekends he'd leave at the same time, to cycle down to Beaconsfield and back. She had come to Hilltop to escape. But escape came at a price: the move had cut her off from everyone she knew, from her past, from her own self.

Blue chose her customary seat, the one at the head of the table. Stella began to dread what the girl might reveal. Her thoughts would not follow rhythm or logic; she knew Blue had brought something terrible into her home.

Peter nodded at her, impatient to start. He stayed silent as Stella asked the questions.

'Is your name Lauren Simpson?' Stella said.

'I told you – my name is Blue.'

'And your surname?'

'Cunningham. Blue Cunningham.'

'So your name isn't Lauren Simpson?'

'Not any more. It's true. You can ask my mother.'

'But your name used to be Lauren Simpson?'

Blue nodded.

'Is Lawrence Simpson your father?' Stella asked. She hated the sound of his name, the feel of him in her mouth. Her throat itched and she pulled hard at the neck of her jumper. Her voice rose – half frightened, half furious. 'Did he tell you to come here? *Where is he?*'

'No.' Blue looked surprised by the question, and confused.

'Does he know you're here?'

'No. Why would I tell him I'm here? I hate him.'

'Where is he now?'

'I don't know where he is!' Blue was becoming distressed, her eyes filling with tears.

Whatever Blue had done, whatever else had happened, Stella reminded herself, she was still a victim.

'Are you even listening to me?' Blue said. 'I said I HATE him. I would never have told him I was coming here. The man I told you about upstairs – that was him.' Blue stood up, defiant. 'You can't force me to stay here. I don't have to talk to you.'

'Sit down!' Stella snapped.

'Stella.' Peter interrupted her. He reached out, keeping his eyes on Blue, and put a hand on her arm.

'Blue,' he said, 'this is really important. Have you told anyone where you are?'

'No.'

'Are you one hundred per cent sure? No one at all?'

'I'm sure. I ran away. You don't tell anyone where you're going when you run away.' She was biting down hard on her thumb. All of the skin around the nail was raw and angry.

'Does your father know this address?' he asked.

'I told you – no. I don't understand—'

'When was the last time you saw him?'

'I don't remember.'

'Come on, Blue, think carefully. Take your time.' Peter kept his tone even and unthreatening. He sat with his feet planted firmly on the floor, leaning forward, his hands flat on the table in front of him. He looked casual enough not to be intimidating, he kept any urgency out of his voice. But Stella could see the muscles tensed across his shoulders and his neck. She admired him and she envied him. He was doing his job and he was good at it. She used to be good at hers.

'A few weeks ago, maybe more,' Blue said. 'I'm telling you the truth, I can't remember exactly.'

'Blue – I'm tired,' Stella said. She stood up. 'I'm sick and tired of your lies. Either you can tell me the whole truth about why you've come here, everything – or Peter is going to drive you to the nearest police station. Right now.'

Blue took her thumb out of her mouth. She smoothed down her fringe, and pushed her hair behind her ears. She bit down on her lower lip.

This girl is dangerous, Stella thought.

'Fine,' Blue said. 'I'll tell you everything. I want to anyway. I wanted you to know – that's why I came. But I need to talk to you on your own.'

'Absolutely not.' Peter stood, ready to come in between them.

Blue's eyes were limpid, hypnotic. Stella saw an angel and then a demon.

'She's manipulating you,' Peter said.

Stella took the girl's outstretched hand. They had to trust each other.

'Don't follow us,' she said to Peter. 'We'll only be in the living room. You can wait in the study.'

His face was a mask of tension. 'If something happens to either of you – my career is on the line. I'm begging you, don't do this.'

'I'm sorry,' Stella said. 'I have to know.'

## Session Ten

The bus took forever and so she was a few minutes late for the session. She was all sweaty, from running. And she was pissed off. She sat in her usual chair, legs slightly apart. She took off her ugly black school shoes and her socks and rubbed her feet into his patterned rug. She stretched out her legs and looked down at her feet. She liked the way the bright pink nail-polish looked against the pale skin of her toes.

He said nothing.

'I left a message with your secretary. Why didn't you phone me back?' She pulled her hairband out, letting her hair fall loose around her shoulders and down her back.

'We shouldn't be talking to each other in between sessions unless there's an emergency,' he said.

'Like what?'

'What did you want to talk to me about?'

She looked down at the arms of the chair and scratched at the flowers with her fingernails. She wondered how long it would take for him to let her touch him today. She didn't like having to beg.

'What if I'm pregnant?' she said, only because she wanted to watch him squirm.

He kept his face very still, like he wasn't surprised or anything. 'What makes you think you're pregnant?'

'I'm not. I just wanted to see your face.'

He wasn't giving anything away, he had on his professional face, like a mask. Far away and blank, that was how he looked, even when he was inside her. She was fuming. He had used her, he didn't really give a shit about her.

'I wanted to see you. I didn't want to have to wait so long for my stupid appointment time. And I'm sick of seeing you in here, in this office. I want to go to a hotel. I want you to take me home with you, I want to see where you live.'

Her voice sounded all bitter and horrible and she already knew she was never, ever, going to get what she wanted. Not really. He could make her so happy. The two of them, together for hours, all night cuddled up, not just an hour on the carpet that burned her butt, or squashed up on the chair trying to find a place for her legs. Except that thinking about all of that was making her squirm in her chair. She could go over, kneel between his legs and take him in her mouth. That would make him listen. It might change his mind.

She imagined the two of them in a really big bed under a fluffy duvet. Maybe there could be one of those enormous round bathtubs with the jets and the two of them could get in together. And room service: chocolate brownies and ice cream. It would be nice to do it lying on a soft mattress. Half the time she wondered why she even wanted to touch him. He hurt her, sometimes. Her anger was back again, burning and aching, like a hot metal fist knotted in her stomach. Sometimes she hated him.

'You have to take me to a hotel,' she said.

'You know that's not going to happen,' he said.

'I'll tell someone what we've been doing. I'll tell the police.

You'll go to jail.' She bit down along the edges of her thumbnail. She could taste blood.

'I'm going to end our session for today. I'll meet with your mother and discuss what we can do about getting you the right treatment.'

He stood up and walked to the door. She stayed immobilised in her chair, her legs apart, her top gaping open.

'You need to leave now,' he said. His voice was ice cold.

He was in control of everything and he didn't give a fuck about her, he had never loved her at all, not even a small bit. He would do whatever he wanted and she was nothing, she didn't exist. He thought he could get rid of her, he thought he could use her and chuck her out when it suited him. She wouldn't let him get away with it.

She threw herself at him, she wanted to scratch at his eyes that were so far away and so cruel. But she couldn't get anywhere near them because he grabbed her wrists and he was much, much stronger. She tried to get away from him but he wouldn't let go, she couldn't get her hands free.

'You need to calm down,' he said.

Her nails were too short to do the kind of damage she wanted to do anyway. She wanted to see his blood. She couldn't speak but a groaning sound came from the back of her throat. She felt like an animal trying to break out of a cage.

'Deep breaths,' he said. 'Control yourself.'

Her hands unfurled from the tight fists they had become.

'That's better.'

She couldn't bear the sound of his voice. She made the mistake of looking into his heartless eyes and the rage inside her threatened to boil up all over again. The office, the chairs, the desk, the carpet, everything was hazy. Her chest was closing and her heart was racing, she couldn't breathe. She covered her face with her hands and closed her eyes, she was gasping.

'If you sit down and behave,' he said, 'I can give you something that will help you to relax.'

She nodded. *Help me.*

He took hold of her, she felt his fingers, too tight around her arm. He was hurting her, pulling her towards the bed under the window.

'Good girl. Sit.'

He pushed her down. The sheet of paper rustled and fell to the floor. She looked up at the fluorescent lights in the ceiling. She was terrified. She still could not breathe. She told herself nothing bad would ever happen to her here in this room.

'Just keep breathing. Slowly. Slow it down,' he said. His voice promised her relief, but she no longer believed in him. He rolled up her sleeve. She didn't want to see, she turned her head towards the cream wall and closed her eyes tight.

'It won't hurt.'

But it did, the needle stung and burned as it pierced her flesh. She squeezed her hands into fists again, digging what was left of her nails into her palms.

'It won't be long,' he said.

And it wasn't. Within seconds, her breathing slowed and the muscles in her chest loosened, expanding to let the air back in, right down into her lungs. Her heart stopped its bashing against her ribcage. She lay down and he pulled a white blanket up around her. She turned on to her side to face the wall. She could feel the drug rushing through her veins, warming her up, slowing her down.

From a distance, down a long tunnel, she heard voices.

Her thoughts drifted and swirled as if through warm water. People talking. About her. *A few trial sessions . . . hoping for a positive response . . . too anxiety-provoking at this stage . . . a chance to mature . . . severe emotional difficulties . . . Treatment . . . Hardly surprising given . . . a female therapist . . . acting out . . . escapes into fantasy . . . needs to be watched . . .*

She was awake, relaxed, loose and floppy. She turned over on to her side so she could see her doctor. She looked around the room. If he had his way, this would be the last time she was allowed to be in here with him. Her eyes moved across the wingback armchairs with the red flowers, past the patterned Persian-y rug and then over to his desk, dark wood with a green leather top. She saw a photograph of a woman, smiling. She must be the wife.

# Grove Road Clinic, May 2009

Stella walked into the clinic at nine o'clock. Anne was in position, presiding over the front desk, all mascara, razor-sharp haircut and manicured nails. Stella thought about complimenting her, possibly asking who her hairdresser was as a vague attempt to break the frosty atmosphere between them. She could do with some polishing herself. But she decided against it.

In front of Anne's extraordinary cleavage was an equally ample bouquet of pink roses, the buds just about to open.

'Morning,' Stella said. 'Nice flowers.'

'They're for you,' Anne said.

For some reason she couldn't fathom, Anne seemed annoyed.

'Who are they from?' Stella asked.

Anne toyed with the bee dangling helplessly from the chain around her neck. Stella could never understand how she managed to type with those talons.

'Your client brought them in this morning. Dr Simpson. He was here at eight thirty. He waited for you for forty minutes. I couldn't find any record of the appointment. If you do want to book a room, Stella, you need to make sure it's entered into the system or there could be a clash.' She swung the bee slowly from left to right and back again.

'There was nothing in the booking system because I didn't have an appointment scheduled with him,' Stella said. She pushed the roses apart, peering between the buds to check for any sign of a note. There wasn't one. She recognized the vase, it belonged to the clinic. Anne must have accepted the roses on her behalf and put them in water.

Anne continued: 'Eight consultants work here now. *Everyone* has to use the computerized booking system. You can't just assume an office will be available. And I have asked you to ensure that clients are given a signed appointment card.'

'Anne, are you listening to me?' Stella said. 'I told you I did not schedule an appointment with him for this morning. I told him to contact the receptionist if he wanted to reschedule. As far as I know, he hasn't done so.'

'And you *really* need to be careful in care proceedings cases,' Anne said. 'His ex-wife and daughter arrived at eight forty-five for a joint appointment with Dr Fisher. It was potentially a very awkward situation. As it was, Dr Simpson was very understanding about it. Initially he wanted to wait until I telephoned you to find out why you weren't here, but when his ex-wife and daughter arrived, he thought it best that he leave and reschedule for another time.'

What a fucking disaster. She wondered if Max was angry at her too. The mother could lodge a complaint with her solicitor. All parties in the case had been warned about the acrimony between the parents and had been instructed to make sure there was no overlap in appointment times.

'I said: I did not make an appointment with him.' Stella repeated herself to no avail. Judging by the look on her face,

Anne remained unconvinced. Stella reminded herself that she did not have to explain herself. Not to Anne, anyway. But she did have to talk to Max.

'Bin the flowers,' she said.

'They're just about to open,' Anne said. 'What a terrible waste.'

'I don't accept gifts from clients. And you shouldn't have taken them on my behalf.'

'I can accept rudeness from clients,' Anne said, 'but not from staff. I don't like your tone.' Her eyes narrowed. The bee whizzed from side to side.

'I apologize if my tone was rude,' Stella said. In fact she did not feel at all sorry, but she did acknowledge that Anne was not the main problem. 'I'm angry with Lawrence Simpson. Please can you just throw the flowers away. And if a client ever leaves a gift for me again, please do not accept it.'

'You can throw them away. I can't bring myself to waste such lovely flowers.'

'With pleasure.' With a sharp movement, Stella picked up the vase. Water splashed on to Anne's desktop.

Stella hoped she would have better luck explaining the situation to her boss.

She waited in the office on the first floor, door ajar, until she heard Max's door open on the floor above. Voices and footsteps floated by, on their way down the stairs; the front door closed with a loud clack. She needed to catch Max before his next appointment; she dashed up the stairs and tapped on his door.

'Come in,' he said.

For once, she didn't want to. 'Am I interrupting?'

'Not at all.' But he got up from behind his desk, walked over to the door and reached for his coat.

'It's about the Simpson care proceedings.' Stella wasn't sure where to stand. 'Do you have a few minutes?'

'I'm just on my way out. Actually I wanted to come and talk to you about that case today. But I'm due to give evidence in an hour – at the Old Bailey. It's the Vogel case, shaken baby. I think you prepared the background summary for me?'

'I did. Will you be back in the office later? I was hoping to talk to you today.'

'If you don't have anything booked this morning, why don't you come with me? We can talk in the car. It would be interesting for you to see the cross-examination. The psychologist and paediatrician are also giving evidence today.' Max straightened his tie and slipped his arms into his jacket.

She didn't have any clients booked. 'That would be great,' she said. 'I'll just grab my bag.'

She met him at reception, where she imagined a certain resentment lurking beneath Anne's tight smile as she watched them walk out together. Max's car was a shiny, low-slung, two-door affair: a single man's car. A showy car. The interior was clean with a sharp smell of eucalyptus. A copy of *The Times* was at her feet, a half-full bottle of Evian in the cup holder. Nothing else was lying about. As he turned the key in the ignition, *Radio 2* began to play. Max turned the volume down. The steering wheel was feathery light under his fingers as he made a three-point turn. She was silent, watching him, feeling the heightened awareness of being in a confined space, so close to him.

'So – about the Simpson family,' she said. She was anxious that he should believe her version of events.

'I've just seen mother and daughter,' Max said.

'I know. And I understand the father turned up at the clinic this morning, saying he had an appointment with me?'

Max nodded. She wasn't sure he was following, he was concentrating on changing lanes.

'Max, there was no appointment scheduled. I know it could have been a bad situation, him and the ex-wife in the building at the same time. I hope you believe me,' she said. 'Anne seemed convinced it was my mistake.'

She could hear herself, brittle and defensive. Max was probably regretting putting his trust in her, since it was obvious to both of them she was barely keeping her head above water in this case.

'Anne is not a clinician,' he said. 'And it's her job to be polite to our clients.'

*As opposed to being polite to staff members.*

'And of course I believe you,' Max said. 'I think it's quite likely he found out about the appointment I had with the mother and child and made a point of turning up. It probably wasn't a coincidence.'

'I hadn't thought of it like that,' Stella said. She had been too busy imagining everyone held her responsible. She was hugely relieved to have Max's support. She relaxed a little and began to take notice of the world outside his car. They were on the Finchley Road, passing Lord's cricket ground, heading towards central London.

'He left a huge bunch of flowers for me this morning,' she said. 'I'm really annoyed about it. Again – it's like he wants to give the impression that there's some kind of relationship between us that there shouldn't be. I think he's trying to force me into an awkward position, in front of my colleagues. I suppose he wants me to feel the way he feels: embarrassed and humiliated, as if I've done something wrong when I haven't. It's exactly the way he experiences these proceedings.'

'Absolutely. I agree with you,' Max said. He glanced over at her and smiled and she felt she'd passed some sort of test.

She combed her hair with her fingers. She continued talking, thinking aloud. 'I suppose it's an attempt to reclaim some power in a situation where he feels powerless. In his view he's a victim of an unjust system. He's never actually been accused of doing anything wrong or harming the child in any way, and yet he's still being hauled in front of psychologists and psychiatrists to prove he's a competent parent. It's driving him crazy that he's being tarred with the same brush as the ex-wife. And I'm guessing this is the first situation in his whole life where he feels completely out of control.'

Max nodded.

'Max,' she said. 'Do you really believe me about the appointment this morning?'

'Stella, of course I believe you,' he said. 'Why are you asking me this again?'

'I don't know. Despite all my professional psychobabble, Simpson makes me doubt myself. I keep going over it, wondering if I've done something to encourage him, something to lead him to believe there is some kind of intimacy between us. I know he finds me attractive. And I know I haven't done anything to encourage him. He's messing with my head. And I'm reacting just the way he wants me to, I suppose, doubting myself.'

'I think you just answered your own question,' Max said.

Stella rested her head against the smooth leather headrest and enjoyed the feeling of sun on her face. The scent of sharp, oily pine mingled with the richness of new leather. She could get used to this sort of life. For a few moments, she felt much freer around Max, much less self-conscious. Perhaps it was the speed of the car, the sense of being cocooned inside, with him, away from the clinic.

'I have offered him a replacement appointment,' she said. 'But I asked him to contact the secretary if he wants to reschedule – I think that if he's serious about cooperating, he needs to show some initiative. If I do all the chasing, I'm pretty sure it will be another two hours wasted.'

'That's fine, but I do think he deserves to have his side of the case heard. Other than the ex-wife's claims, there's no evidence in any other context to suggest that he poses a risk to the child. I think you have to keep an open mind – she has serious problems herself and we can't take her reports at face value.'

The tone of the conversation had undergone a subtle shift, and now it seemed Max was lecturing her on how to be objective, on how to do her job properly, and she resented it. It was always so fraught between them. And she knew it was all in her mind: she was ultra-sensitive to any perceived shifts in Max's mood, to any veiled criticisms in what he said. She placed far too much importance on each word, on every inflection.

'Of course,' she said. She worked to keep her expression neutral, relieved that he was concentrating on the road ahead of him.

'Listen,' he said. 'Simpson's behaviour goes with the territory. If you're going to work on these reports, it gets uncomfortable at times.'

'I know.'

He thought she had overreacted.

She allowed herself to be distracted, mesmerized by his hand, the fluid movements of his wrist and his fingers on the gears. She wanted to enjoy every second of this time alone with him.

'I had a conversation with the lead solicitor this morning,' he said. 'Simpson has now defaulted on three appointments with the psychiatrist and so he's decided not to offer any further appointments.'

'I can't say I'm surprised.'

Max's right hand rested gently on the wheel. The journey was stop-start, a procession of endless red lights now they had entered the heart of the city.

'So what happens now, if he refuses both the psychiatric and the psychological assessment?' Stella asked.

'The lead solicitor thinks his chances of gaining sole custody are increasingly unlikely. The judge ordered the assessment and obviously won't look favourably on his failure to attend appointments. His ex-wife has admitted herself voluntarily to an in-patient substance-abuse treatment facility and the daughter is adamant she wants to return to live with her mother. The Local Authority is going to put forward a proposal that the child is returned to her mother's care once she completes treatment. His lawyer is informing him of all of this today.'

'He won't be pleased.'

'No. But the pressure might make him a little more enthusiastic about talking to you.'

The car purred down Limeburner Lane. Stella glimpsed the familiar dome of the Old Bailey and the golden statue of Lady Justice, her arms outstretched holding her sword and her scales.

She needed to toughen up. She couldn't be a pushover if

she was going to succeed in the medico-legal cases. Her clients were in distress, angry, abusive, emotionally disturbed. They felt persecuted by the proceedings and by the system, and it was inevitable these feelings would be directed at her from time to time. She couldn't go snivelling to Max every time she didn't like something a client did.

'I'm sorry, Max,' she said. 'I was looking forward to this case. I was probably overly optimistic – I thought I could crack it. I hate letting you down.'

'You haven't let me down. You did your best – you always do.'

He lifted his hand from the gearshift and placed it all too briefly on top of hers. A reassuring pressure. A sign that he cared. A sign, maybe, that he saw her as something more than an employee. She looked down. Flames licked around the edges of his fingers where they touched her thigh.

By five o'clock the next evening, everyone but Stella had knocked off. Max was in court for a second day running and his staff had taken the opportunity to start the weekend early. Once again, Stella was the last to leave. She went through the motions: locking the filing cabinet; checking all windows and lights. Paul's office, as usual, smelt strongly of incense. It was more like he'd been conducting a yoga class in there than a therapy session. Stella lifted one of the sticks out of the wooden holder just to be sure. It was completely cold. She sat down in one of his armchairs, imagining herself to be his patient, telling him her deepest, darkest secrets, her fantasies. It didn't feel right. He seemed nice enough, but rather timid behind his John Lennon glasses, as though he was easily shocked. She could never open up to a man in socks and sandals.

In the waiting room, Stella found a copy of *The Times* and decided to take it with her to the pub, to read while she waited for Hannah to turn up. Stella was always early, Hannah was habitually late. She checked and double checked the locks on the front door of the clinic and set the alarm. Gravel crunched under her heels as she crossed the empty parking lot. At the gate, she turned left, heading for the Duke of York.

'*Dr Davies.*' The voice came from behind her, just as she reached the corner.

She turned around. Lawrence Simpson was right there, close enough to reach out and touch her. It was too much of a coincidence that she should bump into him just outside of the office. Clearly, this was not a chance meeting.

'Are you following me?' she said. She held her over-stuffed bag in front of her, like a shield.

'I was hoping I might catch you,' he said. 'Are you walking across to the station?'

Stella wasn't about to share any personal information, no matter how trivial, and so she didn't answer. He was staring at her: at the newspaper under her arm and at her heavy bag crammed with her laptop and yellow files – which strictly speaking were not supposed to leave clinic premises. But he was not to know that.

'I have a few things I want to say to you,' he said.

'You can talk to me in my office, during a scheduled appointment.'

'I know this seems pathetic – me following you, trying to get a few words in. I wanted to say I'm sorry about the confusion yesterday. I'd asked my secretary to make the appointment on my behalf – there must have been some miscommunication.'

'Right,' she said. Her bag weighed a ton. She shifted it on to the other shoulder. People were passing, leaving work and heading for the underground station or the restaurants and pubs beyond.

'I'm leaving for a conference tomorrow,' he said. 'I'll be away for two weeks.'

'I can't delay the report. I'm due to submit on Thursday. I'm sure your solicitor has told you about the deadline: it has to be in before the final hearing.'

He had already had several chances and multiple missed appointments with various professionals involved in the case. He had wasted her valuable clinical time by walking out of his appointment early and he gave no sign he understood she might have been put under pressure by his refusal to co-operate. She had to stick to her deadlines, no matter how he behaved.

'I know it looks really bad,' he said. 'All these missed appointments.'

She wondered whether his lawyers had briefed him, and if he knew already that he had little or no chance of succeeding. That must be why he was there: a last-ditch attempt to salvage his case.

'How about this evening?' he said.

'I beg your pardon?'

'Any chance of making up the missed appointment this evening? I don't suppose you could fit me in?'

'The clinic doesn't offer after-hours appointments,' she said.

'Please. I know I screwed up. I'm asking you because I'm desperate. I don't want to lose my daughter.'

It was strange and – if she was honest – gratifying, to see him with his arrogance stripped away. To see him beg.

Behind his shoulder, she spotted Hannah walking towards them. She was already at the corner of the next block.

'Sorry,' she said. 'You've had plenty of time since the last appointment to contact me.'

'I know. I find it terrifying – the interviews with you.'

Stella was a small person, much shorter than he was and at least a decade younger. 'Most people do not find me particularly terrifying,' she said.

'I'm begging you,' he said. 'I'm serious. I can show you my itinerary, I'm not making this up. My solicitor telephoned me this afternoon to say that I've ruined my chances by missing all these appointments. I just want one chance to put my case forward, to show the judge I'm serious.'

If she completed the interview that evening, she had a chance of gathering the information she needed to write up a comprehensive report that would be helpful to the court. She imagined Max's joyful response when she told him she could charge her full hourly quota for the report. And ethically, completing the assessment was the right thing to do. A full psychological assessment would be in the child's best interests, and preferable to handing in a report with the equivalent of an 'I don't know' about the father's personality. Admittedly, she felt a slight thrill, at the thought that she might be the first professional who succeeded in getting under Simpson's skin.

She hesitated, trying to decide.

Sometimes bending the rules worked. As Max might say.

'If you really want to understand me,' he said, 'then you have to meet me halfway. Surely you want both sides of the story before you reach an opinion? I'm not going to do your ridiculous test. But there are some important things I think you should know. And things about my childhood that might explain – things I haven't told the social worker.'

He dangled the carrot, luring her closer.

Hannah gave an expansive wave. She had almost caught up to them.

It was in the best interests of Lawrence Simpson's daughter for Stella to get a full psychological profile before a decision was made as to who would win custody.

'Hi!' Hannah swooped on her, planting a big, flamboyant kiss on her cheek. She looped her arm through Stella's and turned to give Lawrence Simpson a large grin. Hannah's skirt was short and her heels high and she looked fabulous. Stella tended to cover up, to dress down, to avoid unwanted interest from her clients. She should get Hannah to dress her, then Max would have no choice but to take notice.

Stella deliberately did not introduce her client.

Hannah held out her hand. 'I'm Hannah,' she said.

'I'm Lawrence.' Simpson gave her friend a disarming smile and a handshake that lasted longer than strictly necessary. 'I was just imposing on Dr Davies, hoping to poach some of her precious time to discuss a case.'

'Do you work together?' Hannah asked.

Stella could see her friend's mind ticking away. Stella had been alone a long time; Hannah would be ecstatic if she thought she had met someone promising.

'Sorry, this isn't a good time,' Stella said. She pulled on Hannah's arm, turning away.

But Hannah managed to extricate herself. 'It's no problem,' she said. 'You two go ahead. I'll go for a run, which is probably a much better option for me than the three glasses of wine I'm about to drink if we go to the pub.'

Stella tried to formulate a protest, an exit strategy without seeming rude or breaking confidentiality, but she was too slow.

177

'Thank you so much,' Simpson said. 'I really appreciate this.'

Hannah grinned as she waved goodbye and rushed away, keen not to interfere with what she must think was a promising encounter.

'Join us later,' she called out. 'We're going belly dancing again. Izzy's still pregnant. If she doesn't go into labour in the next two days they're going to induce her. She's desperate.'

Simpson laughed.

Stella was resentful and she was tired. She deserved to have her nights to herself, at the very least. And she would rather be drinking a glass of wine than interviewing Simpson.

She took a breath as she switched back to work mode. She didn't want Simpson following her in to the clinic, watching her as she turned on lights and hunted down her assessment materials. She needed some time alone to get her head straight and go through her interview schedule. 'Can you come back to the clinic in half an hour?'

'Of course,' Simpson said. He put his hands in his pockets and ambled away towards the small café in the underground station.

She regretted caving into his pressure to bring the appointment forward at such short notice. But she had no choice now but to go through with the meeting. If she didn't, Simpson would no doubt report her to his solicitor immediately, undermining her credibility.

## Hilltop, 1 a.m.

'You've got what you wanted,' Stella said. 'It's just you and me.'

The bucket chair wanted to swallow Blue whole as she sank down low into the sagging leather cushion with her feet tucked tightly underneath her.

Peter was livid. Stella had left him no choice but to wait in the study.

For the time being, her need to know the facts had vanquished her fear. She had to know if Blue's visit had anything to do with Lawrence Simpson. She was determined to stay rational.

She took a breath, steadied herself, adjusted the neck of her jumper. Reminded herself that Blue had suffered, too.

'Blue,' she said. 'I know you've had a difficult time, I believe everything you told me earlier – about your mother and father. I'm sure you had a good reason to come and see me. I want to understand what's happened so that I can work out the best way to help you.'

'He's my doctor,' Blue said. 'Or – he used to be my doctor, but now he won't see me any more. That's why I came.'

'You're talking about your therapy sessions with Dr Fisher?'

Blue nodded. She was determined to avoid talking about her father. Stella had to find some way to exhaust her resistance, or at least to expose some sort of inconsistency in her latest version of events.

'Why did you start seeing him?' Stella asked.

'My mother thinks I have problems.'

'And why is that?'

'I did some stupid stuff at school. I used to cut myself. My GP wanted to send me to some place but they had a really long waiting list so I think she asked Dr Fisher to see me as some kind of favour. I don't know why he said yes, because we don't have any money.'

'And in your sessions – did he prescribe medicine for you? Or did you talk too?'

'Mostly we talked.'

'But was it Dr Fisher who prescribed your pills for you?' Stella asked.

Blue nodded.

Max must have believed she was either delusional or bipolar. Adolescent psychiatrists were notoriously difficult to find; he must have felt obliged to step in and help. But still, she couldn't quite get her head around it. She was furious with him: for not discussing it with her first. For not thinking about the implications.

'The pills you take – they're sometimes prescribed for people who have hallucinations, or delusions – who see or hear things that aren't really there. Has that ever happened to you?'

Blue bit down so hard on her thumbnail that Stella saw a small smear of blood at the corner of her mouth. Blue didn't seem to notice, she chewed harder on her raw skin.

'Did you hear me?' Stella asked.

'I never heard or saw things that weren't there,' Blue said.

'Stop it,' Stella said. 'You're hurting yourself.'

Blue moved her hand away from her mouth. She began to pull at the loose threads at the bottom of her T-shirt. 'I know things about him that even you don't know.'

'Is that so.' Stella tried to manufacture an expression of concern, of interest.

Blue could not stay still. She fidgeted, and pulled her knees up to her chest, hugging them tight. There was an incessant pulling and biting, her thumb was back in her mouth.

'I didn't know if I should tell you,' she said. 'I wanted to meet you, to see what you were like. I thought I'd hate you.'

'You've lost me,' Stella said.

'I liked going to see him. I liked the way he listened to me. And the way he looked at me.' Blue looked up at Stella, checking for a reaction.

'I didn't just like it – I loved going to see him. When he wouldn't see me any more I was gutted. It wasn't fair. I knew he was married. I saw his wedding ring and the picture of you on his desk. I thought – if I couldn't see him, then, I don't know, I wanted to see you.'

Blue put her knees down, and leaned forward. 'It wasn't just talking. I think he's scared I'll tell people what happened, what he did. Maybe that's why he won't see me.'

The girl was toying with her.

Stella studied Blue's face. Her pale pink lips were shaped as a perfect cupid's bow. She was a sensuous, pouting creature, a child with curves of an adult. Beautiful Blue.

'Patients often fantasize about their therapists,' Stella said. 'It even has a name, it's called transference.'

'It's not in my head.'

'Sometimes these fantasies are so powerful, they seem so

real, that patients start to believe the fantasies are true.'

'You sound just like him.'

'I'm sure he was kind to you. I'm sure he listened to you and spent hours of his time alone with you. That can lead to strong feelings, especially if your father didn't give you the love you needed.'

Blue shook her head. 'No.' She leaned forward, her hair hanging loose and wild around her face and her eyes smouldering. 'I love him. And he loved me back. Things . . .' Blue lifted her gaze, looking intently at Stella, her eyes defiant. 'He touched me,' Blue said.

And suddenly, Stella wanted to laugh. Blue's claims were ludicrous.

'It wasn't just once. We did things.'

Lying was like breathing to this girl. That's what Stella told herself.

'I thought I'd hate you,' Blue said. 'But I don't.'

Stella wanted her tablets. She wanted to swallow a precious, blue, diamond-shaped piece of oblivion. She wanted to escape so fucking badly. The girl was delusional. She must be.

'What exactly are you saying – that you had sex with him?' Stella said.

Blue nodded. She was staring at her, pleading with her eyes. What did she want? Comfort? Absolution? Understanding? When there was nothing, no response, no softening of her face, Blue looked away.

'This a very serious allegation. Do you understand? This is not a joke, this isn't some stupid prank like the ones you've pulled at school. My husband took you on as a charity case. You said yourself your mother has no money. He's been kind to you because he's a good man. He's also a brilliant psychiatrist. I'll bet he paid for all your medication as well? Because if you'd waited for an appointment on the NHS you'd still be bloody waiting. Or off your head, psychotic probably, in a secure adolescent unit. So he takes you on – out of kindness. And now you thank him by lying to get inside his home and making up vicious stories.' As Stella spoke, her anger was unleashed and grew larger. 'You're sick. You're really sick.'

*You and your father.*

Blue shook her head. She pushed herself backwards, cowering in the corner, as though Stella would hurt her. She was mute, but the bright blue of her eyes made Stella frightened. She was Lawrence Simpson's daughter, through and through. She had been manipulating Stella all along. Blue had come to Hilltop to destroy her life, or the little that was left of it.

'So now what?' Stella said. 'What do you want from me, Blue? You came here to hurt me and to try to destroy my husband, my marriage. So now what?'

Blue's eyes filled with tears. 'I don't know.' She was weeping now, playing the victim, and Stella couldn't stand the sight of her. She got out of her chair and stood in front of the fireplace, turning her back on Blue. She closed her eyes, leaning her forehead against the cold cast-iron mantelpiece. She should have let Peter deal with her.

She sensed Blue coming closer, standing behind her. She could feel her breath on her neck.

'I was the one who wanted it,' Blue said. 'I wanted him. I made him touch me. He didn't want to at first but I needed him to touch me.'

'You're a liar,' Stella said. 'Or you're crazy. Either way, I will never believe you.'

Now that Blue had started talking, she wouldn't stop. *Touching herself, unbuttoning her top, crawling over to him on her hands and knees, opening his fly . . . climbing on top . . . locking the door.*

Stella kept her eyes closed, her back turned. Blue's words wormed their way inside her brain, burrowing into her thoughts and her gut. She should never have let her in. Hilltop was the one place she was safe, and now Blue would contaminate it all. She wanted to destroy the last thing Stella had left. Max. Her marriage.

Blue pressed her face into Stella's back and twisted her arms around her waist. Stella would not turn around. Blue's forehead dug harder into Stella's shoulder, her arms gripped tighter.

'Please turn around,' Blue said. 'I need you to see—'

'Get away from me!' Stella dug her fingers into Blue's arms and wrenched them loose. She turned and shoved her away. Blue stumbled and tripped over the jade Buddha squatting on the hearth. She stayed on the floor, on her hands and knees, her head down and her hair covering her face.

'Why are you doing this to us?' Stella asked.

'He can't stop seeing me. He can't throw me away like a piece of junk. I'm not nothing!'

Blue was a beast, crouched on her hands and knees. Crying. Unhinged. Unpredictable.

To look at her made Stella frantic. The thought of Max in his office, alone with her, unable to contain himself.

It wasn't true.

Stella put her hands over her eyes but images of Blue and Max were all over the inside of her eyeballs. The consulting room she knew so well, the armchairs, the antique rug, her blonde hair falling forward, her perfect breasts, her creamy skin, her blazing eyes, her desperate need to be loved. Stella's stomach twisted and she felt she was going to be sick.

Blue's hands were on her again, around her knees, clinging on. 'Please look at me,' she said. Stella tried to pull away from the ugly, chewed fingernails but Blue held on. 'I did want to hurt you. But I don't any more. I just want you to know.'

Blue wouldn't let go. Stella wanted to lash out, to kick her, to slap her and to see red welts blossom across the side of her face. She would love to strangle her. She couldn't take it any longer. She reached down and grabbed a fistful of hair and yanked Blue's head back, yanked hard until her arms loosened and she let go of Stella's legs. Then Stella moved away, a safe distance, leaving her weeping, still crouched on the floor, pleading.

'I'm telling the truth,' Blue said. 'I promise. I just want you to believe me.'

'You lied to get into my house and you haven't stopped lying since. You'll never get anywhere *near* my husband again. I'm going to call Peter in here and he is going to take you to a police station. From there you'll most probably be sent to a secure mental hospital where they'll lock you up. So you can forget about Max. You can even forget about seeing your mother.'

She looked straight into Blue's scared, desperate eyes, feeling the pleasure of the pain she had inflicted.

This was her house. Max was her husband. She wasn't going to be pushed around by a teenage runaway. She could see now the benefits of the chemical cocktail of restraints the girl had been taking. Clearly Max had good reasons for prescribing what he did.

The girl's eyes darkened. She was staring at her with an

unsettling mixture of pity and defiance. Blue stood, straightened her jacket, pushed her hair back. She took a step backwards. Then, she knelt down and lifted the jade statue of Buddha with both hands. She raised it over her head, and ran. She flung the statue right at the window.

The sound of shattering glass pierced the snow-dampened morning.

Blue grabbed hold of the sides of the window frame, crying out as glass pierced her palms. She propelled herself through and staggered forwards, her small feet crunching over glass shards and slipping against the frozen snow.

# Ladbroke Grove, Friday 7 January 2011, 11 a.m.

Her mother started calling her Blue when she was six years old. She had changed her name just like that, without asking if she minded, without telling her why. Her real name was Lauren. She was named after her father, a long time ago, back when her parents didn't hate each other's guts. Lauren Simpson.

Her mother lied to her. She said she had always wanted to call her Blue, because of her eyes, but Lauren knew the real reason. Her other name reminded her mother too much of the man she hated.

The name change was the first time she could remember being really pissed off with her mother. There were other things, too: she drank, she came home with men who stared at Blue funny, she was sick all the time, some days she couldn't get out of bed.

But mostly, Blue hated her father. For leaving them and for not sending any money. And she hated him even more for coming back, for making them hope, and then making everything worse. He would never, ever, leave them in peace. Each time, it would start the same way. The judge would force Blue to go out with him for the day. He was supposed to pick her up and drop her off somewhere far away from the house, at a neutral place. Their home address was supposed to be a secret. Instead, her mother would tell him where they were living, would let him inside; she would dress up, with too much lipstick and perfume. After a while, the arguing would start. And worse.

It was doing her head in. Her mother promised her she wouldn't invite him in next time, promised she wouldn't even come to the door when he dropped Blue off, but she always did.

Blue loved her mother, but her mother drove her crazy.

She was in her bedroom, with the door locked. Her mother didn't like it when she locked herself in, but then her mother wasn't home to complain. Her room was so tiny, just about big enough for a single bed and a side table and a small chest of drawers with a television on top. Her mother's room was slightly bigger – you could fit a double bed in it but there wasn't much space left to walk round it. The bathroom was under the eaves. You couldn't even stand up straight if you wanted to shower. Lucky neither of them was very tall. There was never enough money to get to the end of the month. Some came from her father, but her mother complained: it wasn't enough, he always gave it too late, he made her do things before he'd hand it over, he would only give it to her if she let him come to the house.

Blue was supposed to be at school. She was supposed to have her appointment with *him* on a Friday afternoon. She opened her phone and dialled the number of the clinic.

'Grove Road Clinic, Anne speaking.' Fake cheerfulness, fake friendliness, same as her fake boobs. She felt her own – they weren't as huge but there was a good handful, and they were nice and firm.

'It's Lauren,' she said. 'I'm supposed to have an appointment this afternoon. At four. So – I think maybe it was
cancelled but I really need to come in.'

'You couldn't have had an appointment today,' she said.
'Doctor's away at a meeting.'

'Where?'

'Is there something I can help you with?' She sounded
more impatient than helpful.

'I need to talk to him. Can you give me his mobile phone
number?'

'That won't be possible.'

'Is that what he said or what you say?' Blue pulled her legs
up to her chest, wrapped her arm around her knees and
rocked back and forth. 'I need an appointment, it's urgent.'

'I'll check for you,' she said. 'I'm just popping you on hold.'

Stupid music was coming through the phone. She felt a
small spark of hope.

'He said to make an appointment with your GP if you need
anything. Do you understand?'

'*I'm not fucking stupid, am I?*' She slammed her phone
shut and hurled it at the wall.

She kept rocking. She had to see him. She had to get him
to help her. She rocked harder, pushing herself back and forth
with her heels. She could go into the bathroom and get her
mother's razor, those blades were a bitch to get out, but she
could do it. Or she could smash one of the picture frames and
use a piece of glass. If she cut herself up, then he'd have to
take notice. Blue pushed up the sleeve of her top and had a
look at her arms, all criss-crossed with thick white lines. She
hadn't been cutting herself since she'd been seeing him; her
arms looked better than they used to.

She was frightened that whatever she might do to herself,

he wouldn't care anyway. She was nothing, she didn't exist. She may as well be dead. She wanted him to suffer. She wanted him to feel what it was like to be in pain. She pulled out the envelope from her bag. She had taken it off his desk while she waited in his office when he had been late for their appointment, like he sometimes was. *Hilltop.* She had memorized the address and the postcode, but she had taken the envelope with her, anyway. She wanted something of his, to keep. She had taken his pen, too; it was inside the envelope. She rolled it between her fingers, smelt it.

She hated being alone and she hated waiting. She changed out of her school uniform, into leggings and trainers and her leather jacket.

She left the house and headed for the tube station. Tiny flakes of sleet fluttered around her, landed on the concrete pavements and disappeared into nothingness. She felt much better when she was out of the house, moving. She tucked her hair up inside her beanie so it wouldn't get wet. Tiny white snowflakes bounced off her cheeks and her eyelids. She felt full of energy.

By the time she was halfway to the station, the snowflakes had grown bigger. When they reached the ground, they turned black and sludgy under people's feet. The sky was threatening and dark. Blue began to be aware of the cold in her hands, her fingertips had turned bright red. She pulled her beanie down low to cover her forehead and her ears. She tucked her hands into her pockets and walked on, head down. She wasn't wearing socks and her ankles felt like blocks of ice. She walked faster, trying to stay warm. She considered giving up and going home, where the heating was on, but by that time she'd crossed over the traffic lights and she was already at the entrance to the station.

She grabbed a tube map: she needed to get to the Metropolitan Line. All she had to do was make one change at Baker Street, it was easy.

She touched her Oyster card to the yellow circle and waited for the beep. The barriers swung open and she made her way down the steps and on to the windy platform. When the train arrived, it was old and it smelt bad. She sat down on a worn velvet seat and put her feet up. Some fat old guy in a puffy-looking coat gave her a dirty look. She leaned her head back and looked out of the window. Snow eddied and swirled, covering the train tracks.

# Grove Road Clinic, May 2009

Lawrence Simpson was predictable. He rang the bell of the clinic precisely thirty minutes later.

The carpet on the stairs was spongy and silent under Stella's heels and the air in the empty clinic seemed to hover uneasily around her, as if she were an intruder. Anne's desk was pristine as always. Her pink-striped mug stood next to the empty vase.

Stella pulled her blazer tighter around her as she opened the door. At least it was still light.

'I really appreciate you going out of your way for me,' Simpson said. He was on his best behaviour: charming and humble.

Stella nodded. She led the way up the stairs, once again uneasy, with Simpson behind her, looking at her. She paused at the open doorway and ushered him into the office ahead of her.

'Take a seat,' she said.

She wondered if she should close the door of the consulting room – it wasn't strictly necessary as there was no one else in the clinic, but she closed it anyway, out of habit. She stayed a moment with her hand on the door handle. She wished she wasn't alone with him, in the empty clinic, with the fast-fading light outside.

While she delayed, Simpson chose the chair she had sat in during the last interview. Usually she would have placed her clipboard down, in a pre-emptive strike, but she had forgotten and he had seized the moment. His long legs were already tightly crossed, his restless fingers tapping at the arm of his chair.

Stella sat in the chair opposite. 'We have sixty minutes,' she said.

One side of his mouth curled up into a smirk. 'Busy night ahead?'

She looked down at her list of questions. 'I thought we'd start again, take the interview from the beginning,' she said.

His fingers were still drumming a beat against the armrest.

'What's your understanding of why the judge has asked for a psychological assessment?' she said.

'As I've explained to you, it really has nothing to do with me. My ex-wife has trouble being a competent parent. I want a chance to take over, to do it properly, to give my child a stable home.'

It was the identical response he had given the last time. Stella despaired. He hadn't changed his attitude to the assessment. *Of course* he hadn't changed. It was only her pride, and some inflated sense of her talent, that had made her offer this useless appointment. She was too invested in this case. She had always had a soft spot for medical professionals. It was her downfall.

'She was very beautiful when she was younger. My wife. She's let herself go.'

'You mentioned that the last time we met.'

Her eyes flickered to the window. She just wanted this interview to be over. He was so defensive that she would never gain anything useful from talking to him. He had wasted her precious time again, deliberately. She was damned if she was going to sit through another session of his complaining about the ex-wife.

'Complaining about your ex-wife is not going to help you,' she said. It was the end of a long day, and her irritation showed.

His jaw clenched.

'Are you prepared to talk about yourself at all?' she asked, although she already knew the answer.

'Why bother?'

'I beg your pardon?'

'You've already made up your mind. You know I have no chance of gaining custody. This time round, anyway. Does it give you pleasure, *Doctor*, watching me suffer?'

She was fed up with him. She wished she was out belly dancing, listening to Hannah's laugh. She wondered why on earth he'd been so insistent on the appointment.

'Earlier today,' she said, 'when we talked outside, you mentioned some new information that you wanted me to know about. Something you thought was important to include in the report?'

'Do you have any idea how humiliating this process has been for me?' He leaned forward in his chair.

'I'm sorry you see it that way,' she said.

'Are you really?' His face contorted, filled with frustration and contempt. 'I shouldn't be in a psychologist's office. This entire process is an insult. Your questions are an insult. This is an invasion of my privacy and it's entirely unwarranted.'

The appointment had turned into a sparring match. It was even worse than the previous two. She was at a loss for words, she knew there was nothing she could say that could salvage anything. He guarded his inner life like the crown jewels. The way he was behaving now, his anxiety and irritability replaced with outright hostility, she was damn sure he had good reason to conceal what went on inside his head. There was likely to be a lot he did not want professionals to find out about him.

'Then why did you insist on this appointment?'

'Because I have nothing to lose.'

'I don't understand,' she said.

'You were going to do a hatchet job. I've watched your face when I talk, when I try to explain things to you. You don't listen. You're a condescending bitch and you don't listen.'

She wanted him out of the office, out of the building, as soon as possible. She stood up. To hell with the report. Simpson wasn't going to engage with the assessment. He had never had any intention of doing so.

'I think we should end the interview,' she said. She acted as though nothing was wrong; as though she wasn't intimidated.

Simpson remained seated. He uncrossed his legs. 'Not yet,' he said. 'Let's talk about you, first.'

She rested her hand on the back of the armchair and resisted the urge to wrench open the door and leave the room.

'I'm a GP,' he said. 'As you well know. I have access to the centralized database. I've had a look at your medical records. All of them. Going right back.'

'That's unethical. You don't have permission to do that.'

He gave her a scornful smile. 'Quite an interesting life you've had.'

'My life is not under scrutiny here.' She wondered how much he knew. Everything. He must know everything. It was all in her records. 'What's your point?'

'I think you know,' he said. 'If anybody needs a shrink, surely it's you?'

He stood up, taking his time. He took a step towards her. And then another.

His eyes frightened her. They narrowed and glinted. She was looking at a viper.

*Run*, her gut screamed. She was paralysed.

And then it was too late. He moved quickly. And he stood with his back to the closed door, blocking the exit.

'When you agreed to this appointment,' he said, 'you already knew I didn't have any chance of getting custody. So, basically, you wanted to fuck with me.'

His solicitor must have told him there was no hope.

'No.' She shook her head. 'I wanted to make sure my report was comprehensive. I believe that's in everybody's best interests – yours and your daughter's – no matter what the judge decides.'

His eyes did not change, did not soften. He didn't believe her. There was no way to get through to him. He turned, locked the door.

'What are you doing?' She would not show her fear, she wouldn't give him the satisfaction. She could hear the frantic beating of her heart.

He had his back to the door, feet planted slightly apart, hands at his sides.

'Unlock the door, please,' she said.

He pulled at his tie, loosening it. His forehead was shiny

with sweat; a drop trickled down the side of his face. If she wrote this up in the report, his chances of ever getting custody would be finished. He must know that.

He wasn't planning to leave her in any state to write anything.

His ex-wife had said he would choke her, his hands around her throat. He would strangle her, long enough for her to lose consciousness but not long enough for her to die. He was a sadist, he enjoyed torturing her, she said. But no one wanted to believe her.

Stella had told no one about this last-minute appointment.

'You wanted to humiliate me,' he said.

'That's not true. You *begged* me to give you this appointment.' She shouldn't have used the word begged. He blinked, and in the split-second shift of his expression she thought he would rush at her, lash out at her.

She stayed very still.

His fingers flexed; opening and closing. Warming up. She was terrified that she was about to find out how his ex-wife had suffered.

There was a panic button on the wall behind the desk, she could lunge for it – but it would not help. It activated an alarm behind Anne's desk and Anne was not there. The clinic did not offer after-hours appointments.

She could tell Simpson she would write whatever he wanted her to in the court report, but she wasn't under the illusion that he was stupid enough to believe her.

*Stay calm.* She tried to slow her racing thoughts, her heartbeat, she tried to push down the panic. *Breathe. Think.* If locking the door was an impulsive act, she still had a chance. But if it was premeditated, she had no chance at all of getting out of the consulting room unharmed. She thought back to their meeting on the street corner. She didn't believe he had asked her to meet him in order to murder her. She could have told anyone they were meeting, it was too risky. In his own twisted way, Simpson loved his daughter and he wouldn't want to destroy his chances of having some sort of relationship with her.

Her best chance was to convince him that there was still time to get out of the situation without incurring too much damage.

'Dr Simpson,' she said, 'if you open the door right now, I can accept that locking it was an impulsive mistake that you immediately regretted. That you had no premeditated intention to intimidate me. I know you're under tremendous stress, and that your solicitor has given you some very bad news. You're not yourself.'

She hoped she had given him a way out.

His pale blue eyes had turned to black. They were filled with hatred. 'Don't talk down to me as if I'm a moron.'

He wasn't listening to her. He wasn't rational.

'Even if you can't get custody, don't do something stupid that will cost you your chances of having contact with your daughter and building up a relationship over time. You told me you've never done anything wrong as a parent. But if this door stays locked, you're keeping me in here against my will and it won't matter how good a parent you've been up until now.'

He didn't move. If she tried to go towards the door, she would have to go closer and she did not want to be within striking distance. She backed away. She retreated to the desk, packed her interview schedule and clipboard into her tote and slung it over her shoulder.

She walked towards him. 'Please move out of the way,' she said.

His backhand caught her, across the jaw. She stumbled, holding her face. The shock was worse than the pain.

'I used an open hand that time,' he said. 'But I can hurt you more.'

'What do you want?'

'I want you to cooperate.'

She pressed her hand harder against her jaw, which had begun to sting.

'Men used to look at my ex all the time. You're an attractive girl too, attractive enough to get any man you want. I can change that.' The right side of his mouth curled upwards again, into a twisted smile of fury and of anticipation.

*Blame the victim.* That's what they had all been doing to his ex-wife.

'I can smash up your face until it's so fucking crooked no man will ever look at you, let alone touch you. You're young, so you'll live that way a long time. They can help with plastic surgery these days, but it never quite looks the same. Or – if you behave yourself – I can hurt you in places it won't show.'

She wouldn't beg for mercy because it wouldn't help. He was a man with no soul, no conscience. But she had found out too late.

'Would hurting me be worth the sacrifice? You would lose contact with your daughter and you'd go to jail. There'd be no chance of a second family with your girlfriend. Why would you do that to yourself?'

'You know,' he said, 'you're absolutely right. But I'm not going to lose any more than I already have. I'm just going to do something for myself, a reward for what I've had to put up with. And I know you won't tell a soul. I told you, I've seen your medical records. You'll do exactly what I tell you. And you won't talk.'

She didn't back away, she faced him full on, squaring her shoulders. She reminded herself to breathe.

He was so sure of himself. But then he had been abusing his ex-wife for years and he had got away with it.

'You're going to see what it's like to be fucked over,' he said. 'Literally. If you behave it won't hurt as much.'

He would hurt her for pleasure as much as revenge.

She didn't want to be scarred. She didn't want to feel pain. She wanted out, with the least possible damage.

She coughed. She almost choked on her own spit. She couldn't hide her fear any longer. He had promised he would not hurt her too badly if she did not resist. He might be lying. He might change his mind. But whatever else happened, she wanted to live. She was thirty years old and she had already managed to stay sane ten years longer than her mother. She was going to make it out of this room. Whatever it took, she was going to make it out alive.

Simpson was dangerous. He was in control.

'I'll cooperate,' she said.

Once she had decided to do whatever he told her to, she felt slightly calmer. He could do anything to her body, but he couldn't get inside her mind. And after him, she promised herself, no one would ever have this kind of power over her again.

He pushed his face against hers. He grabbed at her breast, pinching and twisting. 'What's your first name, *Doctor*?'

She tried not to pull away.

'Stella.'

He let her go.

'Take off your clothes, Stella.'

Stella was still in her suit: linen jacket and trousers, a white shirt underneath. She blocked her real self off inside, behind a high brick wall, and she undressed. She took off her shoes first, and placed them neatly beside her chair. She folded her jacket, balanced it over the back of the chair. She had to lean against it for support because her legs had turned to jelly. She removed her shirt and her trousers. She hesitated a moment in her underwear. He waited, his face impassive. She took off her bra, her knickers.

Bastard. She wanted to take hold of something blunt and heavy and batter his face to a pulp. For some reason, she pictured a hockey stick with pale wood and a pink handle – perhaps it was one she'd used at school. In her mind's eye, she bashed his face, over and over again, taking pleasure in the taste of blood that splattered against her cheeks and her mouth. The rage kept her upright as she waited for him to tell her what to do.

'Lie down on the examining bed,' he said.

He took photographs of her, naked, her legs spread. 'I will always have these. You never know when or where they'll pop up on the internet.'

*So what? One female body looks much like any other. It doesn't matter. It's only a body.*

'Turn over. All of your future clients will be delighted to know you so intimately as I do. On your hands and knees.'

What a way to find out that everything his ex-wife said about him was absolutely true. His abuse was premeditated and cruel. Simpson was a sadistic psychopath.

She did not move, did not protest, did not try to run, or to escape. Was that wrong? She didn't know. She believed him capable of anything. Capable of killing her if she ignited his murderous rage. Time moved slowly, each second dragged itself out longer than the last. She was cold, she could feel goosebumps along the exposed skin of her arms and legs and along her spine.

'Don't move. You're doing very well. Being obedient suits you so much better.' She heard fumbling, a soft tearing. Please let that be a condom packet, she thought. She knew what would come next.

## Hilltop, 1.20 a.m.

Shards of glass lay at her feet and the living room was flooded with wet, cold air. Peter was running, the thick soles of his boots trampling over sharp edges, grinding glass into her golden Chinese rug.

'She smashed the window,' Stella said. 'And ran out.'

'Why?'

'I frightened her. I threatened her.'

Peter gave her a look she didn't like. She deserved it, she knew.

'How big is this garden?' he asked.

'Huge. An acre.' Stella fumbled with the stiff key, unlocked the patio doors and pushed them open. 'We have to find her. She'll freeze out there. I think she's hurt.'

There was more glass on the ground outside, and a trail of shallow footprints. Red droplets were scattered across the snow.

Peter seemed to be responding ever more slowly as her own urgency grew.

'What's behind those trees?' He pointed to the back of the garden.

'Nothing,' Stella said. 'I mean – a fence runs along the

back of the woods and along the sides, between us and the neighbours. I don't think she can get out.'

She remembered she had wanted to cause the girl pain; she saw her fingers wrenching at Blue's long hair, forcing her head back. Something terrible was going to happen to Blue and it was her fault.

'There's a pool,' Stella said. 'An old, empty swimming pool. She won't know it's there. If she's running, if she doesn't see it—'

They stood shoulder to shoulder at the shattered window. The lights only illuminated a few metres of white, after that, everything was blanketed in silvery-grey darkness.

'Find a torch and a first-aid kit,' Peter said. 'Which direction is the pool?'

'Behind the trees, on your left.'

He walked out on to the patio, testing the slippery ground.

'Don't leave me alone.'

'Then come with me.'

But she was paralysed in the doorway and she did not move a muscle.

'And blankets. Get some blankets,' he said. And he turned and left.

She was at the open threshold, exposed. Anyone could get at her. She pressed her fingertips along the edges of the broken window pane, against the small, pointed spikes.

The garden was silent as the snow dampened all sound.

If Simpson wanted to get to her, he would have come for her last night, when she was alone with Blue. Why wait until Peter's car was standing in the driveway? She wouldn't give in to paranoia. Simpson had finished with her eighteen months ago. She had not heard from him since. It was over.

The living-room temperature had dropped and the

radiators were scalding hot, useless, as they battled the freezing air. English goddamn Heritage. If those windows had been double-glazed, Blue would never have been able to smash the glass. And that stupid Buddha – so ugly and so heavy. It had belonged to Max's mother and it was the one thing he had insisted they bring with them when they moved to Hilltop. The statue lay, fat and intact, on the frozen patio.

Stella felt a tingling across her skin, a nervous energy. It was becoming harder to stay still. She moved away from the window. She found a torch and the first-aid kit in the kitchen. She found her coat and pulled on her trainers. Then she went back, to wait at the open doors.

She trusted Peter to find Blue, to bring her back in one piece. Please, let her be in one piece.

The pool was large, six metres by four metres. She and Max had talked about restoring it, or at least covering it over to make it safe, but there had been no need. Stella never ventured into the garden.

She had let her temper and her bitterness get the better of her. She had failed a child.

She should have kept Blue safe. The girl was as much a victim of Lawrence Simpson as she herself had been.

Stella forced herself to take one step over the threshold. And then another.

The patio was frozen and slippery and she couldn't keep her balance; her feet slid out from underneath her. She tried to catch her breath as she hit the ground, the small of her back slamming against the bottom of the step and winding her.

She started to shake. Her heart raced, so fast it might break. Her breathing became shallow and she began to pant as the muscles in her chest seized up. She was alone, exposed. Helpless. She was going to die.

She pressed her hands against the freezing cold ground and managed to get her balance. She struggled to her feet. Blue's bright red blood formed a trail in the pristine snow. She could make out two sets of shallow footprints on the white-carpeted ground, leading towards the semicircle of trees.

There was no way she could make it across the open garden.

Her heart was still thundering. She forced herself to breathe. Slower. Deeper. She looked back towards the house, at the safe, bright lights of the living room.

She heard a scream.

Please let Blue not be lying at the bottom of the pool, broken.

Then silence. A terrible stillness.

She could see terrible things. Blue, mangled on a cushion of white, her limbs bent at odd angles.

Tiny icicles pricked Stella's face, it was snowing again. The cold was bracing, so intense it became all she was aware of. Her palms stung where they had pushed against the ice. The skin under her nails was on fire. Her toes were numb.

Another scream slashed the still, white garden.

Stella oriented herself towards the sound. A figure emerged from the line of trees. It was too far, there were too many shadows, she couldn't see who it was.

'Peter?'

She took a step backwards, towards the house.

## Grove Road Clinic, May 2009

'That wasn't so bad?' His voice was saturated with pleasure.

She was on her hands and knees looking at the magnolia-painted wall of the consulting room. The muscles in her arms and hands ached from holding herself up, her knees hurt where they pushed against the hard bed. She was too scared to move until he gave his permission.

'I'd guess you haven't done that before,' he said.

She thought she might be bleeding because a raw, sharp pain pierced from back to front. She imagined that behind her he was smiling. Seconds ticked past. She guessed he was carefully removing the condom and he would take it with him.

'I'm impressed,' he said. 'You didn't scream. Hardly made a sound. There's K-Y Jelly here on the doctor's stand but I didn't think you deserved any.'

At least she didn't have to look at him.

'Get up.'

She stood. She didn't dare go for her clothes. Her mouth was so dry she did not think she would be able to speak, there was a disgusting taste on her tongue, her throat ached. Her legs were unsteady, they didn't want to hold her up. She would not let him see her cry.

He unlocked the door, his back to her. She scanned the room, the desk, for something heavy – anything she could use against him. There was nothing, and even if there had been, she had no strength. She leaned against the edge of the medical couch, closing her eyes for just a second. Standing up had made her dizzy. But she was still in one piece. Just about. She held on to the hope that her ordeal might soon be over, that he would be satisfied with his revenge. But she didn't believe he would simply let her go.

He waited for her at the open doorway, relaxed. He had all the time he wanted, he knew they would not be disturbed. He had no weapon, no gun and no knife. And still, she was terrified of him. She was confused; whipped and subdued and sore. He took hold of her upper arm, gripping hard as he pulled her towards the bathroom. He held on to her while he pulled the shower curtain aside.

'Get in,' he said.

She was shaking, but she managed to lift both legs over the edge of the bath, not to fall.

The spray of cold droplets pierced her skin, like needles. She was shaking. He picked up the bottle of hand soap from the basin, unscrewed the lid and poured it over her head and her shoulders.

'Scrub,' he said. 'I'm watching. Everywhere.'

She did as she was told. There was too much soap and it lathered easily. At least the water was warmer now. She wanted to scrub every bit of him off her; she didn't care about DNA. She rubbed the soap over her closed eyes and pressed her fingers hard into her scalp. She washed her arms, breasts, stomach and between her legs. She was careful not to look down. She feared she would see blood across the white enamel of the bathtub. She didn't want to know.

She held on to the handrail, unsteady, fixing her eyes on the grey lines between the white tiles, as she reached down to wash her feet. She wondered if she had been punished enough or if there was worse still to come. She wanted to crawl away somewhere, into her flat, put the chain on the door and pull the curtains shut and just hide and never come out.

Simpson turned off the water and handed her a towel. She was grateful for the small gesture of kindness. She had no intention of running away or fighting back. She was weak.

'My daughter is too old to be adopted, so she'll probably stay with her useless mother or go into long-term foster care. I'll still have contact with her. In a few years, she'll see what a weak, useless bitch her mother is, and she'll come back to me of her own free will. And there's nothing any one of you meddling cunts can do about it. And you'll have your memories of me.'

She saw his fingers curl into a fist, but he checked himself, relaxed his hand, pushed his fringe back from his face. His jaw was still tight. She was sure he ached to hit her, but he wouldn't want to leave any marks easily visible to the world.

She wrapped her arms around her chest.

She was very cold again, the shaking grew worse. The pain between her legs was acute and blood trickled down her legs. She felt sick at the thought of the damage. She was in shock. She couldn't push down the nausea any longer, she dropped down and retched into the toilet bowl. She stayed there, kneeling, relieved to be looking away from him.

'Tell the A and E team it was a bit of rough sex with a one-night stand,' he said. 'That's what I'd recommend anyway.'

She nodded.

He gave her one last appraisal as she knelt in front of the toilet, in pain, trembling, naked, grasping at the edge of the bowl. He ran his fingers through his fringe one more time and then turned and left the bathroom.

She managed a few deep breaths. The pain throbbed so much she felt she was split in two. She had no strength.

She gathered herself together, a second or two, then crawled to the door. She reached up and turned the lock. She sank to the floor, grasping at the too-small hand towel, pulling it tight around her shoulders, putting her head between her knees to try to stop the room from spinning. She thought she heard the front door slam shut, but she couldn't be sure.

There was no window. She had no watch so she couldn't tell how much time had passed. She lay down on the tiles, curled on her side. Her thoughts slowed, her limbs became heavy and then all she could think of was water. She needed a drink of water. She wanted to stand up and turn on the tap, but she didn't have the energy. She craved a nice hospital bed with crisp white sheets and lots of painkillers.

Her hip and shoulder ached where they pressed against the cold, hard floor. The overhead light reflected off the white tiles. She must have slept, a little. She sensed she was alone in the quiet building. She pulled herself up to a sitting position, staying there until her head cleared. She reached up to grip the basin with her right hand. She gasped at the sharp stabbing between her legs as she tried to stand. She bit her lip until the pain eased. Her legs were weak, but they held her upright. She closed her eyes, stayed still for a second to check she would not fall. She didn't want to think about the pain or the damage that might have been done. She needed a doctor. She so badly wanted her clothes. She unlocked the door, waited a second, opened it. The passage was in darkness. She felt safer in the dark, she'd been exposed enough. The photographs. They might be up on the internet already. Simpson had won. She had submitted to him completely. He had ensured that she would forever be vulnerable; degraded. *It's only a body.*

Stella felt her way along the wall to the office and once inside she moved slowly in the dim light that filtered through the shutters. She did not want to see this room ever again. She just wanted her clothes. They were still there, folded over the arm of the chair. She dressed, taking care to make only small, slow movements.

Her bag was still propped against the desk where she had left it. She slipped her feet into her shoes. Even the low heels were a source of pain, so she took them off again and put them into her tote. She put the bag over her shoulder, still holding her mobile phone. The building remained hushed.

She was sure she was alone.

She trailed her hand along the wall again, until she reached the top of the staircase. The thick pile was comforting under her feet as she made her way down, carefully, one step at a time, clutching the banister for support.

She walked to the front door and pulled on it to check it was locked. Simpson had shut it when he left and he wouldn't be able to get back in. She fastened the security chain, then hobbled over to a chair in the waiting room and thought about what to do. Through the slats in the blinds, she could see headlights passing on Grove Road. The only number she could remember was 999 so that's what she dialled. After one ring, she disconnected the call. There was another number for non-emergency matters, but she couldn't remember it. She didn't want to talk to strangers. She didn't want anyone else examining her, hurting her, humiliating her.

Her eyes had adjusted to the murky light and she could see perfectly well. She still had no idea what to do. She moved to the sofa and drew her legs underneath her. She considered staying that way until Monday. She thought of her privacy and of her career. She needed advice.

After a few rings, he answered. She wondered where he was, on a Friday night. If he was out with Hannah and Izzy and the rest of her friends.

'Pete,' she said. 'It's Stella.'

'Stella,' he said. He sounded pleased to hear from her.

She was silent, she couldn't think what to say.

'Are you all right?' he asked.

'Listen – can you come and see me?' she said.

'Sure.'

'It's not what you think. I need some advice. And please don't tell anyone else.'

'OK,' he said. 'Tell me where you are.'

While she waited for him to arrive, she ransacked Anne's neatly ordered drawers, looking for painkillers. All she could find was paracetamol. She managed to swallow a few. She needed something stronger. She wasn't bleeding any more, that was the important thing, her clothes were dry. Any damage was on the inside.

She had bad cramps. She went back to curl up on the leather chesterfield in the waiting room. She had forgotten to ask where Peter was and she didn't know how long it would take him to get to the clinic. She wanted him to hurry. She felt as though she'd been in a car accident, battered and bruised and raw.

At ten o'clock she heard a car pull up on the driveway at the front of the building. She peered out: Peter was climbing out of his Golf. She walked gingerly to the front door, took off the shiny brass chain and turned the large brass lock.

'What's happened to you?' he asked, when she peered out.

'Come in.'

She switched on the light in the hall, but used the dimmer to turn it down to the minimum setting. She supposed she looked pale, but she didn't think Simpson had left any marks. She couldn't find any words, it was exhausting, to have to tell him, to have to live through it all again.

'Could you please make me a cup of tea?' That was all she could manage. 'There's a kitchen at the top of the stairs – it's small, you'll find everything. Milk and lots of sugar.'

He did as she requested without asking any questions and she was relieved. But she wondered if it had been wise to telephone a police officer. The last thing she felt like was explaining. She pulled a small cushion over her lap.

The tea was milky and not too hot. He had to hold the cup steady for her. The sweetness helped to steady her, to stop her head feeling so light it might lift off her shoulders. He sat facing her on the sofa, solid and dependable.

'What were you doing when I called?' she asked.

She needed a little more time.

'Studying for my DI exam on Monday.'

She nodded. She had dragged him out to St John's Wood when he should be at home studying for the most important exam of his career and now she didn't want to tell him what had happened.

'You look like you need a doctor,' he said.

'I just need a few more minutes. To sit here.'

'It's OK.' He was patient, but observant too. She took

another sip of the milky, sweet tea. She felt better, safer, now that he was with her.

'I'm sorry about this,' she said.

'Don't worry about it.'

She felt a little less weak, a little less like she might keel over at any moment. 'Did you always want to be a policeman?' she asked.

'Since I was fifteen. I came home from school and our house had been broken into – they smashed a window at the back. My mother's jewellery was taken, nothing valuable, but everything she'd inherited from her mother. The house was a total mess. And the worst part was that our cat ran away. I found her lying in the road, hit by a car. I was so angry. I just wanted to go out and find them and get revenge.'

'And here you are,' she said.

Her mug was empty. She had automatically placed it on top of a magazine, so there would be no stain on Anne's wooden coffee table.

'Do you want another cup?' he asked.

She shook her head.

'Are you ready to talk?'

She told him then, in detail – as though she were writing it up in a report. Dispassionately. Everything. The most degrading parts. She tried to speak as though it had happened to someone else and not to herself and to stay clear and calm.

Peter put his arm around her shoulder and squeezed. She wasn't afraid of his touch. He put his lips to her forehead.

'I'll come with you to the police station,' he said. 'I'll stay with you. They'll get you a doctor.'

'I haven't decided yet – if I want to report it,' she said.

'The quicker you do, the quicker they can pick him up.'

She took a deep breath, let it out slowly. 'I need to think about it,' she said. 'That's why I called you first. I want to know what will happen if I do report it.'

He kept his arm around her shoulders and she leaned into him.

'I'll take you down to the nearest station – Swiss Cottage. We can ask for a female police officer. You'll tell her exactly what you told me. They'll get a doctor to examine you and take swabs for DNA evidence. They'll want to treat the clinic as a crime scene, they might find evidence here. But we need to act quickly in case the bastard decides to run.'

'I don't think he will. There's a court case in progress, he's trying to get custody of his daughter. And he thinks he's safe.'

'Did he threaten you with anything?'

'He said he'd put photographs on the internet. And that he would say that we had a relationship – something that would imply that I'd violated my ethical code. He'll say it wasn't a scheduled appointment, that I invited him here for sex after hours. We once bumped into each other in a restaurant, he bought me a drink, there were lots of witnesses. Long story.'

'You don't have to explain,' he said. 'Are you ready?'

The shivering had begun again and the entire surface of her skin was burning, at the same time, she was freezing cold. The last shreds of her dignity would be shattered under the bright lights of the police station, everybody would know. The careful façade she had created behind her title – *Dr Davies* – would be stripped away. It would be her word against his. They would dredge up her history. An interview at the police station, followed by a court case, would be an extended version of what she had gone through upstairs at the hands of Lawrence Simpson. It wasn't worth it. She had had enough. She couldn't bear any more. She was hanging on to herself with her fingernails, keeping herself together when she felt she would collapse, would fly apart, would finally crumble and give up.

'You're in shock,' he said. 'Another half an hour won't matter. I'll wait with you.'

'I'm so cold,' she said. He sat close, reached over and put both arms around her. She wanted to stay that way, and never have to move and never have to remember. She fixed her eyes on the deep red leather of the chesterfield. Hundreds and hundreds of buttons began to swirl in front of her.

'Do you want me to call someone for you?' he asked.

'No one. I don't want anyone to know. I'm sorry,' she said. 'I can't go through with this. I'm not going to report what happened.'

She could report what Simpson had done to her, but the public ignominy would be shared between them. One way or another, she would be called in front of an ethics committee. Her photograph might appear in the newspapers and the professional persona she had worked so hard to earn would rupture. She knew how short prison sentences for rape could be – and that was if they even secured a conviction.

She had a choice: she could keep her mouth shut, withdraw from the Simpson report, carry on with her life. Pretend.

'Stella, it's not my decision to make but I think it's critical that you go to the police. Tonight.'

'If I go to the police,' she said, 'then I can't revoke my statement, can I? They can investigate, even if I ask them not to.'

He nodded.

She shook her head. 'I can't.'

'Technically,' he said, 'I could report this myself.'

'You wouldn't do that to me.' She looked him straight in the eyes. 'Tell me you won't do that.'

'I know you're in shock,' he said, 'but it's important that you make a police report.'

'You're saying that because you're a policeman.'

'I'm saying it because I care. It's the best thing for you. He's still out there, he could hurt someone else. And if he's not arrested, you'll live in fear.'

She pulled away. 'Pete, we've been friends for years, but you don't know everything about me.'

The churning sensation in her stomach was settling and so was the buzzing in her head; all of it was quietening down. Her lower back still ached and so she leaned back and carefully lifted her feet one at a time, putting them up on the coffee table. She thought about how much Anne would hate the sight of her feet on the magazines.

'I need to talk to my boss. He's a psychiatrist. I need to get another perspective. I need to think about what it's going to do to my career if this comes out.' Her voice sounded stronger, but when she looked down, her hands were still trembling. She couldn't remember Max's mobile number, even though she knew it off by heart.

'Can you dial for me?' she asked.

She handed Peter her phone. 'Press the green button,' she said. 'Then press *M*, his name comes up first: Max.'

## Hilltop, 1.30 a.m.

The window had exploded; she hadn't expected it to be so loud. Glass everywhere. She hadn't meant to smash the window. She couldn't remember why she'd done that. Sometimes, her anger got the better of her. Her crazy part. Hate was everywhere inside her, like fire, burning her alive.

She ran for the trees at the back of the garden. The cold hit her, like a blast from a gun, burning her eyes and her mouth and her ears. She had forgotten how bad it was outside.

Shit. Fuck.

He was calling her, coming after her.

She had made a really bad mistake. All she wanted was to get home again, to her bed. To her mother. There must be a way out of this place. But once she got inside the trees there was only blackness. She didn't know what to do. She couldn't see; she couldn't find a path. Only dark. Black, freezing cold. She had to slow down. She counted ten, small shuffling steps, holding her hands out straight in front of her. A million needles were poking into her palms. Her knees buckled and she sank down into the soft cushion of snow.

'BLUE!'

The police don't help. They don't believe a word you say.

The freezing air pierced and stabbed her face. Her hands stung so badly it was driving her mad. All she wanted was to lie down. If she stayed out in the snow, she knew she would give up; she would go to sleep and probably die. She had wanted to smash that stupid fat green statue straight into the wife's head.

They would take her away from her mother. Again.

She hated Max Fisher. She hated him most of all. She wanted a knife, to slice up her arms and let the rage and the cold bleed out of her. She pushed her raw hands into her pockets, feeling carefully for the piece of glass: a long, thin triangle.

But as the cold took over, the fire inside her faded. She gave up. She put her head between her knees and waited. She would let them do whatever they wanted to her. She didn't want to be out in the snow. She didn't really want to die. She wasn't crazy.

She heard him, coming closer, his boots crunching. She closed her eyes. Invisible. He just stood there. He didn't try to grab her or anything.

'Let's go back to the house,' he said. 'You don't need to be frightened.'

She lifted her head and held out her hands. 'I'm bleeding.'

He bent down to take a look. She lifted her arms, higher. He lifted her up.

She reached around his neck and laid her head on his shoulder. She closed her eyes, pretending it was him. His hands were around her waist and under her knees. She felt like she was about six years old. He walked, slow and steady, and she felt peaceful, being carried. It was so quiet.

He stumbled, trying to climb up the slippery steps of the porch and she clung on tighter.

A bright light burst through her eyelids. She blinked. Stella was standing next to the fucked-up window, shining a torch right at her. She looked terrified and she looked like she was sorry. She'd turned white and she was breathing like she was having an asthma attack or something.

'I didn't mean to frighten you,' Stella said. She got a sick look on her face when she saw the blood. 'Are you in pain?'

She left her face pressed against the policeman's shoulder. 'She didn't get very far,' he said.

Just inside the house, he put her down. She preferred being carried. She wasn't going to help them; she wasn't going to make it easy. She let her legs go limp and refused to walk. Stella came closer and held one of her arms, he took hold of the other. She slumped between them, so they had to half lift, half drag her. The house was a mess. Totally fucked up. It was cold inside, too.

'The study,' Stella said.

They dragged her, all the way through the living room, across the entrance hall and into the study. She tried to make herself heavy. She wanted Stella to suffer. She wanted to make her pay, for calling her a crazy liar.

The window in the study was tiny: long and narrow and placed high up on the wall. There was no way out.

When they let go of her, she stumbled, dropped to her knees. Her clothes were on fire. She pulled at them, trying to get her arms out of her jacket; she threw it off, everything was tangled, she couldn't get her legs out, she was jerking all over the place.

'Blue, stop.' Stella held her down. Her voice was kind and soft.

Now her skin had turned clammy and cool, the burning

had gone away but the snow was back inside her and she couldn't get warm. Her blood was leaking out, all over the place.

The two of them wrapped a blanket around her and lifted her into a deep, soft chair.

Stella rubbed her arms and her back. 'I think she has hypothermia,' she said. 'We need to keep her temperature stable.'

They were smothering her, in blankets. Blood was flowing, from the cuts on her hands, soaking all the way down, all the way right inside, down into the chair.

The policeman pulled at her arms, straightening them out, examining the bits of glass in her hands, pushing her sleeves up, staring at the old scars too. He had gloves on. She watched what he was doing with the tweezers, but it was like watching somebody else's body, someone else who was bleeding. She felt nothing.

Stella looked away. Like she was about to faint.

'I don't think there's too much damage,' the policeman said. He was lying, pretending to be cheerful. 'A few glass splinters. I'll take some of them out and clean the cuts with disinfectant. Then you'll need to see a proper doctor.'

'The nearest emergency room is a thirty-minute drive,' Stella said. 'Longer if the roads are iced over.'

He held her arm, stretched out straight along the arm of the chair, his fingers tight around her wrist. He didn't flinch as he stabbed the sharp tip of the tweezers into the cuts. She hoped he knew what he was doing. Slowly, he took out a sliver of glass. It stung when he pulled it out, she pressed her lips together but she was moaning. He did it again, the sharp tip of the tweezers into her bloody hands, over and over again. It took for ever. When he had finished, he laid the tweezers down on the towel, next to the bits of glass. Stella swooped in and took them away. He bandaged her hands and wrists. He was useless, her fists were so thick she looked like a boxer.

Her blood was splattered all over his shirt. His jeans were soaking wet.

Stella sat on the arm of the chair and tried to stroke her hair. She let her. Stella felt sorry for her. Stella wasn't a bad person. Blue would fight for Max too, if he was her husband. She wouldn't want to believe anything bad about him either.

There was noise, from the entrance hall. Someone was coming through the front door.

'I'm home,' he said.

It was him. The feeling of warmth spread through her, flowing from deep inside her belly, up through her arms and down to her toes. Fizzing. Like champagne.

## Hilltop, 2 a.m.

Her husband stood at the door of the study. He had his coat slung over his arm and he was holding his medical bag. He was calm and composed and he looked right through her, as though she were invisible.

Nobody moved.

Blue huddled under a blanket. Stella perched on the edge of her chair, still feeling the adrenaline rush of her brief foray outside the house.

'Peter?' Max said. He was apparently more surprised to see her old flame than he was to see Blue.

Peter was leaning against her desk, his arms folded and his shirt smeared with Blue's blood. He nodded. He didn't rush forward to offer Max a handshake.

'Stella called. She asked me to come over,' Peter said. 'What brings you home at this hour?'

Max placed his bag down on the floor. He did not move any closer. He did not embrace her. It wasn't the presence of unexpected guests that held him back; it was never really any different when he arrived home. Stella had learned to live with the distance between them.

She saw the scene through Peter's eyes: a man disinterested in his wife. Detached.

She wondered if Max would care, if he knew, about the kiss with Peter. She could only hope there might be a flicker of jealousy somewhere behind his inscrutable exterior. He knew they had slept together, once. But she could barely summon the energy she needed to delude herself.

'You're still with the police?' Max asked.

Peter nodded. 'I am. I take it someone from the Met police tracked you down. Asked about a patient of yours who's gone missing.'

'This girl arrived at the house tonight.' Stella placed her hands on Blue's shoulders, as if to bring attention to the most unexpected person in the room. 'She says her name is Blue. I understand you know who she is, and you know the family—'

'Why is it so cold in here?' Max asked.

'Because there's a gaping hole in the living room,' Stella said. 'Our guest threw your mother's Buddha through the window.'

'I see.'

'She says she's your patient.'

Max nodded. 'Was,' he said. 'Was my patient.' He seemed to feel no need to explain. The anger simmering in Stella's solar plexus grew larger.

'Blue cut herself on the glass from the window,' Stella said. 'Pete's been trying to patch her up.'

Blue had perked up at the sight of Max. She was alert and upright in the chair, the blanket had dropped down around her waist. She was staring at Max as though her life depended on it. Her hair was still wet with snow, her hands were grotesque, swollen with white dressings, bloodstains seeping through the bandages. A smile spread across her face and lit up her eyes as she gazed at him.

Stella knew just how she felt.

After a few moments Blue couldn't contain herself, she ran straight at Max and buried her head in his chest.

Max was embarrassed. He pulled at her arms, loosening them, trying to extricate himself.

Her 44-year-old husband would never fall for the charms of a disturbed teenager. Even one as seductive as Blue. Surely.

'How did you get my home address?' He held her at arm's length.

'On the internet,' Blue said.

'How did you really get my home address?'

'I saw it on an envelope in your office.'

Stella could see Blue's mood sinking in the face of Max's coldness. Her damaged thumb hovered around her mouth and she slunk back to her chair, sulking.

'How could you do this to me?' Stella asked. 'How could you get involved with her without telling me? She could have brought her father here with her.' Her voice was tight, strained.

Peter stayed well back, looking between the three of them. His expression was like thunder. Stella despised herself for involving him again. He was still trying to help her and she was still beyond rehabilitation. And this time it could cost him.

'Stella, this is *not* the time.' Max used the same tone for her that he used for Blue. Concerned, but condescending. He turned his back on them, as though hoping they might have vanished by the time he turned round again. He ran his hand over his hair. He lifted his bag up on to Stella's desk and began to search inside it.

225

'She needs to be treated in hospital. And we need to leave soon,' Max said. 'They're expecting more snow and soon I won't be able to get out of here. The driveway and the hill will be impossible.'

'I was hoping you might be able to talk to her,' Stella said. 'You're her therapist – the person she's most likely to respond to. I need to know if her father is behind this visit in any way.'

He shook his head, still not looking directly at her. 'Nothing she says is reliable. The critical thing is that they get her medication stabilized. She needs admission to a psychiatric unit.'

'I want my jacket,' Blue said. She had regained her colour.

'Are you cold?' Stella asked. 'You can have one of my jumpers.'

'I just want my own jacket.'

Stella found it for her on the floor behind the chair. Blue squeezed her bound hands through the sleeves. She walked over to Max and stood right in front of him. Expecting something.

'I'm going to take you to a hospital,' Max said.

Blue turned her small face up towards his.

Stella felt sad for her. Blue should be enjoying her beauty, in love with a boy her own age; happy. Not inside Hilltop, tormented.

'I want you to tell them what happened,' Blue said. 'Tell them that we were together – loads of times, in your office. That you couldn't keep your hands off me.'

She smiled up at him, a pale, crazed angel.

'Come on,' Max said. 'Sit down.' He spoke gently as he pulled her hands firmly away from his jacket and guided her back to the chair. 'The drive across to the hospital could take up to an hour. I'm going to give you an injection before we go. It will relax you and also help with the pain in your hands.'

'I don't want an injection,' Blue said. Her thumb was in her mouth and her eyes were glossy with tears. But she stayed still, waiting, as Max prepared two syringes and balanced them in a kidney-shaped cardboard dish, on the arm of her chair.

'Is this really necessary?' Stella said. 'She's already medicated to the eyeballs and I gave her a sleeping pill last night – is it safe to give her more drugs?'

'Look at the state of her,' Max said. 'While you two have been in charge, she's smashed a glass window and shredded her hands. Do you really expect me to take the risk that she might hurt herself again? The drive to A and E is hardly going to be a picnic in this weather as it is.'

He had a point, Stella had to admit. It seemed typical of Max, somehow, to come in at the end stages, to take charge and to make everyone else feel incompetent. She trusted him to do the right thing, but he could be so self-assured that he verged on domineering. Clearly he did not welcome any interference.

Stella felt ashamed at how she had failed the girl – again. She had already let Blue down once before. Her report had gone out without the crucial finding that Simpson was a psychopath. She had not reported Blue's father to the police and so he had been free to continue to torment his family. Blue deserved to get the help she needed.

Stella would have to wait until Blue was safely in hospital to get any details out of her husband.

'I don't like injections,' Blue whimpered. She squirmed in the chair, tucking herself deep into the corner and pulling her knees up.

Peter was staring at Max with an expression of open dislike. But he too did not interfere between doctor and patient.

Max ignored Blue's distress. He reached down to push up her sleeve. 'It won't hurt too much,' he said.

Blue twisted, pulling away from him. She swiped at Max's hand, sending the needles, ampoules and the kidney-shaped dish clattering to the floor.

Stella didn't see where the piece of broken glass came from. Blue clutched it in her injured hand, holding the tip right up against Max's throat, over his pulsing Adam's apple. Blue strained forwards, her teeth bared in an ugly grimace, pushing the small glass shard deeper and harder into his flesh.

Stella could not speak or move, her throat had closed, her muscles had seized up.

Max. She was about to lose him.

Peter was only an arm's length away, ready to lunge at Blue – but waiting – for what?

'I love you,' Blue said. 'I could kill you.'

She took a deep, shuddering breath as she scraped the shard upwards until it rested against Max's lips. For once, Max had nothing to say.

Peter spoke: 'Blue, just put the glass down. Step back. We'll find a way to help you. I promise.'

Blue kept the glass just where it was. 'I won't hurt him if he tells the truth,' she said.

'What truth?' Max spoke softly, through clenched teeth. He looked a smaller man than Stella had remembered, stripped of his authority and his carefully measured distance and his medical bag.

'That I'm not crazy,' Blue said. 'That I'm not a liar. I want *you* to tell them.'

Out of the corner of her eye, Stella glimpsed Peter inching forwards. She stayed very still, dragging her eyes back to Blue's face. She willed the girl not to lose it completely. It wasn't too late.

Blue moved the piece of glass down again, to Max's Adam's apple. She moved it from side to side, slowly, caressing him. He held his breath, stared at the ceiling.

Lawrence Simpson's face floated in the air in front of Stella. His dilute-blue eyes, the sadistic smile, his exquisite pleasure in her shame and her powerlessness and her suffering. Like father, like daughter. She threw her full weight at the girl, pushing her away from Max. Blue screamed as she went for Stella's face. Stella ducked, covering her head with her arms. Blue was panting and sobbing. Stella couldn't see, couldn't grab hold of the bandaged hands before the shard of glass slashed at her again. *Please, not my eyes.*

But Peter had the girl now, pinned against him, holding her arms at her sides.

And Blue was quickly subdued. She didn't struggle; the glass simply dropped from her hand to the floor.

'I think you'd better take that jacket off and give it to me,' Peter said. He stood behind the weeping girl and kept a firm grip around her as she shrugged the jacket off one side and then the other until it dropped to the floor at her feet. Stella checked the jacket for any more weapons. The zipped compartments were empty, except for a small mobile phone, which she removed and pushed into her back pocket.

They had Blue stretched out on the floor. Stella pinned her legs down and Peter held on to her wrists.

Max was unfazed as he retrieved his paraphernalia from the floor.

'Are you all right?' he asked Blue.

Blue nodded. Her cheeks were wet with tears.

'What is that stuff?' she asked Max.

'I should have explained it to you properly before,' he said. He held up the small glass vial: 'This one will help you to relax. The other one is a tetanus shot. It's very important you have that so you don't get ill from the cuts.'

Stella felt tender towards him, and proud, as he worked to contain the frightened girl.

'OK,' Blue nodded. She was trying now, to be good and to be brave. For Max.

Max prepared to inject his trembling patient. He lifted the needle and a few drops of fluid spurted from the tip. He pressed on her arm with the flat of his hand. Cold steel pierced her supple skin. As he pressed down on the plunger, the girl flinched with pain and gave a small cry and then covered her mouth,

Stella felt a rush of nausea as Max withdrew the needle. He wiped away a droplet of blood. He lifted the second syringe.

Her rational, sane self did not question his innocence. And yet Blue's words kept playing over and over again in her mind.

His patients trusted him to do no harm. Max could do anything he liked to Blue, she was at his mercy.

He was her husband and she loved him.

When it was over, Stella and Peter let Blue go. She pushed herself up to a cross-legged sitting position and stretched out her arm. She stared at the droplet of blood that formed in the crook of her elbow and at the thick bandages around her hands. She wiggled her ravaged fingers. 'I want my mum,' she said.

Stella reached out and rubbed Blue's shoulder. Blue had no idea what lay ahead. With her history and her behaviour over the past few hours, she would not be going home for a long while. If ever. No professional would release her into the care of her mother after what she had disclosed. Stella felt terribly sad for her. What a life.

'Good girl,' Max said. 'We'll give the injection a few minutes to work, and then we'll get going.'

Blue lay down on the floor, holding her arm. She closed her eyes.

'She looks semi-conscious,' Peter said. 'I thought you said it was some kind of muscle relaxant?'

'She's fine,' Max said. He began to issue instructions, barely looking at Blue. 'Can you get her something dry and warm to wear? And can you do something about taping up that broken window? And see if you can get hold of an emergency window-repair service. We need to secure the house.'

Stella got up to do what Max had asked of her, but she felt uneasy. She had become accustomed to watching over the girl and it didn't seem right to leave her side.

Max was Blue's doctor; she was safe with him.

Stella looked from Blue to Max. She could not be swayed by the girl's bizarre and lurid allegations. She had to trust her husband, and do as he asked of her. He was all she had.

## Grove Road Clinic, May 2009

Stella and Peter waited in an awful silence for Max to arrive. Stella was thinking about how she would explain what she had done, and the risk she had taken. The scandal could destroy the clinic. The practice would for ever be seen as the centre where someone was raped, or perhaps worse – where a psychologist slept with a patient. The investigation would no doubt close down the clinic while forensics combed the offices and interviewed the staff.

She had not resisted, she did not have a bruise on her. Lawrence Simpson could say whatever he liked. He could say, truthfully, that she had invited him over to the clinic in the evening, on a weekend. He could say she had wanted to be alone with him, he could point out he was unarmed. He was not an unattractive man and she was young.

She wondered how Max was going to view the situation. One way or another, she had broken boundaries and paid the price.

She shouldn't blame herself. She had voiced her concerns about Simpson to Max. She hoped he would have faith in her, would be loyal to her, would believe her story.

Peter sat close by, but a space had opened up between

them. She could feel that he wanted to talk to her again, about reporting the crime, and she knew he wanted to rush her off to a police station, but he held back.

Once again she heard the rush of tyres against gravel as Max arrived in his Mercedes. Stella sat on the chesterfield and listened to his key in the lock and the sound of the door opening. She had interrupted his precious weekend, and this would not be a welcome intrusion. She hoped he wasn't angry. She might have single-handedly brought his practice to its knees.

Max looked confused at the sight of the two of them sitting on the sofa in his reception area in the middle of the night.

'Peter's a friend,' Stella said. 'And a police officer. That's why I called him.'

'What's happened?' Max asked. Not angry, but concerned.

Stella was grateful he had come, and relieved. She needed his advice – she needed him to tell her exactly what she should do. If she was lucky, he might be able to help her through this with both her sanity and her career intact.

She looked down at her scrubbed-clean fingernails as she talked. She was careful to speak slowly, she didn't want to vomit all over the cream medical-centre carpet. She didn't want to go through the ordeal again, she wanted to retreat down a long dark tunnel, to somewhere distant and peaceful, but she forced herself back.

'I gave Lawrence Simpson an after-hours appointment. We were alone in the building. He raped me and he also took some photographs of me naked which he has threatened to put up on the internet. Photographs that look as though I was enjoying myself. He has said that if I report what happened, he would deny it was rape, he would say it was consensual. He knows he's going to lose his custody battle. I was his parting shot.'

'Are you injured?' Max asked.

She nodded. She didn't want to cry.

'We need to get you to a doctor,' Max said.

'I can't face hours in A and E.'

'I know a private GP. I can call her to come over.'

'Yes, please.' She was so thankful to have him taking care of her.

Peter's lips were moving as he spoke to Max, but there was only the sound of waves in her ears, drowning out his words. She was frightened they might leave her alone in the room. She could not bear to be on her own. Max left, but Peter stayed. He sat on the opposite end of the sofa, watching Stella stiff and upright and closed off from him. Max returned with a white medical sheet, the kind they used in the consulting rooms. He tucked it round her and then he held out two pills: 'One's for the pain, the other is a tranquillizer,' he said.

She reached out for them. She didn't care what they were, she would swallow anything to escape. Max handed her a glass of water and watched as she forced the pills down her throat. She rested her head on the arm of the sofa and stayed still, to keep the drugs down. Maybe the hospital would give her a bed for a few days. She couldn't imagine ever going to sleep alone in her bed, in her empty flat.

With the two men in the room, she felt safe again. But she also understood that this false sense of security would soon come to an end. How could she go back to work, while Simpson, or others like him, lay in wait? Paranoia was setting in already. Was it paranoia? Was it illogical to draw the conclusion that nowhere was safe? Bile pushed upwards;

she focused all her attention on her breathing, trying her hardest to keep the pills down.

Max said she was in shock, she shouldn't be pressured. Peter said the rape must be reported, a brief statement, it was important. She could give a full statement later. Peter said the clinic was a crime scene, nothing must be touched until the forensics unit arrived. Max looked angry. The two of them weren't getting along.

'She needs a doctor who can examine her and take forensic evidence,' Peter said. 'Once the shock wears off she may well want to report this. The evidence shouldn't be lost.'

She didn't want to make any decisions or take any action.

'I'll get someone to examine her,' Max said. 'But it has to be her decision to report what happened.'

'What have you given her? She's in no fit state to report anything.'

'She's in shock. I couldn't leave her that way. She deserves some relief.'

'You're concealing a crime.'

Peter kept saying her name: *Stella, Stella, Stella, Stella.* He wanted her to wake up. But it was too late. She was drifting, away from herself and away from the room. Her eyelids were so very heavy. She knew she should listen, but she couldn't hold on. The pills were pulling her down to a place where everything was hushed and muted, and she didn't have to be terrified or ashamed.

She woke up alone, in a strange bed.

She was blunted, empty.

The doctor Max had called had been an attractive woman in her late forties, very blonde with a short skirt and knee-length boots. She had reassured Stella: the damage was not too great, certainly not permanent. There was bruising and some tearing but not so much that it required stitches. She had prescribed a short course of antibiotics. To Stella's relief, the examination was over quickly. She had heard the woman talking in low tones to Max in the hallway before she left.

The large bed had blue-striped sheets and a plain square-edged headboard covered in navy cotton. The room was a good size, with high ceilings and sash-windows. The beige roman blinds were closed, but sunlight filtered through. There were lovely exposed floorboards on the floor. One built-in cupboard, one chest of drawers, no frills.

Max was at the door. She had never seen him dressed in casual clothes, he was always in his suit and tie. Now he was in front of her in jeans and a black T-shirt.

'I convinced your boyfriend to let me take care of you for a bit, while you're still in shock,' he said.

'He's not my boyfriend.'

She tried to push herself up to a sitting position, but when she moved, the sharp pain was back. She gave up and lay back down. She looked down and saw she was wearing the same clothes as last night.

'How long was I asleep?' she asked.

'Some of last night is probably a blank, because of the shock and the tranquillizers. I brought you back to my apartment. I thought it better to let you sleep here. Your friend was very keen to get you to a police station last night but I didn't think you were up to it.'

'Thank you,' she said.

'Is there anyone you'd like me to call?'

'No,' she said. 'I don't want anyone to know. You can't tell anyone without my permission.'

As she lay, half propped up in Max's bed, careful not to make any sudden movements, she thought that if no one knew, then it could be almost as though it had never happened. Even in her own mind, perhaps. She didn't want to talk about it, she didn't want to report it and she didn't want to see some other doctor who was only interested in taking swabs. Her body would heal. She would work to erase everything from her mind.

'Of course I won't tell anyone without your permission,' Max said.

'Good.'

'Peter seems to feel very strongly that you should report what happened.'

'What do you think?' she asked him.

Max approached the bed. 'Can I sit down?'

'It's your bed,' she said. It was all so ironic. She had wanted this for so long, to be inside Max's apartment.

'It's my guest room, actually.' Max sat on the edge of the bed, careful not to come too close. He looked ill at ease, as though he had to deliver bad news.

'You know how these rape trials go,' he said. 'The reality is that it will be his word against yours. There are no witnesses, no hard evidence. He'll claim you liked rough sex. I hope you understand I'm not saying this to upset you, but I know that these trials can be more traumatizing than the rape itself. And the sentences – well – it might not be worth it in the end. I think you should know what you're getting yourself into if you go to the police.'

'I thought the same thing.'

'I'm not discouraging you from reporting what happened. But I think you should take a realistic view.'

'I don't want to involve the police. I don't see the point. I screwed up so badly, Max. I was so naive, seeing him after hours without letting anyone know. With him being a GP – I just did not see it coming.'

'You aren't responsible,' he said. 'I was your supervisor on the case. I should have taken your concerns more seriously. Don't start questioning yourself – that's playing right into his hands. That's just what he wants.'

'Tell me the truth – are you angry?'

He came a little closer and leaned back against the headboard. He held out his arm: it was an invitation. Stella let herself go, let herself snuggle in against him. He rested his arm across her shoulders.

'I had a client once,' he said, 'it was while I was still a registrar, and I treated her as part of my psychotherapy module, at a residential unit. I saw her in my office, twice a week for a month. This patient lay on the sofa bed, looking at the ceiling, terrified and not saying a word, week after week. Eventually I couldn't take it any more, the rigidity and the coldness of it all. I felt angry that we'd somehow taken the heart and soul out of our treatment. Maybe because of our own fears about getting close to people, to protect ourselves. So one session I suggested we go for a walk. There was a park, with a small lake. Being outside was healing.'

His voice soothed her.

'And?'

'She started talking. And when she cried, I put my arm around her. None of what I did was in a textbook. But she responded. And if you read Freud or Jung, you'll find they broke quite a few boundaries between doctor and patient that today we would find shocking. The point of this rambling story is that I was lucky – my treatment worked. The patient got better. You did something outside of the textbook and it went badly wrong. It doesn't make you a bad psychologist, or a bad human being.'

She wondered if he meant any of what he said, or if he was just trying to appease her guilt.

'I've been working with these people for years,' she said, 'assessing risk. And I know it sounds stupid, but it never occurred to me that something like this could ever happen to me. It was as though I deluded myself into thinking I lived in some sort of separate universe from my clients. But now I know I don't. And I can't go home on my own.'

'You don't have to go home,' he said. 'You'll stay here. As long as you like.'

'I didn't mean it like that. I wouldn't do that to you. I just need to find somewhere that's safe. A roommate, maybe. One that never goes out. A Rottweiler, preferably. What I mean is, I wonder if I could have an advance on my salary to check into a good hotel for a while? Where there's someone on reception twenty-four hours. Unless you can think of a better option?'

'Listen to me,' he said. 'You told me you were worried about Lawrence Simpson and I didn't take it seriously enough. So please let me help you, let me make it up to you. You're not in any fit state to make decisions. Let me take care of the practicalities for a while.'

She nodded, grateful. Max genuinely did not seem to blame her for being unprofessional, or for inviting potential disaster into his clinic.

She looked around, at the striped sheets, the linen headboard, the strip-wood flooring and the high ceilings. She would take up the offer to stay. She was overwhelmed, with relief and with longing, that he would stay next to her, stay holding her.

239

'I'm going to get another pill for you,' he said. He moved away. 'You don't need to be brave about it – you don't need to suffer any more than you have already.'

She wished, instead, that he would ask her more about her suffering. But she nodded, she would take what he offered. The pill would dampen her pain, would hold her in its arms and she could bury her thoughts and her aching spirit.

When she woke up, it was dark and she was alone and she began to shiver. All of her joints ached and her head pounded with pain. For days, she heaved and heaved into the toilet bowl, her stomach contorting and lurching. She was running a fever, but at the same time she was freezing cold. She was in so much pain, inside and out, that she imagined death to be a relief.

Max would appear in the doorway at the times she thought she couldn't bear it any longer. In one hand, he held a glass of water, in the other, her pills.

# Stella and Max

Stella knelt in front of Max as he sat on one of the kitchen chairs. She reached up and loosened his tie, she undid the top buttons of his shirt and then she dabbed at the scratches on his throat with an antiseptic wipe. The wounds were only superficial.

He was looking up at the ceiling.

'I'm sorry,' Stella said. 'I underestimated how disturbed she is. She could have killed you. I feel—'

He pushed her hand away, as though swatting at a fly. 'What were you thinking, when you let her in?'

She turned away, tossed the wipe into the dustbin. She'd had a long and eventful night, maybe she was imagining his derisive tone. He must have thought he was about to have his throat slashed. He was entitled to be angry at someone and he could hardly be angry with a mentally unstable, vulnerable teenager.

Or perhaps he had been angry at her for a long time, angry at the burden she had become. Perhaps he hadn't been aware of it himself, until now.

Stella could feel the cracks in her carefully constructed version of reality beginning to rupture.

'I could hardly let her freeze to death on the doorstep, could I?'

'I'm not blaming you – I'm just surprised that you would let a stranger into the house while you're here alone.' He peered at her over his glasses. 'After everything.'

He looked at her, with the affectionate, protective expression she adored. Or else, she was imagining the expression she wanted to see.

'I know,' she said. 'But on the other hand – I didn't know she was Simpson's daughter. I don't understand, Max. How could you have anything to do with any member of the Simpson family? Why didn't you talk to me about this first?'

He ran his hand over his head, in the gesture she so loved. His eyes shifted to the kitchen doorway and beyond, where Peter stood over a sleeping Blue.

'Can you look at me when I'm talking to you,' she said. 'Please.'

'It's been difficult, Stella, to discuss anything with you in a rational way.' His eyes kept flickering down and away. 'I consulted with her a couple of times as a favour to her mother. Things have been extremely difficult for them since the court case. I didn't think it was a good idea to tell you. I didn't think you could deal with it.'

'But you did think it was a good idea to treat both mother and daughter in a case already fraught with complications?' She stood up, so that she was looking down on him. He was determined to look at the floor, rather than at his wife.

'Let me rephrase that,' she said. 'In a case that was already thoroughly fucked up and where crucial information was withheld in the court report provided by *your* clinic.'

He didn't answer her.

'What the hell were you thinking when you took them on

as clients?' She deserved an answer. She deserved his attention. She had to fight the urge to collapse, to give up. 'How could you get involved with this girl and her mother without telling me? What if she had told her father our home address? What if he had followed her out here?'

'What have you taken tonight?' Max asked.

'Answer me. *What the hell were you thinking?*'

'I asked you how many pills you'd taken.'

His cool, controlled voice incensed her. He was so detached, so indifferent. She wanted to scream at him, to shake him, until he responded to her, but she knew she had to stay rational if she was to have any chance at all of connecting with him. She didn't want him to dismiss her as panic-stricken or out of control or irrational.

She took a deep breath and sat down on the chair next to his. 'I took diazepam – a couple of extra tablets. And I drank some of your leftover wine. I took my antidepressant.'

It wasn't easy to contain her agitation, but she managed. 'I still want to know why you treated Lawrence Simpson's wife and daughter without telling me.'

'You've behaved like an invalid for eighteen months and all of a sudden you expect me to treat you like a responsible adult?' This time there was no doubt about the contempt in his tone, and it stung.

'Sometimes I wonder, Stella – if you stay locked in this house because you're afraid of Lawrence Simpson, or if you stay locked in here because it's the best way you have of controlling me? Do you have any idea what it's like for me, living this way? I don't know how much longer I can do this.'

She had seen in her marriage only what she could bear.

She wasn't going to break down. She wasn't going to cry or beg or plead. She held herself rigid.

243

Perhaps he was being unfair – perhaps he wasn't. She had at some point taken a decision to remain helpless and to be dependent on him.

'I'm glad I know what you're really thinking.'

'No,' Max said. 'I'm sorry. That was totally out of line.'

He reached for her hand and gave her a light squeeze and a conciliatory smile. 'Stella, come on.' His expression was softer, and he was the old Max: gentle and charming.

But she had seen something different. He was only human. He was fallible.

Stella put both feet on the floor, to steady herself, and placed her hands on her knees. When she spoke, there was a trembling in her voice which she fought to control. 'Max, I do find it strange that you would start a therapeutic relationship with Simpson's ex-wife and then his daughter – instead of simply referring them on to someone else. It does look like – it seems as if you might have had some agenda, as if you might have been trying to control the situation . . .'

She paused, waiting for a reaction. A discussion. But Max just looked numb and tired. She kept going, hoping to break through the barrier between them. 'Maybe you've been affected by all of this too – emotionally, I mean – more than you realize. Maybe your decisions haven't been entirely rational. I've been completely dependent on you, isolated out here, while you've had to deal with all of the fallout and keep the clinic going.'

'You know I would never put you or anyone else in a compromised position.' His tone was gentle, but he was condescending, talking to her as though she was a child, or one of his patients.

'But you *have* put us all in danger,' she said. 'You have to see that. Simpson's daughter found out where we live. She ran away from home to try and make contact with you. She's obsessed with you, she fantasizes about you. She came here because she was angry at you for rejecting her, because you refused to see her or to talk to her. And the medication she's on—'

He stood, abruptly. 'I think it's safe to put her in the car now,' he said.

Stella stood in his way. 'Listen to me, Max. The girl has made these allegations and she's likely to repeat them. You heard her: she claims you had a sexual relationship. Talk it through with me, Max. Tell me exactly what happened between you and Blue – what was the relationship like, in the therapy? Was there some kind of eroticized transference?'

'Stella, she's delusional. A fantasist. If you believe her version of events there really is no hope for us.'

Stella felt herself shrinking, at the warning in his words. 'Don't,' she said. She wouldn't survive, without him. She could no longer imagine it.

'She needs to be in a secure unit.'

'A secure unit? Do you really—' Her mouth was dry once more; the words that had begun to flow had dried up.

She thought Max was making a mistake, recommending a secure unit. If Blue was placed with adolescents who had severe problems this would serve only to crystallize any anti-social or criminal tendencies she already had.

'How much more convincing do you need?' Max asked her. 'Would you like her to kill someone, maybe herself, before I take action?'

Stella did not speak. Max was the treating psychiatrist, and Blue's prognosis for recovery was bleak if she didn't get the help she needed.

She wanted her husband's arms around her. She wanted so

much for him to love her. He reached out and held her, tight. Her mouth pressed against his shoulder. She closed her eyes. It was much too soon when he let her go.

'Are you ready?' Max asked, even though Blue was clearly in no state to answer.

Blue did not move and did not respond. She lay in a foetal position on the floor. Peter had covered her with the blanket. Stella wasn't certain whether she was asleep, or just pretending.

'I'm not convinced you should be the one to take her to a hospital,' Peter said. 'If you're not the treating clinician at this point.'

He and Max faced each other, hands hanging at their sides, shoulders slightly tensed and feet apart, as though they were about to begin a sparring match.

'As a psychiatrist,' Max said, 'I have an ethical responsibility to a former patient with serious mental health issues.'

'So do the Met Police.'

'Where are they then?' Max asked, not unreasonably.

Peter did not answer.

'Well, in that case, since I am here and I'm prepared to get the girl the help she needs, I will drive her to a hospital. She needs proper treatment for her injuries and she needs to start taking her medication again as soon as possible – sudden withdrawal is dangerous for her.'

Peter did not move, or change his stance.

'Did *anything* happen in your sessions with her?' Peter asked. 'Even something small, something that in her mind might have encouraged her fantasy that you're in love with her? Anyone can make a mistake. She's an attractive girl. Almost an adult.'

Stella thought Max would finally run out of patience, finally lose his temper, but he did not.

'Please,' Max said. 'It's enough.' His voice was flat, disheartened. 'I listened to her. I gave her my full attention. That's all. And now I'm taking her to a hospital so she can get the treatment she needs.' He pulled on his coat and began patting his pockets as though searching for his car keys.

'Thanks for coming out here to support Stella tonight,' Max said to Peter. 'I appreciate it.'

Max held out his hand; Peter did not take it.

Peter had been ill at ease ever since Max had walked in the front door. Stella wondered how much his feelings for her might have interfered with a fair assessment of her husband's character.

'Which hospital are you taking her to?' Stella hovered next to Blue, who had not opened her eyes.

'St Agnes has an acute admissions unit. I'll take her there to begin with.'

Stella knew there was every likelihood that Blue would land up in foster care for good this time. Her medication might yet again be increased.

'Good girl,' Max said, as he leaned forward and manoeuvred his hands under Blue's arms and heaved her to her feet. Blue's eyes were open and she seemed at peace, relaxed and happy as she leaned against Max.

Peter stood with his arms folded.

'Can you give me a hand getting her into the car?' Max asked him.

Peter did not seem to be inclined to help him. He stayed where he was. Max could barely move, with the girl hanging around his neck.

'Look,' Max said, 'are you going to give me a hand?'

Peter came forward, stony-faced. He took hold of one arm, and Max the other, and together the two men lifted her and walked her towards the front door. Her trainers trailed along the marble tiles.

The entrance hall was as cold as a meat-locker. The chandelier shone brightly and fractured rays of light bounced against the walls. Stella opened the front door on to the snow-cleansed, pitch-black morning. The cold crept underneath her clothes and found its way into her shoes. She was still clutching the blanket that had been covering Blue as she lay on the study floor.

Stella stood at the open doorway and watched as the light in Max's Mercedes came on, and Blue slumped into the passenger seat. Max leaned over her and strapped her in.

Stella found that she had crossed the threshold of Hilltop and was walking towards them. The sharp air cleared her head. She covered Blue with the blanket and tucked her hands underneath it so they would not get too cold on her journey. Her eyelids fluttered, blue-veined and almost translucent.

'Do you want me to come with you?' Stella asked Max. 'I can manage.'

She wasn't sure if Max had heard her, he was already around the other side of the car, in the driver's seat, slamming his door. The engine turned over and the car jerked forward almost before Stella could shut Blue's door. The headlights were dazzling. The tyres slid across the snow, spoiling it, leaving behind ugly black tracks.

Stella turned back to look at the house. Hilltop was lit up, bright like a white beacon, rising up, an extension of the snow on the ground. Her palace: battered and bruised and open to the elements. Peter waited for her, just inside. She pulled the heavy steel door closed behind her. She should have been relieved but instead she found herself agitated and restless.

## Hampstead, June 2009

Stella wanted to erase Lawrence Simpson from her memory and to move forward. But the problem she faced was that the second she stepped out of Max's apartment – or tried to step out – she began to panic. The symptoms were classic, and as a psychologist, she reminded herself she was not dying. But she felt she was. Her chest constricted, her throat closed, her heart thrashed hard and fast in her chest. In a matter of seconds she was soaking with sweat, in her neck, under her arms, in the small of her back, behind her knees.

The door to the street was painted cream and a small frosted window let in some light. The floor was patterned with brown and cream diamonds. Stella would stand, petrified, one hand still on the door handle of Max's place, while she looked out across the hallway that led to the street. She would last all of twenty seconds, then the panic would begin. She would retreat, shut the door, double lock it and secure the chain. She would lean with her back against the wall until she regained control of her breathing and her heart settled down into a normal rhythm. Then she would go back to bed.

Weeks passed that way. Max would leave for work each

day at seven in the morning. She would wake before him and prepare a pot of coffee, the quality of which was a whole lot better than the stuff Anne supplied at the office. Stella would sit with him at the small round table in the kitchen for a few minutes before he left.

He would telephone her three times a day to ask how she was. She watched breakfast television. She slept more than she needed to. She researched recipes on the internet and emailed Max the list of ingredients she needed to cook dinner. He would shop at the Waitrose near the clinic and bring home the food she had asked for. She was a good cook. Over dinner, they barely spoke – they didn't know what to say to each other in the midst of their precipitous intimacy.

Max did not ask her to leave. And he never asked if she had changed her mind about reporting the crime.

Peter telephoned, but she would not take the calls. She watched his name flash across the screen. If she pressed the red button to disconnect the call too early, he would know she was avoiding him, so she left it to ring a while. Perhaps he would think that she was busy at work, that she had resumed her old life. The call would end and a message icon would flash up. She didn't listen to her voicemail. She wondered if Peter had looked for her at her flat, or gone to the clinic, asking for her. If he had, Max didn't say. After a week, he called less frequently and he no longer left messages. After two weeks, he stopped calling. Stella might have been a little disappointed, but it was difficult to be certain under the haze of benzodiazepines muffling her emotions as effectively as a duvet pulled over her head would block out light and sound.

She wondered if there was such a thing as a statute of

limitations on reporting a rape. She was no longer sore and the bruising and tearing had healed. She found she had a talent for repression; she no longer remembered the exact details of the ordeal.

Max told her that Simpson had withdrawn his bid for sole custody. She wanted to believe that in the afterglow, having indulged his sadism and his power play, he would bow out gracefully and leave his child and her mother in peace.

She wanted to delude herself, to believe there might have been some point to her ordeal. She was humbled. *Dr Davies*. What a fraud. Simpson had seen her for the joke she was.

While Max was at work, she combed the flat for clues to who he might be. He had a collection of art house movies and she had made her way through some of them while he was at work: he liked Woody Allen, Almodóvar. She was trying to understand him as much as to entertain herself. His bookshelves were a mix of literary and crime: from Milan Kundera to Robert Harris. She wanted to educate herself about his tastes by reading all of them, but the tranquillizers made her sleepy and interfered with her concentration. Passive television watching was all right, engaging with a challenging text was another story. The point was, though, he was her ideal man, just as she'd always thought: educated and intellectual. Maybe somewhat mysterious. She felt a certain thrill. For the first time, she had penetrated into his personal space.

Stella opened the door just a crack. The chain was still in place.

'How are you?' Peter asked.

'I'm fine.'

'Are you going to let me in?'

She knew it was irrational, the anxiety she felt as she lifted the chain from its slot. They stood in the small entrance hall and she didn't invite him inside.

'I'm sorry I didn't answer your calls. I thought you'd given up on me. I don't blame you.' She pulled her towelling robe tighter and knotted the belt. Since moving in with Max, she didn't bother getting dressed in the mornings, but she was always presentable by the time Max got home.

'You look good,' she said. Peter wore a loose-fitting black suit and a white shirt. The top button was still undone. His hair was cropped shorter than usual. A tie was crammed into his jacket pocket. 'Did you pass your exam?'

He nodded.

'I'm happy I didn't screw it up for you.'

'Of course you didn't.'

She felt a small lump in her throat. The way they stood, so stiff, the awkward way they spoke to each other, it was as though something was lost; as though they hadn't been friends for years. She could barely remember what they used to laugh about when they were together. Rude, stupid, inappropriate jokes.

'That was some second date,' she said.

He didn't laugh.

'Whenever you're ready, I'll come and get you,' he said.

'Ready for what?'

'To make a police report. To go home.'

'I'm not going to report what happened. And I'm staying here, for now.'

'You can't be serious,' he said.

'I'm dead serious. I'm not up for a fight. I'm tired and I'm sick of being poked and prodded and I don't want to be interrogated. And you of all people know there is a good chance the case won't even make it to court.'

'There's a specialist unit for rape victims. They'll help you. It might make you feel better in the long run – even if it doesn't get to court.'

'Please don't quote police propaganda.'

'I'm trying to help you.' He held out his hand, palm facing upwards. She placed her palm on top of his.

'Why is this so important to you?' she asked.

'Stop being so stupid,' he said. 'And stubborn.' He closed his hand around hers.

Peter could be terribly persuasive.

'I don't want to argue with you or to frighten you. But think, Stella: he's out there, free to do as he pleases. He could still fight for custody of his daughter, he could hurt someone else.'

'Are you trying to scare me?'

He reached for her other hand. 'I'm trying to protect you. I think he belongs behind bars.'

'It will never happen,' she said.

'You can't be sure. And this isn't a real life – hiding in this flat. Reality is going back to your flat and feeling safe. If you report what happened, it's a start.'

'I'm happy here.'

'I find that hard to believe. You've worked so hard to get where you are.'

'You're wrong about me.'

Stella was not unhappy in Max's Hampstead Village apartment. Peter expected her to behave like a grown-up, to take full responsibility even when she was the one who had been hurt. But she had chosen Max. And Max did not pressure her. And Stella was tired of fighting.

'I want to be taken care of. Max is happy to do that for the meantime.'

'You're letting him influence you.'

'So what?'

'It will hurt you in the long run. I've worked with victims. So have you.'

Her hands were beginning to feel clammy inside his. She pulled them away, disentangling herself. She dug them back into her pockets. She knew she was being rude and unkind, making him stand in the gloomy hallway.

'Max isn't forcing me to do anything. I make my own choices. None of this is his fault. If anything he's helping me with a bad situation that I was responsible for.'

'You blame yourself?'

'Partly. I made an appointment with a client after hours and I didn't let anyone know. I violated the safety codes of the practice.'

'Has it occurred to you that Max has a lot of influence over you and he's using it to cover his own sorry arse? That he could be sacrificing you for his clinic?'

'That's ridiculous. You're wrong. I know him.'

Peter meant well. He just didn't understand her.

'If anything,' she said, 'Max has shouldered the burden of all of this, having me here. He isn't the one to blame, Simpson is the psychopath.'

'You can't stay trapped in this weird limbo with your boss. You have to face what's happened, Ellie.' He was the only person who knew the nickname.

'Don't.' She didn't want to think about her mother.

'You know I can report this myself.'

'You wouldn't do that to me.' She had to make him understand.

He stood stubbornly in front of her. He was furious about what Simpson had done; his judgement was swayed by his feelings for her. He wanted revenge, maybe more than she did.

'Peter, you have to listen to me. There are things you don't know. About my history. I have good reason to believe that I haven't got a hope in hell of winning a court case.'

He waited. She pushed her unruly hair behind her ears and glanced down at her bare feet. She looked like an invalid.

'I spent time in a psychiatric hospital,' she said. She cleared her throat. 'In my teens. I was an in-patient for a whole year. I have a diagnosis, it's in my medical records – which they will of course request. It will all come out. My mother was schizophrenic and I was in and out of foster care from the time I was born. She was sectioned, several times, under the Mental Health Act. They would force her to go into hospital, force her to take her medication. She'd improve and she'd go into remission, for a few months, even a couple of years sometimes. And I'd be sent back home. But when she started feeling better, she'd think she didn't need her medicine and she'd stop taking it. I don't blame her, it has horrific side-effects. The whole cycle would start again. Each psychotic episode got worse. She was slowly losing her mind and she knew it. The drugs they gave her were almost as bad as the illness itself; in the end it was hard to tell what was worse, the illness or the cure. There is no cure for schizo-phrenia, not really, it's a downward slide. The drugs kill you off in a different way: they make you feel blunted, stop your thoughts, slow down your movements, give you all these terrible tics. It was like my mother disappeared over a period of years. So – when I was fourteen, she killed herself. I found her. I had a kind of breakdown and I was admitted to a secure adolescent unit. I was delusional. I made all kinds of claims that my teachers had raped me and I thought the doctors in the unit were trying to poison me. They thought I was prodromal – that I was having a psychotic episode and coming down with schizophrenia myself. Anyway, it seems I wasn't, because I recovered. But I still have that diagnosis on record: delusional disorder, psychosis.'

Peter had a good way of being quiet. She could see he was taking it all in, thinking about what to say. She supposed it wasn't every day he found out he'd slept with a crazy woman. He reached for her again, and stroked the back of her hand with his thumb.

'That was a long time ago,' he said. 'You were a child. It was only the one episode.'

'It doesn't matter. I'm screwed. I've made these claims before and they were false. I nearly destroyed someone's life – my poor English teacher who tried to help me. So you see: I have no credibility. His lawyers will dredge it all up and use it against me. I know it and he knows it.'

'You've been well for years. You've done brilliantly in your job.'

'I've been rethinking everything. Maybe my choice of career was a huge mistake. I've just stayed, stuck in the hell of my childhood, working with abusers and abused children. Maybe that's what's destroying me.'

He looked sceptical. 'You love your work,' he said.

She was grateful for the pressure of his thumb against the back of her hand.

'The point is, it will be my word against his, because that's all there is. They'll ask for my medical records. They'll want a psychological evaluation. I'm not going through with all of that. It's not worth it. And at the end of all of it, best case scenario he'll get a year or two in jail. I've worked with these cases, I know.'

She held his face, she forced him to look at her. 'Promise me you won't report this. Promise you won't tell *anyone* without my permission. Promise me. I want to hear you say it. Right now.'

It took him a few moments, but he said it: 'I promise.'

He didn't look happy about it, but she believed him.

Her hands dropped from his face. She felt self-conscious, in her robe, barefoot, her hair gone wild. 'I think you'd better go now,' she said. 'I'm feeling tired.'

He gave her a big bear hug. She wanted him to scoop her up and take her with him. She could go back outside and face the world, like a grown-up. But it was a brief spark and it passed quickly. She let him leave and she put the chain back on the door behind him. She returned to the empty flat, feeling a familiar loneliness descending.

Max had given her three bottles of pills. One contained industrial-strength painkillers she no longer needed. The second was filled with tranquillizers and the third with sleeping tablets. According to Max, it was safe to take the sedatives three times a day. Stella allowed herself one sleeping tablet before bed. She needed the pill to wipe out her thoughts and anaesthetize her troubled consciousness. She would close her eyes, put her head on the pillow and sleep without dreaming.

The supply of tranquillizers and sleeping tablets lasted precisely one month. Stella had assumed that when the pills ran out, her time would be up and Max would expect her to return home. He might also expect her to return to work. Stella had no idea how she was going to manage any of it, since she still had not been able to take a single step further than the front door of his Hampstead flat. She decided not to think about her future prospects. She hoped each day that the panic attack would not come, testing it out at exactly eight in the morning, after Max had left for work. Each day, she experienced the same set of symptoms. On the twentieth day, she gave up hoping.

The night of Peter's visit, she experimented with taking half a sleeping pill instead of a whole one. Falling asleep wasn't so difficult. It wasn't the usual plummet into blissful oblivion, but the dose was enough to relax her, and after lying with her eyes closed and forcing herself to stop ruminating – about how she would ever live alone again, about naked photographs of herself surfacing on the internet, about her job – she drifted down to sleep.

At two in the morning, she sensed something. A presence, moving, at her bedside. She crept out of bed and cowered at the side of the chest of drawers, closing her eyes, like a child, hoping she was invisible. When she opened her eyes, the darkness in the room was absolute. Blackout blinds blocked out any brightness from the streetlights and she could see nothing. She held her breath and stayed completely still. He was in the room, moving towards her. She felt him brush past her, his flesh, cold and scaly like a reptile, grazing her shoulder. She was terrified.

As her pupils adjusted, benign shapes of furniture emerged from the darkness. She knew the intruder had been a nightmare, but the racing heartbeat and the terror remained as she crouched with her head in her hands, waiting for something terrible to happen. She managed to stand, went into the bathroom and splashed water on her face. She felt better, but she couldn't bear to be alone. Softly, she opened the door to Max's room. She felt her way over to his double bed and eased her way in under the duvet. He lay with his back to her and she spooned up behind him. He adjusted himself slightly and then his hand took hold of hers and pulled it up to his chest.

## Hilltop, 3.30 a.m.

Stella doubted she would find a window-repair service willing to come out to Hilltop any time soon. As she rummaged through the cupboards to find masking tape and black bags in order to attempt some makeshift repairs, she came across her boxes of pills, as she had known she would.

She could not last one minute more. She lifted the box of benzodiazepines. One would take the edge off her restlessness, would pull her back from the cliff-edge, would keep her paranoia at bay.

She swallowed. She didn't care that Peter was watching.

In the living room, he wrapped a cushion cover around his hand and smashed out the remaining pieces of glass from around the sides of the window frame. Stella cut open a few black bags and together they stretched them across the open space and taped them to the sides. It was pretty much a hopeless endeavour: the wind battered the thin plastic membrane and it was obvious that the temporary fix would not last long.

Peter was still covered in Blue's blood. It was all over his sleeves, and down the front of his shirt. 'You look terrible,' she said. She managed a weak smile.

'Thanks. I've been in touch with the Met,' he said. 'Simpson's ex-wife has given them some more details about what's been going on.'

He did not seem as furious with her, or as disappointed, as she had feared. Maybe, despite his antipathy for her husband, Peter was relieved that Max had taken responsibility for the troubled girl.

Stella reached up and held the corner of the plastic bag steady as Peter put on yet another layer of masking tape. The minute she lifted her hand, the wind began its assault on their work.

'After Simpson . . . attacked you,' Peter said, 'it seems the relationship with the new girlfriend didn't take too long to break down. Apparently he is back to his old ways – he's been stalking his ex-wife, with emails and phone calls, sometimes following her when she leaves the house. She claims he tormented them, drove her back to drink after she'd got her life back on track. She didn't bother to report him. She doesn't have too much faith in the police.'

'That's what Blue was trying to tell me last night. Except that she didn't tell me the name of the man she was describing, or that he was her father.'

Even with the help of tranquillizers, she didn't know how much more of this conversation she could take. 'Why are you going on about this? Don't you think I feel guilty enough already? Yes. You were right. I should have reported him.'

The roll of masking tape was empty and Peter dropped it to the floor.

'I didn't mean it like that,' he said. 'The point I'm trying to make is that Max has been treating Blue, as well as her mother. He probably knew. And yet he didn't mention to you that Simpson is still at large. Don't you find it strange that Max has had contact with the family the whole time, without telling you?'

Yes, she did find it strange. More than strange. Max had broken boundaries by treating both mother and daughter – while married to another of Simpson's victims. Stella couldn't get her head around all of the implications, there were so many potential pitfalls. And yes, Peter was right: Max's decisions were questionable. But then she hardly had a right to sit in judgement, when she had been so utterly passive. She herself had done nothing at all to try and resolve anything. At least Max had tried to do something to help mother and daughter.

The plastic bin liner flapped, frantic, as the wind tried to break the fragile barrier between the inside and the outside world. It wouldn't hold much longer.

'I'm not saying this to scare you,' Peter said. 'Because I really don't think that Lawrence Simpson sent his daughter out here. It doesn't make any sense. But I think something else is going on. Do you want to hear my theory?'

'No,' she said.

'I think Max agreed to treat Blue and her mother so that he could find out how much they knew about Simpson's attack on you. I think Max was scared that Simpson might – for whatever reason – tell his wife what he'd done. Simpson might have wanted to scare Blue's mother into giving in to his demands for custody. And if Simpson could show that he could control you, then what chance would his wife have? And he's a sadist – so he might not have been able to resist boasting about his victory. He might have been tempted to show those photographs to someone.'

He glanced at her, looking stricken. He regretted his

comment about the photographs. 'I'm sorry,' he said. 'It's lack of sleep. I'm even less tactful than usual.'

'It's OK,' she said. 'I'm not that fragile. And I already worked out that Max might have had his own reasons for wanting to treat Blue and her mother. And I've already asked him about it.'

She enjoyed the look of surprise on his face.

'And?'

'He denied any ulterior motive.'

'What a surprise. And don't you find it amazing that his practice has stayed squeaky clean through all of this?'

The corner of the plastic bag came loose. Neither of them bothered to try and fix it back into place. Stella wondered why she was so angry at Peter.

'I think you're wrong. I believe Max meant well, I believe he genuinely wanted to help Blue and her mother. He does like to be in control, but that's not a crime. So do I. So do you, for that matter. He's been under huge stress – he's carried the pressure of both my mental state and the survival of his practice – and so he took on too much. Yes, he can be over-confident and, yes, he thinks he has to take responsibility for people he cares about – I think he thought he could help Blue and her mother at the same time as keeping an eye on them. But somehow it backfired, and the girl has become fixated on him.'

'So that's your excuse for him this time?'

'It's not an excuse.'

'He's your blind spot.'

'He's a man who has a strong need to be in control. Sometimes that's his weakness.'

'He's a control freak who likes to play God.'

'He's my husband.'

'Ellie, please. Can't you think about this logically, objectively – from a professional perspective? Max must have been concerned that Blue's mother would find out from Simpson himself that you and Max had, by omission, concealed information in your report. If she had got desperate enough, she could have gone to the police. I think Max knew exactly what he was doing. I think he was desperate to stop what happened to you from getting out, and from destroying his practice and his reputation.'

'I know you're only trying to help. I know you care about me.' Stella heard herself and she sounded condescending, like Max at his worst. She didn't mean to. 'It's a huge relief, to accept that Lawrence Simpson wasn't behind all of this, but as for the rest, there's too much conjecture.'

'Funny that you and I reached exactly the same conclusion. Even if it is just a theory. Don't you think?'

Stella moved away from him. She collected the cushions from the sofa and tried to stack them on the windowsill in front of the broken window, but they all fell straight back down to the floor. She gave up.

'There's no proof,' she said. 'We could be completely wrong.'

'I can't think of any innocent explanation why Max would choose to get involved with that family.'

'Isn't it fair to say you've never liked Max, and this has nothing to do with Blue or her father? It's about me.'

Having given up on window repairs, they were standing in front of the fireplace, staring at the wizened logs in the hearth as if hoping a fire might magically ignite.

'Max took advantage of your feelings for him,' he said. 'To keep you quiet.'

'That's not true. I became dependent on him because I didn't want to deal with my own trauma.'

'He convinced you to do something terrible.' His voice rose as he became angrier. 'He encouraged you to conceal a crime. And it had consequences – not only for you, but for Blue and her mother. Max thinks of his own interests – and only his own interests. He puts himself first, always.'

She placed both hands on his shoulders. 'Calm down. Let me be clear. For the last time – Max didn't make me do anything.' Her hands dropped. 'I'm sorry. I was always in love with Max.'

'The problem is, Max doesn't act like a man in love with you.'

The compassion in his eyes made her pain worse. 'Sometimes he needs a break – from me and my agoraphobia and my post-traumatic stress and my tranquillizers.'

'How long are you planning to stay a victim?'

'You're a policeman, Peter, a rescuer. I thought you liked victims. I thought you liked coming out to rescue me now and again.'

'I thought you were tough. I thought you were a survivor.'

'You can't understand what it's like to be raped.'

Despite all the pills, she was agitated; her voice was too loud. She was angry. She wanted to be left alone. She didn't want to be alone. She was lonely.

'I tried to get you to report what happened. I thought that was the first step in getting your life back.'

'That's what you thought. But it wasn't what I wanted.'

'And being locked up in this concrete monstrosity is what you want?'

'*It's a modernist fucking icon!*'

He tried to put his hand on her arm, but she shrugged him off. He knew how to put together a convincing argument. It was part of his job. His words were getting inside her, confusing her.

'Are you so sure there's no truth to what Blue said?'

Stella didn't want to listen any more. She wanted to get away. She wasn't entirely sure where she wanted to go; then she realized she wanted her bed.

'It's so cold in here. I'm going upstairs. I need to lie down,' she said.

'Look,' Peter said, 'your life is your own business but at the very least you must see that Max should not be allowed to go on treating that girl without a second opinion?'

She crossed the frosty entrance hall and grabbed hold of the steel tubular railing. It stung her fingers, as though she'd grabbed a piece of ice. She didn't look back. The higher she climbed, the more the numbness took over.

'I'll stay until the glass-repair people get here,' Peter called out. 'I'm sure they can board up the window. The house will be secure.'

Still, she did not turn around. She did not want to see him. She kept climbing, putting one foot in front of the other.

Bloody hell. Her bedroom. She had forgotten the wreckage Blue had left behind. Stella weaved her way through the chaos and the debris on the floor. She picked up her duvet, shook it out and laid it across the bed. One pillow was still in place, but the other was missing. She soon spotted it, stuffed into the fire grate.

The girl was a demon.

One pillow would have to do. She just wanted her bed. She shook it, fluffed it up and removed two long blonde hairs. She didn't need any reminders. She lay down on her back and closed her eyes.

Something hard was digging into her backside. She reached under the covers and felt around, but there was nothing there. There was something tucked into the back pocket of her jeans. Blue's phone.

## Hampstead, July 2009

Five weeks after Stella had been living in his Hampstead flat, Max came home late for the first time. Her chicken in lime coconut curry sat cold and untouched on the Aga. She wanted to hurl it into the dustbin, but then she couldn't bear to throw away something she'd worked so damn hard on. So, it sat, congealing. Stella simmered. She flicked aimlessly through the television channels. He was with a woman. It was only so long, she supposed, that he could embrace a celibate lifestyle with an unwanted, much younger colleague camped out in his flat.

He couldn't be seeing anyone. Stella had expected, at the very least, that he might have an emergency or two – a suicide, or an overdose – that would mean he had to stay out late. But he must have passed any emergencies on to a colleague, because he was always home on time. He had completed the Simpson report himself and he had arranged with Anne to cancel all of her other commitments. He always came back to her at the same time each night: eight o'clock. He would let himself in and then he would come and look for her. She would be in the kitchen, standing over the cooker. He would approach her and give her a friendly peck on the cheek. Sometimes he would squeeze her shoulder as she stood with her back to him. The cooker was the nicest one she'd ever used. Judging by how pristine it was, he had never used it himself.

She spent her nights in Max's bed. She would get there first, swallow her pill and then drift away, alone. He would join her much later. It was hopeless. She should get the hell out of his home and get on with her life. She couldn't leave. She didn't want to any more. She had a taste of what it was like to have him coming home to her each night. And it was good. She felt a surge of happiness each time she heard his key in the front door; for her, it was the sound of possibility. When he was with her, she felt almost calm, almost happy. The walls of his home were her safety during the day, his presence was her security in the evenings.

Max did nothing to indicate that he desired her. He had a sense of duty towards her. He saw her as a victim. She was his responsibility, nothing more. She suspected that having her near by and taking care of her was his way of dealing with his guilt. Were she more pessimistic, she would have wondered if it was also a way to avoid liability: legal, financial or professional. But she was not entirely cynical.

By nine thirty Stella was on edge. She went into each room, making sure the windows were locked and the curtains shut tight.

He walked in at ten minutes past ten. Stella looked up sullenly from where she sat on his sofa, her arms crossed and legs folded underneath her. He was not bound to her in any way, he could stay out the whole goddamn night if he wanted to and, furthermore, he had every right to bring other women home with him. He was probably frustrated as hell and couldn't wait to get rid of her. He must see her as damaged goods.

'Sorry I'm late,' he said. His tie hung loose around his neck. His suit jacket was uncharacteristically rumpled. He took it off and tossed it over the armchair. Stella wanted to pick it up, to smell it, to check if it carried a scent of perfume.

'Have you been with someone?' she asked. She squeezed herself tighter.

'It's very strange,' he said. 'This situation we're in.'

'A woman?'

He ran his hand over his head. She could never be sure if he was pleased or dismayed to come home to her. She knew so little about him.

He sighed.

'Is there any dinner?' he asked. He was polite as ever.

'There is,' she said. 'But it's cold.'

For the first time she felt she might give up, walk out, there and then, find her way back to her old life.

The table looked beautiful. She had found a pair of heavy silver candlesticks at the back of a kitchen cupboard and these were now in the centre of the table, candles flickering. She had placed sprigs of lavender, cut from the pot next to the front door, in a vase.

'Anne's getting married,' Max said as he sat down. 'That's why I was late. We went to have a celebratory drink – at the Lamb and Eagle.'

'Anne – from the clinic?'

'Yep.'

'Who is the lucky man?' Stella asked. As she served him a plate of cold chicken in lime coconut curry she had the urge to laugh. Everything seemed absurd: the cold food, the candles, the lavender.

'Delicious,' he said, although he hadn't put a single thing in his mouth yet. 'Did you ever meet Chris Marshall? His wife was a patient at the clinic. I treated her for depression when she was in the last stages of breast cancer. That's when he and Anne met.'

'How romantic. Dying wife and all.'

'Anne's had a hard time too, you know.'

'No, I didn't know.'

He had lapsed into silence. Max looked tired more often than not, lately. He seemed older and less optimistic than the picture of him she carried in her mind. He smiled less often. His enthusiasm for life, his passion, appeared to have faded. If she had been infatuated before, now she loved the real him.

'How has Anne had a hard time?' she asked.

'Four years ago her husband died of pancreatic cancer. From the time he was diagnosed, he only had another six months. She was devastated. It was around the time we opened the clinic and I think work was the thing that really saved her sanity, kept her going.'

'I had no idea. She didn't talk to me much. I don't think she ever liked me.'

She was pleased to see that he was eating the chicken.

'Have you lived in this flat a long time?' she asked.

'Twelve years. I grew up around here – my mother's still in a retirement home on Finchley Road.'

She had never dared ask personal questions before.

Max was opening the bottle of Chardonnay she had placed between the candlesticks. She wondered if he drank to deal with her constant presence. While he grappled with the cork, she said: 'I'll need another prescription.' She said it calmly and then held her breath.

'Of course,' he said. 'I'll get it filled for you in the morning.'
He filled his glass, and then hers.

Stella knew the basics of behavioural theory. She knew she was teetering on the edge of agoraphobia and should not be allowed to fall over the precipice or it would be extremely difficult to claw her way back up to a normal life. Part of the problem, Stella suspected, was that she did not want her normal life back. She was sick of a normal life. She was happy, cocooned in Max's flat. Nothing bad would happen to her inside. She knew she was going crazy.

There was another question she wanted to ask him; something she had thought about, over and over again.

'Max, why do you think he chose me? There were so many others involved in the case – the social worker, the parent support worker, his solicitor. Why me?'

'You're a young, attractive female, for one thing. He felt persecuted by the entire legal system and he fixated on you as a target for his rage. That's it.'

'I must have done something to make him choose me.'

'That's what he wants you to think. You were the easiest target and the most satisfying for a sexual sadist. He's the criminal. He's responsible. Not you.'

She wanted to get up and go to him; she wanted to sit on his lap and have him hold her, like a child.

'I don't want this to come out,' she said. 'I don't want any of my colleagues to know and I don't want the clinic compromised. And if I'm honest – I don't want to take any chances with my registration being threatened in any way – if Simpson makes some sort of counter-allegation.'

'Nobody has to know unless you want them to. As far as the staff at the clinic are concerned, you're on indefinite compassionate leave. I've found an associate, he's junior – straight out of uni – but he's prepared to work at the lower rates they're proposing.'

'I'm so grateful. I've caused you so much trouble. It's just that if I'm not at work, I don't expect you to pay my salary, and then I have no idea how I'm going to pay my rent—'

'Shhh,' he said. He lifted her glass of wine and handed it to her. 'I want you to stay here as long as you need to. If you're happy living with me.'

She took a long, cool sip. She was in Max's apartment, sitting next to him, alone with him. A part of her was pleased, even under the worst possible circumstances. Insanely pleased that she finally had him to herself. Perverse. But true.

'I'm in love with you,' she said.

She felt good. She had laid herself bare and she had told the truth. Her position was clear. He was free to ask her to leave at any time.

'Right,' he said. He did not look surprised. 'I'm flattered. But I'm not about to take advantage of you. Not now.'

'Pity.' She refilled his glass.

The equilibrium in the Hampstead flat shifted. Stella felt herself to be at home. Max relied on her to be there; for what, she wasn't entirely sure. His mother died, two months after she moved in. His father had died when he was eight. Like her, he had no siblings, and he was alone. She resolved to try to cut down on the tranquillizers during the day; to try to find her way back to where she was before. At the same time, she was happy with where she was. Max said nothing about her leaving. She fantasized about what it might be like to live in the apartment as his lover.

\*

Anne's wedding took place at an eighteenth-century house in Hampstead. Burgh House, on New End Square, was mercifully close to Max's apartment and it took them all of five minutes to walk there.

In the days leading up to the ceremony, Stella became increasingly paranoid. She was plagued by absurd thoughts. She wondered why Anne had chosen a venue so close to where Max lived. Had she spent time in Max's apartment at some point? Had Anne and Max once lived together? Was that how she had stumbled across Burgh House, tucked away down New End? She was drowning in mistrust. She told herself, over and over again, she was experiencing an anxiety reaction, because she would have to go out for the first time in months. It would pass.

'I know I'm hopeless, but please can you stay with me the whole time we're at the wedding?' she asked Max.

'Of course. It will be my pleasure.' He grinned and she had a precious, fleeting glimpse of the old Max.

She had visions. Everyone would have seen the photographs where she lay spread-eagled, degraded. Perhaps Max had seen them already, and hadn't told her, to spare her the pain. She saw Simpson, waiting for her: leaning against the wall outside the block of flats; sitting at the pub opposite; standing at the gates of Burgh House; sitting amongst the guests. Everywhere.

As long as she had Max at her side, she was safe. That's what she told herself.

'Do you think it's all right if I double my dose of diazepam? Just for today?'

'Absolutely,' Max said. 'Although you probably won't remember too much about the wedding.'

Remembering the wedding was the least of her concerns.

In the wood-panelled music room, as she walked down the aisle, Anne looked beautiful in vintage lace over a satin slip. A string quartet played. Stella floated with the music, on wave after gentle wave.

One of the bridesmaids was an attractive teenage girl, with red hair down to her waist and a little upturned nose. She wore a tight satin mini-dress. Even with the double dose of diazepam, Stella imagined Max was staring at the girl.

There was no way she could manage the reception or the mingling. Max was understanding and he didn't seem sorry to leave. Perhaps weddings were not his thing either. He had his arm around her, supporting her, and she leaned her head on his shoulder as they walked the short distance home. She didn't look around her, at the people walking past. She pretended they didn't exist.

'I've been thinking about what I'm going to do,' she said. 'I'm not going to sponge off you for ever. Since I've been living with you I haven't spoken to a single one of my friends because I know what they'll all say and I don't want to hear it. But I've spoken to Peter a few times. He texted yesterday, to tell me that Hannah's flatmate has moved out and she's looking for someone to share with. She's my oldest friend and I trust her. Peter thinks I should move in with her; he wants me to tell her what happened. She could give me some support, while I sort out some kind of treatment plan.'

They walked, close together, arm in arm, at a sluggish pace. Max pulled his tie from side to side, loosening it and letting it hang down around his collar.

'I think it's not a bad idea,' Stella said. 'It would be the first step in – you know. Hannah's a psychologist, she'll understand if I'm acting weird for a while. I'd have to deal with both her and Peter nagging me to report what happened. But I'm sure I can fend them off.' She managed a smile.

Max had gone quiet. He had stopped walking and was staring down at the pavement.

'So? What do you think?' she asked him.

'Do you find me strange,' he said, 'single and childless at forty-three?'

'No,' she lied.

Yes, she had wondered about him: single and childless and no long-term relationships, as far as she knew.

'What about you?' Max asked. 'Do you ever think about getting married?'

'Sure,' she said. 'If I ever manage to leave your flat. And it would depend who asked.'

She was leaning against him, his arm was casually around her waist and she was in a pleasant sort of haze, disinhibited; she didn't care what she might say to him, what she might reveal. 'Why are we having this conversation?' she asked.

'I like having you live with me.'

'Really?'

'I don't want to take advantage of you. I wanted to wait. But I don't want you to move out without knowing.'

'Knowing what?'

'That I think about getting married,' he said.

'You want to get married – in general? Or you think about marrying me?'

The pills made her bold.

'I don't want you to leave,' he said.

'You don't have to marry me to get me to stay.'

'I know.'

'But if you asked me to marry you then I would say yes,' she said.

He kissed her on the top of her head.

In hindsight, the proposal seemed more bizarre than romantic.

## Hilltop, 4.10 a.m.

Peter was on the sofa, on his back, his eyes were closed. The living room was freezing and the black bag flapped uselessly at the broken window.

Stella was panting, she had run all the way back down the stairs. 'Are you awake?' she said, looking down on him.

He sat up, blinking. His hair was in disarray, some of it standing on end. His cheeks and his jaw were shadowed with stubble.

'What now?' he said.

'We have to go after them.'

'Why?'

She attempted to smooth down his hair as best she could with her fingers. She needed him to look alert and authoritative.

'I didn't tell you this,' she said, 'but when I was alone with Blue, just before she smashed the window, she told me – well, basically the same thing she said to Max – but in a lot more graphic detail. She said they had sex. During their therapy sessions. And I was furious and told her she was lying and that she'd be locked up. I said all kinds of terrible, stupid things. And that's why she ran off.'

'And?'

'I thought about what you said. And so I had a look at her mobile. I found something. And now I need to get to the hospital. Can you just – not ask any questions? Just take me to the hospital, I have to get there before he admits her.'

Stella didn't wait for his answer. She rushed towards the front door, pulled on her coat and threw his towards him. He caught it. She was pleased; he was wide awake and his reflexes were in good working order.

'You're leaving the house?' he said.

'I've taken a couple more tranquillizers.'

'Is that safe? You've been swallowing those things like Smarties.'

She shrugged. 'Let's go before I change my mind. Or pass out.'

She remained rooted to the spot, to the cold, marble floor.

Peter walked past her. He opened the front door, turned back and held out his hand.

Stella looked around, one last time. She walked a few steps forward, flicked the switch, turned off the chandelier. She thought how much easier it would be to stay inside the house and inside her marriage. Nothing had to change.

But she couldn't drift through the rest of her life with her eyes shut and her curiosity strangled by chemicals.

Her legs were stiff. She couldn't move – towards Peter, towards the open door. The temperature was dropping even further.

'I'm sorry,' she said. 'You go. You'll have to help her.'

Peter looked pissed off. He wasn't exactly a champion of passivity. She didn't use to be, either.

'I give up,' he said.

She didn't blame him. She had given up long before.

The emergency glass-repair man would come and the window would be repaired and the house would be secure again. In the meantime, she would be safe and sound, locked inside her bedroom.

'Right, that's it,' Peter said. 'I've had enough. You need help as much as she does.'

He moved towards the door. She closed her eyes. She didn't want to see him leave.

She felt him come back and take hold of her hand. She resisted, tried to push him away. She lashed out, tried to get him to let go; but he was holding on, determined. She felt she would explode. With her free hand, she slapped his face. Hard.

Then she drew away – he looked as if he was about to hit her back. But he rubbed his jaw, moved it from side to side a few times.

She was breathing, deeply. Her chest was clear and open. She could still feel the strength in her arms. She wanted to hit him again, just to feel the power surge.

'I can't leave.'

'Yes, you can. All you have to do is put one foot in front of the other. Don't think about it. Just walk.'

The door of the jeep was stiff, she had to heave it with all her strength to slam it shut. The car smelt faintly of cigarettes and the floor was littered with empty take-away cups.

Peter eased the car over the icy driveway and nudged out on to the top of the hill. The road and the pavements were gone, submerged under a sea of white. Stella gripped the door handle.

'Sorry I hit you,' she said. 'That was meant for Max. I'd like to kill him.'

'No problem,' he said. 'Try not to do anything crazy while I'm driving.'

They inched down the hill, the tyres struggling to grip the frozen road. The car slid forward, jolted, stopped. If the wheels lost their grip, they would go spinning out on to the open road below.

'Typical,' Peter said. 'Your road is the steepest one in this whole goddamn area.'

When they reached the corner of Victoria Avenue, Stella found she could breathe more easily.

'Which route would he take?' Peter asked.

'Turn left.'

They turned into Chenies Road, where traffic had melted the snow and the road was an open strip of black.

'Right at the roundabout,' Stella said. 'Can you go faster?'

'Do you have some sort of plan for when we reach the hospital?' he asked, glancing across at her.

'Don't look at me. Watch the road. Just pull up outside A and E,' she said.

They turned right at the massive Tesco superstore, and then left on to the road that would take them to the motorway. There were no other cars around, and the speedometer climbed to sixty miles an hour. The jeep hugged the curves, Peter's hands strong and steady on the wheel. The streetlights turned the snow in the fields bright yellow. The headlights illuminated road-kill: a guinea fowl and then the remains of a rabbit. Max, probably, she thought, leaving small animals dead in his wake.

Snow was falling, gently, drifting across her line of vision. They flashed past whitened trees; the sky and ground seemed to blend into each other. Stella imagined a small figure slumped against the door of the passenger seat, fair hair pressed against the window.

Hilltop was further and further behind her, but she was not disintegrating. Yet. Although her limbs were beginning to feel strangely heavy. She might have overdone it with the pills. She had to keep hold of her rage. She had to focus on her husband's betrayal, to propel herself forwards. She could see it, frame by frame.

# Max and Blue

They were flying. The car smelt expensive. It smelt sexy. It smelt of him, of leather and sharp aftershave.

Blue felt much better. She could hardly remember why she'd panicked yesterday, why she'd rushed out to find his house, why she'd been so desperate. She could see that she needed to be more patient. He was married, after all, and he was still her doctor. He had to be careful. She understood now why it had been so important to him to keep it a secret. She was sorry she had told anyone. She chewed on the skin around her thumbnail. The wife didn't believe her anyway.

She looked at his profile. He was frowning, concentrating on driving. He must see now that he also needed to be more careful. He knew now what she might do if he refused to see her. She wasn't about to lie down and let him walk all over her.

The car slowed down. He pulled off the main road and drove up a small side bit until they were hidden behind a row of frozen trees. It felt weird, very quiet. There were no other cars.

He turned off the engine but his hands still gripped the

steering wheel. He was just staring, out of the front window.

Blue began to feel nervous.

'Why are we stopping?' she asked him.

She was getting a bad feeling. 'What are you doing?' she said. 'Answer me.'

But he wouldn't talk to her. He was angry: about what she had said to his wife. He was going to punish her.

She undid her seatbelt and tried the handle, it wasn't locked. She got out of the car and slammed the door. She thought about running.

The headlights died and she was left in the cold and the dark.

She had stepped into a deep pile of snow, her trainers were completely covered. The blanket Stella had tucked around her was inside the car and now she was freezing. She wrapped her arms tight around her chest. There was no point trying to get away from him. She would get back into the car and say she was sorry.

As she reached for the handle, she heard the locks clicking. She grabbed at the door, pulled and pulled at it.

She banged on the window with her fists. 'Open it! Please! I'm so cold. Please!'

The engine came to life and the car began to move.

He was going to leave her.

'Don't! Please!' She ran after the car, screaming and begging although he would not hear her. She had pushed him too far, he would hurt her now, make her pay for what she'd done. She slipped on the ice, her knee smashed down underneath her. She squatted down, and rocked, back and forth as she watched him abandon her. The tears were wet and warm against her cheeks.

But the car stopped.

She jerked to her feet and ran, pulling at the door handle and finding it still locked. Her knee throbbed with pain.

She stood with her hands pressed against the window, in the cold. Trembling. Freezing. They had taken her jacket, her bag, her phone. She had nothing

He watched. The glass was burning her fingers but she did not move. He waited a long time, watched her cry. Then he leaned over and pushed the door open and she climbed back in. Her hands had turned a furious red, her ears were on fire. She was shaking with cold, even with the blanket now back around her shoulders. Soon she would have a big fat bruise on her knee.

'Have I ever done anything except help you?' he said. 'Didn't I give you what you wanted?' His eyes were red-rimmed. He frightened her.

She nodded. Everything outside was so strange. The sky was silver, even the trees were glowing. She understood now. He could do anything he wanted with her.

'Why did you go to my house tonight, Blue?'

'I don't know,' she said.

'Yes, you do.'

'I phoned your office and they wouldn't let me talk to you. I was angry. And lonely. I wanted to be with you; I wanted to see where you live. I wanted to see your wife. I thought – if I told her what happened – maybe she'd leave you. Maybe – I don't know. I wanted to punish you. I wanted you to know what it feels like.'

'And? Are you happy now?'

'No. Your wife doesn't believe me. She really loves you. And she trusts you.' She shifted around in her seat. The windows had misted up and she couldn't see out any more. 'Do you love her?'

'Of course I do.'

She didn't believe him.

'Do you love me?' She breathed in deep, she wanted to keep the smell of him inside her for ever. 'I don't want to be alive if I can't see you any more. Please. I'll do anything.'

He put his head back and laughed. 'You are a piece of work, Blue.'

He uncurled his white knuckles from around the steering wheel and stroked her icy cheek. He ran his fingers across her mouth. She parted her lips and kissed the tip of his thumb, then caught it between her teeth. She was still shivering.

'I'll never not love you,' she said. 'I won't give up. I won't stop. Please don't be angry. I could have made them believe me, if I wanted to. But I didn't. I'll tell them I was lying – what I said about us. At the hospital.'

'That would certainly make life simpler.'

'I'll tell them you just tried to help me. That nothing ever happened. I'll do anything you tell me.'

'Baby girl,' he said. 'Are you still sleepy?'

She was tired and the cold was inside her bones, but she was starting to feel happy.

'I don't want to go to hospital. My hands aren't that bad.'

'You have to.'

'Let me stay with you.'

'You ran away from home and you talked to my wife. The police are involved now. I have no choice. I have to take you to hospital.'

She bit down on his thumb. He leaned his head back.

'I'm not letting you go,' she said. 'I'm yours now. You can give me as many jabs as you like. They wear off.'

She sucked on his thumb.

'Let's be clear about what happens when we get to the hospital,' he said. 'If you tell any more stories, you know what happens. Even if someone does believe you – they will put you in foster care.'

She nodded.

'Can I trust you?'

'Yes. I promise.'

'All you need to do is agree with everything I say. Tell them how sorry you are that you made up those lies.'

She nodded. Sucked his thumb deeper into her mouth.

'We can play this down,' he said. 'It'll all blow over quickly – I'll tell them that I understand you came out tonight to find me because you were looking for help. You made a mistake, of course – coming out to my house – but in a way, it was a healthy choice: coming to find your doctor, instead of cutting yourself. I see it as progress. Such a good girl.'

'And then?' she asked him.

'And then no more running away. No more dramatics. I'll try my best to convince them to discharge you back to your mother's care.'

'When will I see you again?'

'We have to be careful. If you talk about what happened between us again then I'll have no power to help you. Do you understand?'

She nodded. 'I promise.'

He put his hand on top of hers. He squeezed. He un-ravelled the bandages and covered her bleeding palm with kisses. He knew he was hurting her. And even when he hurt her, it excited her. She felt perfectly happy. She could make him want her. She could have him back. They were the same, she and him. They belonged together.

She felt sorry for his wife, she really did.

## September 2009

Hilltop stood at the top of a hill, on a road called Victoria Avenue. The house was proud and awkward, two storeys high, a startling white and unapologetic in its modernist glory. The black-framed windows seemed to look down condescendingly upon the neighbours: rows of mouse-brown sixties brick terraced townhouses.

Stella felt an immediate connection with the strange house that seemed so utterly out of place.

Max drove past the low, curved front wall and along the crescent-shaped driveway. She was pleased to hear gravel crunching under the tyres of the Mercedes; if she lived here, she would always be able to hear footsteps or wheels approaching.

Sandra, the estate agent, was parked at the top of the drive, ready and waiting. By the looks of her sporty gunmetal convertible, the property market in the area had not been too badly affected by the recession. Sandra was a petite woman in her fifties, wearing a tailored suit and bold red lipstick. Stella shook hands politely, feeling like a teenage impostor pretending she could afford a mansion. Max evidently could, as a result of a sizeable inheritance from his mother's estate.

Just inside the steel front door, Sandra knelt down and

removed her stilettos. Stella followed suit and took off her pumps. She was hovering, suspended above herself once more: several pills and a lot of coaxing on Max's part had been needed to get her out of the Hampstead apartment. Now, with her husband at her side, at the threshold of a new life, she felt almost contented.

'So you're newlyweds!' Sandra said.

Stella smiled. Max did not remove his shoes.

'Congratulations,' said Sandra.

The wedding had been a brief, no-frills affair at the Marylebone register office. Stella remembered swallowing a cocktail of pills and having nothing suitable to wear. In the end, she chose a plain linen shift. In her darker, more insecure moments, it wasn't entirely clear to her why Max had accepted her impulsive proposal. But he had. And now he walked, several steps in front of her, into the entrance hall. He did not look back to see if she followed. Stella wondered if Sandra had noticed the absence of honeymoon-like enthusiasm or affection.

Her new husband peered upward at the spectacular chandelier that cascaded down the curved concrete steps. She wanted to feel his hand warm on the small of her back as they explored the house. She walked closer to him, until they stood side by side. 'Are we really going to buy this house?' she asked.

He could not tear his eyes away from the chandelier.

Sandra offered Stella a glossy brochure. Hilltop was pictured on a day saturated in sunshine.

Stella wondered about Max's decision to bring her to live in this house that was so stark, so severe, with an absence of soft curves. He would keep the flat in Hampstead, but they would live here. *You need a complete change. Post-traumatic stress disorder. Agoraphobia.* Her thoughts drifted, she was so often lethargic, only half awake. I'll be like Rapunzel in the tower, she thought. She would be glad to leave the city; she could have a fresh start. She imagined she had entered a very beautiful cage.

Contracts were exchanged within eight weeks.

After six months of living in their new house, Max moved into the guest bedroom. He said he did not want to wake her when he left early each morning for the clinic on Grove Road. Stella found it difficult to sleep without him next to her. She would stay up into the early hours of the morning, watching television. Every morning after Max left for work, Stella pounded the treadmill. She dreaded his departure and she hated being left alone. The endorphin rush enabled her to get through the solitude.

A security system was installed. The most important aspect was the sensor that would emit a loud, foghorn-like noise if anyone breached the perimeter of the property. For the most part Stella felt safe, inside Hilltop, up on the hill, looking down at the green treetops.

# Accident and Emergency

Peter pulled up right outside the entrance of Accident and Emergency, behind an ambulance. Stella fumbled with her seatbelt. She jumped down from the car, not stopping to allow for thought, and rushed into the squat, grey building, through the automatic glass doors.

In the waiting room, people in various states of illness, intoxication or injury were lined up on plastic chairs, but there was no sign of Blue. Max must have wielded some influence to wangle his way up the queue.

Unless he had taken Blue somewhere else entirely. The churning in the pit of her stomach intensified.

Stella approached the tired-looking nurse behind the plate-glass window. 'I'm looking for my husband,' she said. 'He came in with a teenage girl, maybe fifteen or twenty minutes ago?'

'Name?'

'Fisher,' she said. 'Dr Max Fisher.'

'They're waiting for the triage nurse now. You can go through.' The nurse pointed to a door on the right. Perhaps she assumed Stella was Blue's mother. Stella kept moving, hoping the diazepam would hold her on an even keel, would not fail her. She needed more time. Peter was parking the car, who knows how far away, and she couldn't risk the delay. She approached a blue door, knocked and barged in without waiting for an invitation.

Blue was hunched on a chair, staring at the floor, swinging her legs. Her suspicious blue eyes stared out at Stella. She did not look pleased to see her.

'I'm so glad I found you,' Stella said. She felt a tremendous warm wave of relief. Blue was awake and in one piece, she was safe.

Max sat upright in the chair next to Blue, distant behind his black-rimmed glasses and his beard. He too did not appear overjoyed at her sudden appearance. Stella thought she saw irritation flit across his face, but he was quick to conceal his response.

'Can I help you?' The triage nurse, in her crease-free uniform, was young, she couldn't be more than twenty-five. Her hair was pulled back from her face in a tidy braid. Max would have her twisted around his little finger in no time at all.

'Are you Mum?' the nurse asked.

She inspected Stella over the top of her wire-rimmed glasses and Stella realized how unkempt she was.

'No,' Stella said. 'I'm a psychologist.' It was the only thing she could think of to say, by way of explanation for her sudden appearance.

'I'm assessing the patient,' the nurse said. 'Can you wait in the waiting room?' There was no sign of Peter. Stella faltered, unsure how to proceed. She could not leave Blue alone with Max. She stayed planted in the doorway, trying not to tremble or sway. There was a list of emergency numbers tacked to the wall above the telephone. Surely child protection services must be amongst them.

'It's very important that you contact social services straight away,' she said to the nurse.

'Stella—' Max said.

'A police officer is on his way, he'll be here in a few minutes,' Stella said. 'Please contact child protection services immediately. This girl is known to them. She needs her social worker here as soon as possible.'

The nurse looked uncertain. She glanced at Max, as if for guidance. Stella repeated herself, loudly. 'You need to call child protection services right now. This child has disclosed domestic violence and emotional abuse. I suggest you review your protocol and follow it – quickly.'

The nurse looked at Max once again. 'Social services are already on their way,' she said. 'Dr Fisher has already informed us about what needs to be done.'

Max kept his composure. He sat, relaxed in his chair.

Stella was thrown. She wanted Max away from Blue. He could say anything; it would all be written down in her records.

'I have to talk to you – alone,' she said to Max. Each word was an effort.

Max got up. 'It's all right,' he said to Blue. 'Just stay here with the nurse.' He put a reassuring hand on her shoulder.

The sight of Max's hand, heavy and grotesque, on Blue's small body, inflamed her. She had the urge to lunge at him but she restrained herself.

Blue was nodding and smiling up at Max. She seemed serene, quite unperturbed. Stella wondered what Max had said to her in the car: what he might have promised, or threatened.

Stella backed into the corridor and Max followed her out, shutting the door behind him. He nodded and smiled at a passing nurse.

'What are you doing?' His voice was low, controlled.

'I know what you've done to her,' she said.

She looked into his eyes, trying to see through, into his soul. He did not look like a monster. He was her husband. Her boss. Her mentor. She had loved him for so long. Part of her was desperate to go back to Hilltop, to pretend. But she had seen what was on Blue's phone.

'How did you get here?' he asked her.

She had her back against the wall and she could feel it, solid against her spine. She swallowed. She focused on her voice, making sure it was strong and clear.

'I need you to tell me the truth,' she said. 'I'm your wife, whatever you've done. You've stayed with me when I've been at my worst – while I've been hiding and dependent on you and on drugs. Maybe I can help you. But you have to let me in.'

He looked at her, blankly.

'This is your last chance to tell me what you did to that girl.'

'How many more pills have you taken?' There was contempt in his voice and in his eyes; he no longer took the trouble to hide what he thought of her.

She was grateful for the hospital wall, with its cracked, tired tiles, still solid and cool against her back.

'Here's another question,' she said. 'Is Blue the first patient you've slept with?' She didn't bother to keep her voice down.

He glanced towards the closed door, impatient. 'Stella – there's a disturbed, distressed young woman in there who needs my attention. Can we do this later?'

She stood up straighter. 'Has it always been adolescent girls that turned you on, Max?'

He blinked. Nothing more. There was no other response to what she'd said.

'Have there been other girls? Were they all patients? Was it always in your office?'

He began to turn away from her. He was going back in, to Blue.

'Wait.' She grabbed at his jacket. 'I can't quite decide. Did you marry me to keep me quiet, to safeguard your precious clinic, or was it because our marriage made you look normal? Or both?' She kept talking, kept hanging on to his lapels. 'Maybe you married me because it was your insurance policy. As long as we stay married, there's very little chance I would do something to damage your clinic. Like reporting Simpson. Or confessing that the report we submitted to the court was less than comprehensive.'

*Where the hell was Peter?* She wasn't strong enough to stop Max from going back into that room. He tried to pull away. She held on tighter. Her voice was unexpectedly loud, unexpectedly clear. 'Did you move me out to Hilltop because you wanted me isolated from my friends? You never tried to help me – you saw that I was becoming more and more avoidant, my life more and more restricted. Why did you keep prescribing those pills?'

An elderly doctor passed them by, cap on his head and stethoscope around his neck, and gave them a concerned look. Max smiled back at him, casual and in control.

'So your mental problems are my fault?' he said.

At least he was engaging with her.

'No—'

'I can't do this any more, Stella. Your jealousy, your

paranoia – it's a cancer that is destroying us. You can't blame me for your addictions or your phobias or your restricted life.'

He shook his head; he looked genuinely distressed.

The corridor reeked of antiseptic and of decay. Stella clung to his jacket as though her life depended on it but her palms were wet and her hands were weak and it was hard to keep hold. Sweat dripped behind her knees.

'I moved you out to Hilltop because I thought your best chance at recovery was to get you away from London, and away from anything that reminded you of the attack. You refused to see a psychiatrist and so I was completely responsible for you. I did my best. Maybe I made the wrong decision, moving away from London.'

She had not known how easy it was for him to lie.

'But for once, Stella, this is not about you. Let me get that girl the help she needs. Can you just pull yourself together and think about someone else for a change.'

She couldn't hold on to him any longer. She let go and wiped her soaking palms against her jeans. The corridor was sweltering. She struggled out of her long woollen coat and dropped it at her feet. Her legs felt as though they might buckle. She swayed back, propping herself up against the wall.

He stepped forward, reaching for the door handle.

'I know that Blue was telling the truth,' she said. 'I know you abused her. I have proof.'

Max hesitated. He looked just a tad less certain of himself.

Stella pushed his hand away from the door. He put up no resistance. She moved in closer. She reached up and put her arms around his neck, so that her mouth brushed his ear.

'She filmed you, with her phone,' she whispered. 'I've watched it. The two of you, in your office.'

She clung on to him, looked over his shoulder, at the empty corridor. She willed herself to stay upright. She willed Peter to appear; or even the nurse. She couldn't let him go, she couldn't let him back into that room. If he was desperate enough, she didn't know what he might do.

She didn't know him at all.

He tried to wrestle her hands away from his neck, but she clung on tighter, leaning into him, collapsing against him. Sweat dripped into her eyes, her vision was blurred. She was breathing too fast, but she couldn't slow herself down.

She closed her eyes. 'The film is grainy because there wasn't much light, but I can see it's you – the two of you, in your office. You're sitting in your chair, Max. Your lovely big, comfy armchair in your consulting room.'

She pushed herself right up close to him. He was very still now.

'She walks towards you. She kneels down in front of you, between your legs. She opens your trousers. I could hear you moan. I could hear what you called her. You called her *Baby Blue*. And then you pulled her on to your lap—'

She breathed him in one last time. Then she unwrapped her arms from around his neck.

'I watched you have sex with a minor. It's statutory rape. You're going to be hauled before the General Medical Council. And then I hope to God you're going to prison.'

She let go. She slumped down to the rubbery floor. She felt faint, and sick.

When Max grabbed her arm, digging his fingers into the soft flesh just above her elbow, she didn't resist. He pulled her to her feet, forcing her away from the triage room, further down the corridor. Someone must walk past soon. Peter would find her. It didn't matter, whatever Max might do to her, at least Blue was safe from him.

'Where is her phone?' He gripped her arm harder. He was hurting her. Her clothes were damp and cold, clinging to her skin. She wasn't frightened, she was heartbroken.

He looked down at his fingers, pressing hard into her arm. He loosened his grip, leaving behind angry red marks.

'You abused her. You committed a crime.'

She saw him crumple and grow more stooped and less vital. 'Please,' he said. 'Don't do this. I'm so sorry.'

She had been fantasizing about him for so long, fantasizing about a man who did not exist.

'Now you're sorry,' she said. 'Now that I have proof. But before I mentioned the video, you told me I was crazy. You weren't sorry at all. You're sorry you got caught, Max. That's all. You lie like other people breathe.'

He stood with one hand pressed against the wall alongside her head and the other gripping her arm, holding her upright. He had composed himself, and he spoke urgently.

'Blue's problems were there a long time before she ever met me. Her personality problems are the reason she worked so hard to seduce me. I promise you I'll see she has everything she needs. I'll pay for a private school, one with a treatment programme tailored to her difficulties.'

Part of her still loved him. She didn't allow herself to look into his eyes.

'If I go to jail it won't make Blue happy and it won't make her better. All I'm asking is that you think about this for a few days – even a few hours – before you make a decision. I want you to know that she was the one that wanted it. I did not hurt her or groom her or force myself on her.'

How warped his mind. He must think his wife a fool.

'You're her doctor. A psychiatrist. You of all people know how vulnerable she is. You know why she behaves the way she does. '

'Stella, she instigated it. She pursued me until I gave in. You've seen what she looks like – in a few months she'll be sixteen, but she looks twenty. Of course I acted stupidly. But things with you have been so – fraught for so long. I was frustrated. I tried to be patient, but it's hard – living with someone who's so dependent, who has an addiction disorder.'

'So it's my fault you fucked a teenager?' If she'd had the strength, if her hands weren't shaking, she would have punched him, right in the mouth.

'All I'm asking is that you think before you rush into this kind of knee-jerk reaction because you want revenge. If you report me, Blue gains nothing. She's safe now. All you have to do is tell social services that she witnessed Simpson abusing her mother. They will stop all contact with him. She'll probably be put in a long-term foster placement, and Simpson won't be able to find her. Don't do this because you're angry at me. Blue doesn't need the trauma of testifying in a rape trial. We can work this through ourselves.'

He was right up close, and all she felt was disgust.

'You're a monster, Max. You took advantage of a sick child. You could have done more damage to her than anyone. You knew what her father was like and you've added another layer of trauma, on top of what that twisted psychopath has already done to her. You're an adult, she's a vulnerable child. That's all. And you can't manipulate me any more.'

She was furious with herself. She was a psychologist, she should have seen the signs. She should have suspected. She should never have put up with the crumbs he threw her way.

'Please,' he said. He reached for her hand, held it, tenderly. 'Don't do something impulsive that we'll both regret. Think about it. If I'm struck off, if I go to prison, what good does it do, Blue? Or you? The medical centre will go under and I'll lose everything, financially. We'll lose Hilltop. We'll lose each other.'

Max pulled up a chair for her. He helped her to sit down, his hand gentle on her elbow. He picked up her coat and draped it round her shoulders.

He knelt down in front of her and placed his hands over hers.

'Don't touch me,' she said. And even then, it was a hard thing to say. If she wanted, she could make him stay. He was hers. The benzodiazepines were waning. She was afraid. She might so easily allow herself to fall under his influence again.

'Where is Blue's phone?' he asked her.

Over his shoulder, she saw Peter walking towards her. The relief was so strong; her breathing eased, she had air in her lungs and space in her head.

'I gave the phone to Peter,' she said.

And finally, as he pulled away, she caught a glimpse of the real Max: heartless and desperate and utterly self-centred. The muscles in his jaw twitched as he ran his hand over his hair. He stood up and turned his back, his hands in his pockets, and walked casually away down the corridor and towards the exit.

*

Stella used the drinking fountain to splash cold water on to her face. She had to stay composed. She had to return to the small, windowless triage room.

When she walked in, Blue would not look at her.

'I'm sorry I didn't listen to you before,' Stella said. 'I believe you. I believe everything you said. About what happened with Dr Fisher.'

'I don't know what you're talking about,' Blue said.

Stella did not try to go any closer, did not try to touch her. The girl did not trust her, yet. 'I want you to know I'm going to make a report to the police and I'm going to tell them everything that you told me. Including the fact that your father has been abusing your mother. They won't force you to have contact with him any more, I promise. There are things I can do. Things I need to tell the police.'

'Where's Dr Fisher?' Blue asked. Her eyes were fixed on the door.

Stella couldn't say which of them had been more deluded: herself or Blue. She stepped forward, venturing a little closer. Blue did not protest. She knelt at the side of the girl's chair, so she was looking directly into her beautiful eyes.

'Blue, please listen to me. What he did to you was a crime. The sex – it was child abuse. If you want to report it to the police, I'll help you.'

Blue's arms were rigid at her sides, her bandaged hands holding on to the seat of her chair. Stella wanted to put her arms around her, but she did not dare. Blue seemed indifferent to what she had said.

'Blue,' Stella asked, 'do you want to report Max to the police? It's a crime, that he touched you when you were his patient. He belongs in jail.'

Blue shook her head. 'You're crazy,' she said. 'He's the

only doctor that's ever really cared about me. He tried to help me. He's the only one I trust. He would never do anything to hurt me.'

They didn't need Blue's evidence; they had proof. Her wishes did not matter.

'I want you to stop talking to me,' Blue said.

'OK. We don't have to talk.'

Stella did not tell Blue that she had seen the video, that she would hand over the phone in her pocket to Peter, that he would deliver the video to the police. Max was right, it would only cause Blue more pain to know what was coming next.

'I just wanted you to know how sorry I am that I didn't believe you before.'

'I don't care what you believe,' Blue said.

'OK,' Stella said. She stood up and tried to smile at Blue, to give her some comfort, but the corners of her mouth were trembling and tense.

The nurse looked out of her depth. She seemed relieved when a small, grey-haired woman with a tag around her neck appeared at the door.

'Hi, Lauren,' the social worker said. 'Let's have a quick chat and then your mum's waiting to see you.'

The nurse and the social worker stood on either side of Blue.

'I'd like to make a statement,' Stella said.

'Of course,' the social worker said. 'I can contact you once we've made sure Blue is settled.'

Blue's arms were still as straight as pokers at her sides, her shoulders up around her ears. She was on her own, with strangers, again. She must be afraid. Stella put her arms around her and gave her a brief, tight hug. Blue let her head rest against Stella's cheek for just a second. Stella touched her face to the beautiful blonde, lavender-scented hair, before Blue stiffened and pushed her away.

Peter was waiting for her, in the corridor right outside.

'What the hell took you so long?' she said.

'Couldn't find a parking place.'

She knew he was lying. She understood.

She reached into her coat pocket and pulled out Blue's phone. She handed it to him. She heard herself sigh. It was over. Her life at Hilltop.

The waiting room had emptied out. Only one large, dishevelled-looking man lay snoring across two chairs. The shift must have changed, there was a new receptionist on duty: a young man with startlingly bright blond hair and tattooed arms. He was staring at his computer screen and ignored them as they walked past his plate-glass window.

The automatic glass doors swished open in front of her. They closed smoothly once again. She had not moved. Peter's hand rested on the small of her back and she tried to absorb some of his courage.

She wasn't ready to go back outside.

She hovered at the exit, safe in the temporary calm of the well-lit waiting room. 'I have nowhere to go,' she said.

'You could come to my place,' Peter said. 'I have a sofa bed – it's yours for as long as you need it.'

She shook her head. There was no way she was sleeping in any house with any man unless she was absolutely certain he wanted to be in bed right next to her.

'I could take you to Hannah's place,' he said.

'Not yet. I haven't spoken to her since that night. I don't even know where she's living.'

Stella pushed her hair back from her face. She needed a shower and a change of clothes. She was very, very tired.

'I want to go back to Hilltop,' she said.

Peter nodded, but his lips formed a tight, disapproving line.

'I need to pack,' she said. 'And then I'm leaving. Permanently. I just need another couple of hours of your time – I promise.'

'Sure.' She could see relief on his face, and hope.

He took a step towards the doors. They whooshed open. He walked right through. Then he stopped and waited for her. She ran forward. She kissed him several times all over his prickly face.

He cracked a smile. Finally.

# Summer

'Do you want me to come inside with you?' Hannah said.

Stella shook her head.

'I'll wait right here.' Hannah opened her car door and stretched her legs. From behind her sunglasses, she gave Stella an encouraging smile.

Stella did not relish leaving the well-worn front seat of her friend's car, but she did so anyway. She was getting better at it: not over-thinking, forcing herself into motion. She walked straight on, a little unsteady on the gravel in her heels, the sun warm against her shoulders.

She stopped to look at the small white-painted wooden sign. *HILLTOP*. She peered behind it. The sensor was still in place, poking out of the overgrown grass.

A convertible, the top down, was parked at the top of the drive. The car was shiny on the outside, immaculate on the inside.

Stella carried on walking, one foot in front of the other.

She could see herself reflected in the undulating steel of the front door: her hair tied back from her face, sunglasses, vest, cigarette trousers. She wasn't displeased.

She rang the doorbell and waited.

Sandra looked just as Stella remembered her, with lively eyes and bright red lipstick. She had a wide, welcoming smile on her face and was evidently delighted to earn sales commission on the house twice within the space of as many years.

Stella was much taller than the estate agent, who was already in stockinged feet. She removed her sunglasses but decided to leave the heels on. They shook hands.

'Mrs Fisher,' Sandra said.

'Please call me Stella.'

Sandra stood back and Stella stepped into her house.

'So you've decided to sell?' Sandra said. Her words echoed inside the dim, bare entrance hall. Only a couple of bulbs were still working, and the chandelier had lost its power to dazzle.

Stella nodded.

The inside of the house was much cooler than outside, and full of shadows. Stella wished she had worn something warmer.

'I have the sales contract with me,' Sandra said. 'Will Dr Fisher be joining us?'

'Dr Fisher is tied up at the moment,' Stella said. 'I have his proxy.'

She was drawn towards the living room, to the window. The garden was bathed in bright sunlight. The grass was overgrown, a cheerful and vibrant green, and the trees were crowded with leaves. Stella looked back into the living room, at the empty space in front of the hearth. She could see a grey sofa, a waterfall of glistening blonde hair and a sharp, mesmerizing face with big blue eyes. She saw Peter at the window, doing battle with a black plastic bag and a roll of masking tape.

'Have you and your husband bought somewhere else?' Sandra enquired. 'Or are you still looking?'

'We're not together any more.'

The last time they had met, Stella had been a newlywed.

'Oh,' Sandra said, taking a second to bounce back from this unfortunate news. 'Are you still living in the area?' she asked.

'No. I've been in a clinic for the last few months. Detoxification programme.'

'Good for you,' Sandra said, encouragingly.

Stella spotted something outside: a rotund shape, peeking out from under the window. The key in the door was stiff and she had to work at it a while to get it to turn. She pushed the doors wide open, and then hesitated, the old familiar tensing in her stomach, her mouth going dry out of habit. She ignored the signs. She stepped outside. The jade Buddha lay on his side on the patio.

'Is that yours?' Sandra asked.

'It belonged to Dr Fisher,' Stella said.

'We did ask the movers to pack everything up, they must have missed that.'

'I only had one guest the whole time I lived here,' Stella said. 'And she threw this Buddha through the window.'

'Oh,' Sandra said.

'She was madly in love with my husband,' Stella said, unable to resist testing Sandra's polite reserve just a little longer. The estate agent was doing an excellent job of not looking shocked.

'I'd like to take him with me,' Stella said.

'Of course.' Sandra looked sceptical as she watched Stella attempt to lift the heavy ornament, swaying on her heels.

The Buddha was no lightweight. Blue must have been in

a fury to have lifted him, to have hurled him through the glass. Stella thought she would like to have even half of her spirit.

'Did you want to take a last look around?' Sandra said. 'To check if there's anything else they've overlooked?'

Stella shook her head.

'Are you sure?' Sandra said. 'You've come all the way out here.'

Stella walked through to the kitchen. She opened the cupboard above the sink, for old time's sake, and because she still longed for the bitter taste of diazepam on her tongue. It was empty. She wanted to go up to her bedroom. Their bedroom. To lie on the bed and see small fluorescent stars on the ceiling and to wait for Max to come to her.

Stella sat the Buddha on the kitchen counter. She reached into her bag and found two sets of keys, both of which she handed over to Sandra.

'You know,' Sandra said, 'I remember thinking you looked so unhappy when I first met you. I thought that was unusual, for someone who had just got married and who was buying such an extraordinary home. The couples I meet generally only start to look that miserable after the first five years or so.'

Stella smiled at her.

The contract signed, Stella struggled out, back down the driveway with the Buddha in her arms. She was sure Hannah wouldn't mind having the cheerful, plump green man squatting at her place for a while. She placed him on her lap and fastened her seatbelt.

She sat back, leaned her head against the headrest, and closed her eyes as Hannah drove with care round the steep bends of Hilltop. She took pleasure in the feel of smooth jade under her fingertips and the sensation of the sun against her forehead, her nose, her cheekbones, her lips. They would be back in London within the hour.

# Acknowledgements

Thanks go first to my brilliant agent, Madeleine Milburn. I have been privileged to have the guidance of a gifted editor, Harriet Bourton, and I am grateful to everybody at Transworld for their commitment to this book and to Sophie Wilson for her early insight and enthusiasm.

I have had several inspirational teachers, and I thank all of them, in particular Tricia Wastvedt and Scott Bradfield. Thanks to Emma-Jane Barton for all your support and encouragement.

My thanks go to Detective Inspector Nick Mervin, who gave generously of his time and expertise, and to psychiatrists Eduardo Szaniecki and Pamela Ashurst, who commented on medication and adolescent mental health issues. The errors are all mine.

Last but not least, thank you to my family for making everything possible.

## ABOUT THE AUTHOR

Luana Lewis is a clinical psychologist and author of two non-fiction books. She was born in Zimbabwe and has lived in South Africa, the Netherlands and England. She shares a home in Buckinghamshire with her family and assorted pets.